MW00770120

# Straight?

## VOLUME 2

# Straight?

## VOLUME 2

**More True Stories
of Unlikely Sexual Encounters Between Men**

## Edited by Jack Hart

alyson books
los angeles

© 2003 BY ALYSON PUBLICATIONS. ALL RIGHTS RESERVED. AUTHORS RETAIN COPYRIGHT TO
THEIR INDIVIDUAL PIECES OF WORK.

MANUFACTURED IN THE UNITED STATES OF AMERICA.

THIS TRADE PAPERBACK ORIGINAL IS PUBLISHED BY ALYSON PUBLICATIONS,
P.O. BOX 4371, LOS ANGELES, CALIFORNIA 90078-4371.
DISTRIBUTION IN THE UNITED KINGDOM BY TURNAROUND PUBLISHER SERVICES LTD.,
UNIT 3, OLYMPIA TRADING ESTATE, COBURG ROAD, WOOD GREEN,
LONDON N22 6TZ ENGLAND.

FIRST EDITION: AUGUST 2003

03 04 05 06 07 **a** 10 9 8 7 6 5 4 3 2 1

ISBN 1-55583-802-2

**CREDITS**
COVER PHOTOGRAPHY BY DARIN LEE.
COVER DESIGN BY LOUIS MANDRAPILIAS.

# CONTENTS

# INTRODUCTION

Q: What's the difference between a straight sailor and a gay
    sailor?
A: a six-pack of beer

Everyone knows that tired joke. But really, a six-pack? For
many of these writers, it took far less than that to nail a hot
straight stud. Maybe the guy was experimenting. Maybe he didn't
have the guts to come out. Maybe he wasn't as narrow-minded as
presumed and was just looking for some fun. Maybe a good blow
job is a good blow job. And who am I to argue if a guy wants to
give or get one?

When I edited the collection *Straight?* in 1998, I was mostly
interested in the allure of inaccessibility a straight—or at least a
seemingly straight—man holds over many of us gay ones. But
between now and then, I've received a fair amount of stories from
truly straight men, who at one time or another felt inexplicably
turned on by another man—and acted on it. Though most of these
stories are the surprise experiences of gay men, I've included a few
straight guys' stories as well. And I'd like to dedicate this collection to them: the straight guys who felt the need to write and let
me know they too had gotten lucky.

Why? Because testosterone is testosterone is testosterone. And
nobody can argue with that.

—Jack Hart

# EN GARDE

**WILLIAM HOLDEN**

"A dvance!" the deep baritone voice commanded. "Very good. Now thrust and glide. Not bad, although you look a little uncomfortable. It would feel more natural to you if your body were in the proper position. Let's take a break and then try it again."

I took off my face shield and sat down on one of the outdoor benches. I was only into my first day of fencing lessons, but already I felt the workout my muscles had received. I'd been intrigued by fencing most of my life but never thought I'd get an opportunity to learn the sport. Then, when I was booking my vacation to Spain, one of the travel agents happened to mention fencing while going over different itineraries I could choose from. I couldn't say no. So here I was. I looked around at the other individuals practicing their stances and attacks. Most of them looked much more coordinated than me. Still, as I thought back over the day's events, I began to realize this vacation was working out better than I'd expected.

I had arrived a couple hours before my first lesson was to begin and was shown around the resort and then to my room. I was asked to meet my instructor at 11 A.M. in Fencing Area 3. He would give me further instructions and my gear.

I arrived a few minutes early and wandered around the fencing area, looking at all of the premarked footprints on the pavement. It reminded me of when my parents had signed me up for dance lessons when I was a kid—a terrible mistake, I might add. I was following the steps when my instructor walked up behind me.

"*Consiguiendo una ventaja, veo.*" The voice came from behind.

Startled, I snapped around and almost lost my balance. "Oh, hi." I managed to say. My face was a little red from embarrassment.

"*Mi nombre es Miguel.*" he paused, looking a little embarrassed himself. "I apologize. I didn't realize you were American until you turned around. I'll be your personal instructor for the next few days." He paused again. "I'm Miguel."

"Hi." I repeated as I walked up to him. "I'm Bill."

Miguel was already in full dress, his face shield resting in his arm. I shook his hand and noticed the firm, tight grip. He looked to be slightly taller than six feet, almost five inches taller than me. His body, hidden by the whites, looked solid and well-built. Miguel had a dark olive complexion, his face rough with morning stubble. His dark hair was shoulder length and still damp from his morning shower. When he smiled, two of the most amazing dimples formed on each side of his face.

"I'm pleased to meet you." He was still holding on to my hand. "Here are your whites. Let me show you where the changing rooms are." We walked into a small building that connected several training areas. "As you can see, we have plenty of lockers to choose from. The showers are to your left." He pointed in the general direction and then continued. "You will work up quite a sweat during our lessons."

"Thanks." I walked over to choose my locker. I've never felt comfortable in locker rooms, so I picked one nearest the showers. It's not that I'm ashamed of my body. I've always taken pride in my tight, hairless swimmer's build. My long blond hair and blue eyes have also been remarked upon by men I've met. I guess I've just worried about getting a hard-on around straight men, so I've made it a point to always shower and get out as quickly as possible. Miguel leaned up against the lockers as I began to undress.

"It's always best to wear as little as possible under the whites." His voice seemed to carry a sense of unease. Then he added quickly, "Clothes can sometimes restrict your movement."

His eyes moved nervously around the room as he waited for me to change. "Are you vacationing with your wife?" he asked, breaking the silence.

"No," I replied as I pulled my shirt over my head. "Actually, I'm gay and traveling alone." The cool damp air of the room surrounded my body. My nipples became erect.

"Oh." He fell silent. "I hope you didn't mind me asking. I just like to get to know my students a little better, before we begin the lessons." He cleared his throat. "My wife always tells me I can come across a bit…how would you say, forward?"

"You're married?" I surprised myself with the question. I had just assumed—or actually hoped—that he was gay. The thought of seeing him without his whites on would have been a definite motivation to do well.

"I've been married six years. She and I met in college and were married within a few months."

I didn't know what to say, so I remained quiet as I finished getting undressed.

"You've got a great body," Miguel remarked. "What I mean is that it looks like you keep yourself in good shape. You should have no problem keeping up with the pace of my training."

I stepped into my pants and then put on my shirt. I fumbled several times with all of the snaps and hooks. "This is going to sound stupid," I said, looking over at him. "But how are these things suppose to be put on?"

Miguel walked over to me and laughed. "Here let me help. These whites can sometimes be difficult to put on when you're not used to them." His left hand trembled as it slid into the front opening of the chest to push the left inside flap behind the right. He looked up at me with those dark-brown eyes and smiled as his hand brushed across my erect nipple. With the folds of my whites properly in place, his hands made their way down in front of my crotch. He began fastening the hooks. His fingers grazed over the band of my underwear as he moved up my stomach and finally to my chest. "There. Now you're ready. Let's get started."

As we walked into the training area, Miguel began explaining the basics. "One of the most important parts of fencing is your initial stance. This is called *en garde*." He took his position opposite me. "You always start out standing sideways from your opponent—like this." He moved his body to demonstrate. "Your feet should be perpendicular to each other, the knees slightly bent. The arm that's holding the weapon should also be bent. The off hand should be held behind you at an upward angle." He positioned himself as he had described. His gracefulness was impressive. "Let's see you try it."

I watched his stance closely as I tried to get my body into position as he had done. With my feet perpendicular to each other, I began to bend my knees. The movement was awkward, and I lost my balance. "Shit," I muttered quietly. "It's harder than it looks. "Let me try this again." I relaxed as much as I could and placed my feet in the proper stance. I could tell I was losing it again and stopped.

"Don't worry. You'll get the hang of it." Miguel started toward me with an amused expression. "Let me help guide your body." He stood behind me and pressed his body against mine. "All right. Just relax. Let me put your body into the proper position. Don't worry if you feel off balance—I'm holding on to you." He wrapped his left arm around my stomach. The roughness of his unshaven face brushed against my skin. "Now move your feet to the proper stance. Good. Now slowly bend your knees. Yes, that's it." His body bent with mine, as if we were dancing to our own private music. His right hand moved down my arm. The strength of it surprised me as he gripped my wrist. "Bend this arm slightly, but don't let the elbow rest against your body."

We stood silently for what seemed minutes as he touched and moved my body. As he spoke he turned his head in my direction, and I felt the warmth of his sweet breath against my neck. My mind wandered, wondering what it would be like to kiss him. My cock twitched as he pulled me tighter in his arms.

"Now that we have you in the proper stance," he continued, "I want you to move your body with me. Don't let your stance be affected by me. You need to learn to keep your body firm and your back straight. Move only with your feet, not your body."

We bent forward and then to the left, ending back in an upright position. As we continued to make our movements together, I felt his cock press against me. The bulge in his pants grew in length and thickness with each forward bend. Through our whites I couldn't determine the size, but I knew he had to be well-endowed.

"You're getting the moves," Miguel whispered as he broke our stance. "Now let's try some face-to-face attacks." He stood about four feet in front of me, his body poised in the *en garde* position. "Before we begin, you need to understand the valid points of attack." He drew his foil and brought it up to my chest. "You can strike the trunk of the body, which is broken into four parts." He brought the point of the foil just under my left nipple and gently moved it across my chest to the right side. "Imagine an invisible line running just below the chest. Then a line running from the neck line down to the groin." He traced this as well, moving the foil in a slow downward motion into my crotch. The tip of his foil gently stroked the length of my all-too-visible erection.

For the next few hours we practiced nonstop. Each new attack and move was repeated over and over until it became almost instinctive to me. Even though my desire to perform well increased as I watched with growing excitement the grace in Miguel's body, I found myself at times missing a step or an advance in order to feel the tip of Miguel's foil strike my body.

"You need to concentrate more so you can anticipate my moves," Miguel said as he made one final attack. "But that's enough for now. Let's get cleaned up and take some time to rest. We'll start back in a couple of hours."

"So how did I do for my first time?" I asked.

He took off his face shield and cradled it under his arm. His black hair was wet from the sweat of the workout. "Not bad for a beginner," he replied with a smile. "You've got great body moves, but we still need to work on your attacks. You seem a little hesitant to strike me." He reached up and pulled off my face shield and handed it to me. "We've worked up quiet a sweat." He pushed back my wet hair. "Let's hit the showers."

Miguel had already begun to unbutton his whites by the time we reached the lockers. I undressed slowly, watching with anticipation as he removed his clothing piece by piece. His chest was muscular. The round nipples were dark and covered by a soft blanket of hair. It tapered to a thin line that ran down his stomach and into the waistline of his pants. I tried not to be too obvious with my admiration of his body, but I found it difficult not to stare. I fumbled around with my clothes and had just taken off my top when Miguel stepped out of his pants butt naked. He had a firm, round ass. My cock pulsed with excitement as I watched him bend forward to pick up his towel—the crack of his ass was covered with a thin layer of dark hair. I wondered what it would be like to run my tongue through it, savoring the taste and smell. My cock was rock-hard, so I waited patiently for him to head to the showers before I took off my pants.

I grabbed my towel and followed only a few seconds behind him. The showers were private and ran along two sides of the opened room, each of them with a full-length door. There was no way to see inside when one of them was in use. I heard the water turn on in one of the stalls and chose the one next to it. As I stepped in, the brightness of the white tiles surrounded me. I closed the heavy door behind me and turned on the water.

With my back to the door, I let the warm water run over my body. I wondered what Miguel was doing in the stall next to me. My hand massaged my erect cock as I tried to imagine him running the bar of soap over his naked body, the lather gathering and mixing with his chest hair. I turned around to let the water run down my back and was startled out of my thoughts by Miguel standing in the entrance to my shower stall. "Shit! you scared me." I stood looking at Miguel's wet body, the towel once again wrapped around his waist.

"I'm sorry," he laughed, but said nothing else.

He stared at my naked body as the water poured over me. Neither of us moved or said a word. My heart was pounding in my chest as my eyes glanced over his body. The silence was killing me. I could tell he was nervous, not sure if he should be here or not. Then he broke the silence.

"I saw you looking at me while I was undressing." He paused. "I kind of liked it. Actually, I liked it a lot." He stood in the doorway for a second, then let the towel drop to the floor. He stepped into the shower and closed the door behind him.

My eyes immediately went to his crotch. He was larger than I had imagined. Even half-erect, his cock looked to be at least eight inches long. His hand tugged at the foreskin, pulling it farther and farther over the large pink head. He stepped closer to me until I felt his breath on my face.

"Your body is amazing." He leaned down to kiss my cheek. "You have to know that I don't make it a habit of this, especially with my students, but when my arms were around you earlier, I don't know, it just felt so good. I knew I had to have more of you."

He kissed me gently on the lips. I placed my arms around his neck and let his tongue inside. We stood there exploring each other's mouths while the warm water covered our bodies. I couldn't believe he was standing there with me. Suddenly, he broke our kiss. "Let's get you cleaned up." He picked up a bar of soap and worked up a heavy lather in his hands. His large, muscular hands were strong as they made their way across my chest. He leaned down and sucked my left nipple into his mouth.

"That feels…so good," I said, running my hands through his wet hair. I gripped his head and moved his mouth up to meet mine. We kissed harder, more passionately as my hands explored his chest. I rolled his nipples between my fingers and pinched them; he moaned, letting me know he liked it.

"Now for your backside," he whispered in my ear as he quickly turned me around and pushed me against the shower wall. With the bar of soap still in his hands, he began to wash my back. He worked my aching muscles with the hands of a pro as he made his way down to my ass. The bar of soap felt cool as he ran it up and down my crack, washing away the sweat of the workout.

"Do you like me playing with your ass?" Miguel asked as he nibbled the back of my neck.

"Your hands feel so good," I told him, then turned my head

around and made contact with his mouth. He kissed me deeply, caressing my chest with one hand as the other continued to play with my ass. As we kissed I felt one of his fingers slide inside me. It moved around gently, stroking the soft lining of my ass. His fingers were long and thick. My body shook as he pushed a second finger inside.

"Bill, you are so hot," he whispered. "I can't believe how you're making me feel. I've never experienced anything like this." He breathing grew heavier; I felt it pulsing on the back of my neck. "Please show me what it's like to be loved by another man."

I turned around quickly at those words. Miguel's dimples were more defined than ever. His face was full of lust. His eyes pleaded with me. I looked down and saw his uncut cock dangling between his legs. I smiled, then lowered myself to my knees. I ran my hands up and down his hairy, muscular legs and watched the water run through his dark bush of pubic hair. The water flowed over his erect cock, covering the foreskin before it rained onto the shower floor. I hesitated for a moment, enjoying the look and texture of his cock. Then I slid my tongue up and underneath his foreskin. The creases of skin covering his soft, silky cock head held the taste of his pre-cum. I savored every drop.

"Suck my balls," Miguel begged as he reached down and held my head in place. I opened my mouth wider to receive his large dick. Inch by inch he forced his cock inside my mouth until I felt the foreskin dangling in the back of my throat. "*Ah, sí. Eso es.*"— Take it all in—"*Eso es.*" I could only moan my reply as slowly fucked my face. His thrusts grew more and more pronounced as he picked up his speed. His pubic hair tickled my nose with every thrust. A mixture of soapy water, pre-cum, and spit formed at the edges of my mouth and ran down my chin.

I tried to talk, to express my pleasure, but all that came out was a muffled moan. He must have understood because he responded with the same soft sounds. My fingers explored his dark, hairy hole as his cock pounded my face. Two of my fingers entered his ass. Its warmth and smooth texture engulfed my fingers as he tightened his muscles around them.

"Your fingers are driving me crazy!" Miguel growled. "I'm going to shoot!" His thrusts came on stronger and faster, his wet balls slapping my chin. When his cock pulled out of my mouth, I wrapped my hand around it. I pumped it hard, watching as the foreskin pulled back and forth from the head.

"Give me that hot cum!" I demanded.

"Fuck, yeah!" Miguel threw his head back as he spouted a thick jet of cum. The heat of his juices sprayed my face, then ran down my neck. I continued to pump his cock as more and more of his cum shot out, the last of it hanging on the folds of his foreskin.

I fell back against the wall as Miguel pushed his way between my legs. He began to stroke my seven inches, running his thumb over the tip of my cock and using my pre-cum as his lubricant. "I'm going to shoot!" I cried out. He leaned in and kissed me as I unloaded hot cum over both of us. I rubbed his chest, mixing my jizz into his wet hair. We stood there together, exhausted as the water continued to run over our bodies.

Miguel looked up and smiled at me. "I can't believe how hot that was." He continued to run his hand over my chest and stomach. "Thank you. You have no idea how much I've wanted to experience something like this. I know it's always been inside me, but I've never allowed it to come out. Until now."

A few moments later in the locker room, Miguel sat down next to me and startled me out of my thoughts. "Ready to start again?" he said as he placed his hand on my leg.

"Sure," I replied as I reached for my whites.

"You won't be needing that." Miguel got up and headed back toward the showers, then turned around and winked at me. A smile appeared on his face as he motioned for me to follow. Miguel was a great fencing instructor, but I guess I taught him a thing or two as well.

# CAUGHT BY A JOCK

### CHRISTOPHER PIERCE

I was on the track team in college. It was hard work, but I loved it: being around all those hot, sweaty, athletic men. It was heaven.

I'd often fantasize about my teammates, wondering what it would be like to suck their dicks or get fucked by them. Frequently, I'd find that by fantasizing while I was on the field, I'd get just the extra boost of adrenaline I needed to complete the course in record time. The other guys would cheer me, clapping me on the back and slapping my ass playfully. I'd just smile at them and think: *If only they knew what helped me along—the thought of them naked!*

Daryl was one of my best friends on the team. He was big and strong, sort of lanky while being muscular at the same time, and a little taller than I was. He had really light blond hair, almost white, with sexy light-blue eyes.

One night after practice I was in the locker room, toweling myself off and getting ready to head out. I liked to take long showers, so by the time I finished up, most of the other guys had already gone home. That suited me fine. Sometimes I'd even jerk off in the shower stall when I knew I was alone.

It was the only way to work off the steam that would build up in me every time I worked out with all those hot, hunky guys.

That particular night I was feeling especially horny. Daryl had been unusually chummy with me all day, rubbing up against me and horse-playing more roughly than usual. It was sexy—damn sexy—but I knew enough not to think too much of it. These guys were my teammates, not my fuck buddies. It was important to maintain our distance.

So I thought.

Daryl was on my mind that night as I dried off. I thought about his blond hair, his square-jawed face, his ice-blue eyes and his strong, muscular body. I might've jacked myself off, but I had an exam the next day and had to get home to start cramming for it.

As I hurriedly rubbed the towel over my body, my eye caught something. It was a flash of white somewhere on the edge of my peripheral vision. I glanced over to it and saw something half in and half out of the locker Daryl used.

It was a jockstrap.

It was one of Daryl's jockstraps.

I dropped the towel and walked over to the locker. This was the first time any clothes had been left out. Normally the guys locked everything up in their lockers before they left.

Gently, reverently, I picked it up. Now, I didn't have a thing about jockstraps.

At least before that night I didn't.

But when I lifted that piece of fabric to my nose and breathed in its aroma, all that changed. As the ripe musky odor of Daryl's crotch sweat permeated my nostrils, I felt my cock stiffen under the towel. It smelled so good—I fucking loved it.

What a treasure to find unexpectedly! It was so wonderful to have that jockstrap up against my nose and mouth. It made me feel like I was a part of Daryl somehow, like I was in some way connecting with him.

The sound of the locker room door slamming open interrupted my reverie. I whirled around, totally surprised—I thought I was the only guy who'd stayed late that evening.

It was Daryl.

Just my luck. We stared at each other for a couple seconds without saying anything. I felt like a kid caught with his hand in the cookie jar.

"What the fuck are you doing?" Daryl asked me, his handsome face contorted in disbelief.

"I...um..." I stammered.

"I knew I forgot something down here," he said. He took a step toward me. I backed up slowly, not knowing how he was going to react. My back hit the wall of lockers, and I realized I was trapped with nowhere to go. "But I didn't think I'd find anyone...especially someone that was playing with my jockstrap."

He grabbed it out of my hand. The sudden move startled me, and I flinched like a junior high school wimp.

"That what's you were doing, wasn't it, man?" he said, his voice rising. I couldn't tell if he was angry or excited or both. "You weren't just playing with it, you were smelling it, weren't you? You were smelling my goddamn jockstrap!"

Daryl put his hands up to the wall of lockers, fencing me in. My burly teammate had me trapped between his thickly muscled arms, and I still didn't know what he was going to do with me.

"Come on, Daryl," I said. "Take it easy." I felt like I was alone with a hungry lion—one false move and I'd be dead meat.

"Well," he said. "If you like smelling it so much, here!" He put his jockstrap up against my face and held it there with one hand. I whimpered and tried to struggle out of the way, but with his other hand Daryl pinned me against the lockers, holding me still.

"Come on, man," he said. "Breathe deep! Take it in! Take in that smell you like so much—the smell of my crotch all hot and sweaty after a night of practice on the track. You know you love it, so just take it in."

Fearful of disobeying, I followed his orders and took another deep pull on the jockstrap. Again, the intoxicating odor of Daryl's groin coursed into me, filling me with his essence. I was a little scared, yet at the same time there was something exciting about being held in place like that, about being in another man's power, the same man whose delicious scent I was savoring through my nostrils.

My cock betrayed me then, hardening up between my legs and standing out, begging for attention. I was still naked, not having had a chance to dress since getting out of the shower, and my erection was painfully obvious. Daryl saw it, and his eyes bugged out.

"You do like it!" he said triumphantly, as if there'd been any doubt. "Look at that. Look at that dick of yours gettin' all hard from smellin' my jockstrap!"

Then put his hands on my shoulders and pushed me down.

"That's it," he said. "Get down on your knees, man. That's what you want, isn't it? To get down in front of me and worship me? I knew it about you from the first day of practice. I knew what you were then, and I know it even more now. You're a cocksucker, aren't you?"

He grabbed the waistband of his sweats and pushed them down. His cock popped out, and was I surprised to see that it was already half-hard! He was getting off on having me in his power like this.

"I know what you want," Daryl said, grabbing his pecker with one hand, gripping it around the thick base. He squeezed it and the head bulged, its plum-shaped corona turning dark pink and squeezing out of the foreskin. "You want this don't you? Admit it, man, admit it!"

Without thinking, I nodded my head. I was too strung out to lie.

"Yes, Daryl, I want to suck your dick!" I said. "I've wanted to suck your dick since the first time I met you!"

"Well, why didn't you say so?" he said as he pushed his cock toward my face. I opened my mouth and took the fleshy rod inside, loving the feel of its masculine strength.

"Oh…" Daryl groaned as I stroked his meat with my tongue. At my touch it completed its erection, hardening in my mouth like a steel spike. It felt so good to have it in there. I immediately started sucking it, running my tongue up and down its length, caressing and stroking the head with my tongue.

I know he liked it because he moaned and rolled his head back.

"Mmmmm, that's good," he said. "You're a good little cocksucker, ain't you?"

"Mm-hmmm," I mumbled around the meat in my mouth. I was happy I was making him feel good—maybe now he wouldn't be mad because of what he'd caught me doing.

If I'd thought smelling Daryl's jockstrap was hot, it was unbelievable to have him right there in front of me in all his glory. He'd just come in from practice so he was still all grimy and sweaty, his body giving off a plethora of odors. It was heaven: olfactory paradise!

While I sucked his dick I thought about the jockstrap: about how it clung to his balls and cock, the same cock I was sucking. I thought about how, when he was running on the track, the jockstrap kept his jewels safe and protected, cradling them and wrapping them up in a cocoon of warmth and safety.

I was so entranced with these thoughts and images that I hadn't noticed myself sucking faster and faster, going up and down on my teammate with a ferocious energy.

"Oh, yeah!" Daryl rumbled above me. "That's it. You got it, cocksucker! This is what you've wanted to do since the first time you saw me."

He was babbling, more to himself than to me. I continued my endeavor, trying to give him the best and hottest blow job he'd ever gotten. I hoped he'd always remember this one.

Maybe I'd even get another chance sometime!

But I was getting ahead of myself and had to concentrate on the here and now—his cock was flexing, I knew it was going to blow soon. The big guy grabbed me by the ears and started to face-fuck me, as if I would try to get away and he had to hold me in place.

As if!

No way. This was a dream come true, and I was going to ride it out to the end, like a surfer on a wave. But a minute later he stopped and pulled himself out of me. I looked up at him, and he was grinning down at me.

"What's wrong?" I asked.

"Nothing's wrong," he answered. "I'm just thinkin' that if you're a cocksucker, then you probably like getting fucked in the ass, don't you?"

I didn't answer immediately.

"Don't you?" Daryl asked again.

"Yes," I said.

"Yes, what?"

"Yes, I like getting fucked in the ass," I said.

"Then ask me," Daryl commanded. I could tell he was really getting off on this power trip.

"Please, Daryl," I said.

"Please, what?"

"Please fuck me in the ass."

"Louder!"

"Daryl, please fuck me in the ass, man!" I said, "I need you to fuck me! Come on, take that big old horse-cock of yours and shove it up my butt hole! I need it, man! Fuck me!"

"Oh, yeah!" he said, "You got it, cocksucker! Get me my works from my bag."

I reached into his locker and pulled a condom package and a tiny bottle of lube from his gym bag. I wondered who else's ass on the team he'd fucked. Daryl took the stuff out of my hand and got himself ready.

Then he put me against the wall of lockers and lined up his cock with my asshole. Usually, I like a guy to warm me up with his fingers, get my hole ready for penetration, but that time I knew we had to hurry. Everyone was supposed to be gone, but there was always a chance of being discovered by a janitor or security guard or something.

Daryl shoved his cock in my ass. Even with lube it hurt, and I let out a little yelp of pain. The jock put one hand over my mouth as he started to fuck me.

"Shhh, cocksucker," he whispered in my ear.

It was quick, dirty, and fast. He thrust himself into me, pulled out, and rammed me again. Within a few moments his breathing sped up and I knew he was ready. I grabbed my own cock and pumped it in my fist.

"I'm cumming, cocksucker," Daryl said. "Can you feel me cum?" And he took his hand off my mouth.

"Yeah, man, I'm cumming too, can you feel me?"

"Oh, yeah!" we both said, and we blew our loads together as our orgasms bloomed inside us like explosions of pleasure. When we were done, Daryl pulled out of me gently and threw away the condom. I got some paper towels and wiped off the lockers where I'd shot my spunk all over them.

When I was done I tried to stand up but lost my balance and almost fell.

"You OK, man?" the jock asked me.

"Yeah," I said. "I just got two workouts today, one on the field and one in here. I'm pretty tired."

Without a word Daryl walked over to me, picked me up, and cradled me in his arms. It was amazing—a gesture of tenderness from such a rough jock. He carried me to the showers and there lovingly washed me and himself. When we were all done, dried off, dressed, and ready to go, Daryl pushed me against the wall and got up in my face again.

"If you ever tell anyone we did this, I'll tell them what you were doing when I came down here, cocksucker," he said.

"You got it, man," I said seriously.

"Good," he said and grinned. "I don't want to have to share you with anyone." And with that he kissed me.

When he took his lips from mine, he gave me another grin, then slung his gym bag over his shoulder and headed for the exit.

"You coming?" he asked me.

# MEMORIES OF AARON

**MAX SOUTHERN**

Aaron stood in front of me, his back turned as he showered. I was trying to conceal the hard-on I had gotten when he had shucked his clothes. As the warm water rinsed our bodies in the communal stall, we made small talk, but I was having a difficult time slinging words together as his farm-boy ass smiled up at me. He wouldn't turn around, so I couldn't see whether he too was hard. I wanted desperately to walk up behind him, embrace his naked body, and make love to every inch of him, yet he had given me no indication that it was safe territory.

His name was Aaron Goldman. We'd met in statistics class my sophomore year of college while we both yawned at the dinosaur instructor. It turned out we had gone to high school together in middle Georgia but had never met. I was a year older than him, and we had hung out in different circles. But in college we hit it off immediately and became friends shortly after classes began. We often studied together. Pretty soon we were hanging out with my residence hall–mates and going to movies and out for pizza.

I experienced a sexual awakening in college. My freshman year I worked up the nerve to have sex with another guy and had gleefully spent the rest of the year experimenting: sucking, fucking, getting my cherry busted by a randy senior. Hell, I'd even had my first three-way. By the age of 20, I'd become quite comfortable with my sexuality and was fairly open about it.

As far as I knew, Aaron was straight. He talked about his girlfriend back home, a cheerleader named Amy. Yet in my fantasies he was just waiting for the right man to seduce him, to take him away from a life of pretense. Against my better judgment I'd fallen for him. In fact, I thought about him day and night: his shy demeanor, his light-brown hair, and the tufts of fur peaking out from his undershirt. He had absolutely no idea how cute he was.

So there we were innocently showering after a game of volleyball. This was my first glance at him bare-assed, and my dick had developed a life of its own. I tried to catch a glimpse of his penis but couldn't, as I was trying to conceal my hard-on. I quickly finished showering and stepped out to dry off. Aaron followed suit and surely had to notice my protrusion below. But we never discussed it.

One evening a flirtatious gay friend of mine approached us at a local pizza joint. "Hi, babe. My, aren't you a cutie," he said to Aaron, grabbing his nipples. No," Aaron said defensively. "I have a girlfriend." It was an awkward moment, and Aaron excused himself shortly after we ate. After that, he didn't return my phone calls and avoided my waves in class. I was devastated, but I knew falling for a straight guy was a recipe for heartache.

One evening about two weeks later, I got a knock on my door. It was Aaron, asking to come in to talk. He'd had a few beers but was still sober. As the night wore on, we talked a lot. Or, more accurately, Aaron asked question after question: When had I first known I was gay? How had my family reacted? He insisted he was straight and had had sex with girls back home. A little past 1 A.M. we ended our chat. I was stunned when he walked toward the door, grabbed the doorknob, then stopped. He looked me square in the face and asked to spend the night.

I didn't know how to react. I was skittish, unsure of his feelings, but of course I agreed. Into my tiny dorm-room bed I tumbled and he followed. I knew we'd have some privacy since my roommate was spending the night at his frat house. Aaron and I were on different sides of the bed, but our skin was almost touching. For a moment we lay there, until finally I reached out and stroked his hair. He didn't seem to mind. Turning to face me, he whispered, "I've never done this before." I slipped his shirt off then slowly ran my hand all over his chest and stomach, thumbing his nipples before tasting them. We stood up and I peeled off his jeans, then his Fruit of the Looms. Eventually we were both naked—and erect. He had a lovely body, with a firm, lightly haired chest and a nice patch of brown pubic hair. I kissed him, and he apprehensively met my lips with his. "I've wanted this for so long," I admitted. He shook a bit as I kissed his neck. I dropped to my knees and dabbled my tongue on his stiff cock. He moaned audibly but still seemed nervous. As I worked my tongue all over his shaft and licked his fuzzy balls, he began to relax and thrust somewhat into my throat. Before long he was breathing heavily, and as I sucked his delicious meat he blew a monster load on my face.

Aaron bent down and touched my erection, then brought it to his lips. It was an awkward and tentative blow job—a novice's one. But Lord, it felt good being with him.

Even after he came, he was ready to go again, so we jumped into the bed, where I placed him on his back and devoured him from head to toe. I turned him onto his stomach, massaged his shoulders, and then centered my attention on his ass. At this point I didn't know exactly what the extent of his sexual activity had been, but I knew one thing for sure: I was the first person to stick a tongue up his ass. It was unexpected; he apparently had never heard of rimming. At first I kissed his cheeks, then slowly moved my tongue closer to his hole until I darted it in. I giggled a bit at his vocal reaction, but I continued to thrust in and out so furiously that his legs quivered as he gripped a pillow.

I wet my index finger and slipped it into his asshole, which made him spring up. I would have loved to have been the first person to fuck his tight ass, but he turned down my request. Still, I wasn't about to let this opportunity pass. I lubed my own hole and slipped a condom on Aaron's stiff dick. I bent in front of him, but he had a hard time working his erection in. So I took matters into my own hands and straddled him, his dick sinking into my cavern. I sat on it a few minutes, enjoying the sensation of him being inside me.

Losing his inhibitions as he penetrated me, Aaron shot up and placed me on my back, slipping his meat inside me. His grinding was slow at first but eventually he picked up the tempo. My legs now over his shoulders, he pounded me silly. I shot a mother load all over my chest while he thrust; a spurt even landed on the bed frame. Shortly afterward he announced he was cumming— again!—and dug his cock all the way in. He collapsed into a big sweaty pile on top of me before repositioning and burying himself in my arms. He slept that way most of the night. The next morning, however, he hurried off abruptly.

Sadly, I never officially spoke to Aaron again. Final exams started a few days later, just before summer vacation. Aaron didn't return in the fall; a friend said he had transferred to another college. Somehow I always thought I'd see Aaron again and we'd discuss our night together. Was he gay? Gay-curious? Or was it just sexual experimentation? I racked my brain, but eventually

I let go and realized my feelings had been more of an infatuation than love.

About 10 years later while I was home for Christmas, I went to the post office to mail a batch of letters. As I was leaving, I noticed a couple getting out of an SUV. It was unmistakably Aaron. Gone were his glasses and timid look. He was very much a grown man—a man with a young woman and an infant. He ambled up the sidewalk ahead of his family and spotted me. For a second he looked and did a double take as it registered. I smiled as he nervously passed by with his clan. As he closed the post office door behind him, however, he glanced at me once again and flashed a big grin, just before I jumped into my Lexus and drove back home to the family I too had forged.

# THE SWITCH

## JEFFREY LOCKETT

In darkness only two things can happen: violence and sex. Being addicted to the danger and excitement of fast sex, I was out prowling for a good time. Through the trees I could just make out the shapes of other anonymous outlaws. It was a hot, sweaty night, and I couldn't sleep; my bedroom was far too steamy and airless. I considered jerking off but opted for something far more interesting. I threw back my cotton sheets and headed off onto Hampstead Heath—by day London's most beautiful park, by night its most notorious cruising ground. It had become doubly notorious since last weekend's raid, when the police had cordoned off the sex arena, combed every inch of undergrowth, questioned the fortunate, and packed off the unlucky into five vans with bars on the windows. Apparently, the police had received complaints. It wouldn't do for upstanding citizens to have to see used condoms and lubes on the paths. Public decency had to be maintained. You know—all the usual crappy justifications. Any sensible person would have stayed at home, but I had an urge to reclaim gay space. Or maybe I just needed to suck dick.

I wandered off the main path, lost my bearings in the darkness, and stumbled into a section of the Heath I didn't know. Keener on finding a way back than tracking the silhouettes of cruising men, I was unprepared for what I stumbled across in a clearing: a policeman. My blood ran cold. He stood motionless. In the silvery moonlight filtering through the trees I made him out quite clearly.

A series of unappetizing pictures flashed through my sleep-deprived brain: my name in the local papers; jeers from gay friends and embarrassing explanations to straight ones. Then I looked again. Was his left hand lightly caressing the crotch of his regulation police trousers? I'd heard about this kind of operation and was about to disappear back into the bushes. But what if his come-on was for real?

From almost my first jerk off, I have spunked to fantasies starring our boys in blue. Could I ever forgive myself for passing up such a hot man-in-uniform opportunity? Frozen by a strange mixture of fear and lust, I looked closer. He was definitely a policeman: silver numbers on his epaulets and the sharp tailoring that makes any man look good. And believe me, this stud needed no help! He had a beefy body, dark hair, thick chunky arms, and legs with muscles built by holding back rowdy demonstrators rather than doing reps on Nautilus gym equipment. I guessed he must be in his late 20s. He had a "I know how to handle myself" look that made my dick as hard as a billy club.

"Don't worry, I need sex too. It's OK," he softly growled. His voice was low and husky—he was so turned on that the words hardly escaped. Still I stood my ground, unsure whether I was being offered great sex or a jail sentence.

He took out his flashlight and shone it into his own face. Steely gray eyes begged me to follow his instructions. Surely in a roundup, the Heath would be swarming with police, not just this lone officer. I decided to go for it!

"Don't be frightened," he said as he smiled and waved his flashlight over his uniform. The buttons sparkled brightly in the beam, and he moaned softly and caressed himself with the light. I couldn't take my eyes off the growing outline of his meaty cock. This was more than I could bear. I had to have him or regret it forever.

Each step forward took an eternity. My heart pounded in time with the crunch of dry sticks under my Doc Martens boots. I could hardly breathe, but I stood right in front of him. I brushed my hand against the harsh fabric of his uniform. There was no explosion of handcuffs from the bushes, just a low moan from my companion.

He switched off the flashlight. With greater confidence, I placed my hand on his cock and looked directly into his cool eyes glinting with moonlight.

"Is this what you want?" I asked.

He nodded.

Something wicked inside me couldn't resist testing him.

"Tell me!" I whispered into his ear.

For an answer, he rubbed his cock against me. My cock throbbed so fiercely I feared it would break through my jeans. Our dicks wrestled for a second. There was no turning back. He tried to push my head down toward a mouthful of regulation blue trousers. But I resisted. I wanted him to voice those animal needs.

"Tell me what you want," I demanded.

"Suck me, please." The policeman was shivering with lust.

"Suck what?" I felt a small surge of power.

"My dick," he rasped.

I needed no second invitation. I dived down, slobbered over the rough material, and tried to imagine how his cock would taste. He thrust up against my tongue and tried to face-fuck me. Though he was even more turned on as he got closer to his goal, he was tormented by the thick barrier between my mouth and his hot cop dick.

He couldn't wait any longer. He pushed my face away, unzipped his serge trousers, and presented me with a heavy, rock-hard cock. The veins stood out along the side, and the red tip quivered. I had to approach this one carefully or white-hot spunk would be pumping over his black boots before we'd even started. Delicately, I ran the edge of my tongue along his throbbing tool and was rewarded with a long sigh. I teased the head and resisted the temptation to close in.

He needed more and he needed it badly. Maddened with lust, the cop took a fistful of my hair and tried with brute force to ram his dick down my throat. I ignored the pain and eased my tongue back down his shaft again, this time really swirling round his circumcised helmet. The sensations were getting to him—he was definitely in the edge zone. I backed off and his prick jerked without me even touching it.

There was a rustle in the undergrowth, and another outlaw emerged into the clearing. The intruder was obviously horrified to discover a policeman with his trousers round his ankles. He was gone in an instant, but it reminded me what a dangerous game I was playing. With a new urgency, I lowered my mouth down the full length of his cock and hit pubes. His moans became loader as I ran my hands all over his uniform. His broad chest started to heave. I shoved my fingers behind his crisp white shirt and deep into a forest of dark hairs. He buried his prick even farther down my throat. My fingers located a nipple and I gave it a harsh squeeze.

With one yell, as piercing as any siren, he began to dump his load. Squirts of sweet cum shot into my mouth—he tasted like fresh doughnuts! It was pure heaven. I swallowed frantically in order to capture the creamy explosion before it could dribble down my chin.

As his breathing became more regular I started to worry again. What if he turned nasty? Before he could fully recover, I disappeared back into the undergrowth. After all, it was just my word against his. Who would the judge believe—the policeman or the cocksucker? Five seconds later, hidden in the darkness, I finally pulled out my own dick. I had been concentrating so completely on my illicit sex partner, I hadn't even touched myself. I leaned back against a tree and start to beat off, but with each stroke I became increasingly angry. How dare he come here and demand sex? What had he been doing while his police buddies rounded up queers and made fag jokes? Having some pervert suck you off doesn't make you "one of those." Incensed, I shoved my dick back in my jeans and zipped up. I had come to the Heath for something better than my own five fingers, and I was damned sure I was going to find it.

I circled back through the bushes. I thought I spotted a familiar shape, but it was a guy carrying a motorcycle helmet. I almost gave up, when walking toward the better-lit main path I found my policeman. He stopped to look over his shoulder, perhaps to be sure nobody saw him emerging from the gay cruising area. It was my chance. I jumped out from behind a large oak tree, grabbed him, and pinned his hands behind his back.

"What?" he spluttered. He desperately tried to turn to get a look at his assailant.

I pulled him back into the murky wood. He struggled hard, but I had surprise on my side. The more he bucked, the higher I shoved his arms and the stronger my surge of pride for so effectively turning the tables.

Threateningly, I whispered the same words he'd used to entice me: "Don't worry, I need sex too. OK."

He obviously recognized the formula because he stopped struggling. I had the upper hand and my dick surged like a racehorse out of the gate. I pushed him onto his knees. He gazed up with something approaching respect. Maybe I could get into this scene full time?

"Undo the belt with your teeth and then pull down my jeans with your mouth," I commanded. He dutifully complied. It took him a while, but I was in no hurry.

Slowly, I guided his head to my groin and, for a moment, held it there just inches away. His chance to worship civilian cock! *Am I the first to invade this virgin throat?* I wondered? I grabbed hold of his hair and pulled it back tightly. Revenge felt good. He let out a moan of agony. With his mouth open, I seized the opportunity to attack with my throbbing hard-on. His inexperience showed when he failed to get his teeth out of the way, but the friction just turned me on even more. How dare he play straight trade? I'd soon turn him into a flaming bottom boy!

With each thrust against the back of his throat, he opened a little wider. He was really getting into this! By now four of my seven-and-a-half inches had disappeared into his eager mouth. Perhaps those lips needed tenderizing a little—maybe that would teach him to spread 'em. I pulled back and started to slap my dick against his cheeks. He groaned. Was it with pain or pleasure? I didn't care. I was in charge this time, and he was just police pussy.

His tongue stuck out lewdly as he tried to reconnect with my prize dick. But I decided it was too good for cop mouth. Instead, I let him have my balls as a consolation prize and forced both hairy orbs down his subservient throat. The sight of a hefty policeman in full uniform crouching at my feet was too much. I'd never felt so powerful, never so turned on. Without even touching myself, I shot my cum in slow arching spurts right over his trousers—white against dark navy blue.

I was not unreasonable: I gave him a tissue to wipe off the stain, and we found a late-night van where they sold coffee and doughnuts. We chatted and I gave him my E-mail address. These days he often comes round for further training. In fact we've both learned a lot. I've discovered policemen really live for doughnuts and hot spunk. And he's discovered the benefits of treating gay men with a little respect.

# TAKING ADVANTAGE

## CHRISTOPHER PIERCE

It wasn't until I had my buddy Craig flat on his back and was fucking his brains out on the stage of an empty movie theater that I realized one of us was being taken advantage of. But was it him or me?

I'd never take advantage of a buddy. Not even if he was totally gorgeous, totally hot, and totally drunk. I'd had the opportunity a few times in my life, and I was proud to say I'd never done it. It never occurred to me that I might be the one being taken advantage of someday—and by someone I never would've expected.

I was 18, out of high school at last and looking forward to college. Myself and a bunch of other friends had gotten jobs at a nearby movie theater to earn some money during the summer. We all hung around together, before and after work. It was fun job—we got free movie passes and flirted with customers from behind the refreshment counter.

Of course, my buddies were flirting with the girls, and I was flirting with the boys.

One of my best friends was named Craig. I'd always felt a

little plain next to him, even though I knew I was pretty cute myself. Craig had always been handsome, but as he grew up he got sexier and sexier, until modeling talent scouts were pestering him to sign with their agencies.

He was over six feet tall, and his body—once lanky and awkward in early adolescence—had blossomed into manhood with every muscle and contour as perfect as those of a Greek statue. His head of floppy blond hair was wonderfully complemented by rich green eyes that almost glowed in the dark, and his face had broken many a heart with its exquisite beauty.

But the model scouts were wasting their time; they didn't know Craig. He had a singular goal—to be a pro baseball player—and nothing could distract him from that dream. He loved the game of baseball more than anything in the world, even more than the girlfriends he always seemed to have. But the girls would come and go; baseball was his true love.

My true love was Craig, even though I'd resigned myself to lusting from afar, seeing as he was straight as an arrow. In any case, knowing my ideal was out of reach just fueled my vivid fantasy life...a life that somehow always included Craig and me fucking each other's brains out.

It'd start with a slow kiss on the cheek, then my lips would move across the angular planes of his face, down to his luscious mouth, which I would kiss, gently at first, then with more force after gathering strength. I'd reach around him, taking him into my arms, holding him close. The warmth of our bodies cumming together would be moist and heady, and one of my hands would slide up into his hair, stroking and caressing its soft fullness. I'd slide my other hand down until I reached his beautiful butt, which I'd massaged gently. Craig's dick would get hard through his shorts, and his erection would be matched by mine.

We'd press against each other, and then I'd drop to my knees, nuzzling his crotch with my face. He'd unbuckle his pants and let them fall, and his hard cock would emerge from darkness into light. My mouth would open, taking all of it inside me, and I'd caress it with my lips, my tongue, my whole mouth. His pulsating rod would energize me, as if it was rejuvenating my life force. The baseball stud would fuck my face, pumping in and out with violent intensity.

It would feel like the realization of a dream. A dream of the night, hot and sticky, full of primeval passion and primitive delight. Craig and I would be sucking each other off; we'd fuck each other, each of us plundering the other, taking and claiming each other with riveting concentration. We would fully consummate our passion, joining together in a bond of mutual love and animal lust, forever.

Right.

Only in my dreams.

But somehow I managed to survive, loving Craig from afar and dreaming of him at night.

In any case, what actually happened was this:

One night all of us employees at the theater had a party. It was on a Friday night, the same day a big movie premiered. It was a sure-fire blockbuster, something about the end of the world and what a few brave souls do to prevent the catastrophe. It was going to make a shit load of money for the studio. That's right, the studio, not the theater. The theater only took home the cash from what the snack counter made; that's why the managers were always pushing us to sell so much popcorn, soda pop, and candy to the customers. When the last showing was over, when the last customer had been chased out of the bathroom and the last empty popcorn tubs had been picked up off the floor, we all looked at each other and gave ourselves high fives.

We were done! It was over! Party time!

The manager was tired, so he left the lock-up keys to his assistant Richard and went home, warning us not to mess up his theater with our party. We assured him everything would be cool, not to worry, to go home to get some sleep so he could be back in the morning for the Saturday matinees. Richard was cool, one of us, so we knew we were going to have a good time. He brought an ice chest of beer and wine coolers from his car, so we were set. The projectionist pumped some hard rock through the theater's PA system, and we had ourselves a party!

I don't drink much, so I got myself some soda and had a good time watching everyone else. Soon enough they were all either wired from the long shifts we'd all worked or spinning from the booze—or both. Various couples formed, and soon everyone was sitting off in dark corners, making out.

Except me, of course. I didn't have a boyfriend and knew all the other guys were straight. Even though some of them were drunk and might be convinced to try some male/male action, I don't take advantage, like I already said. Craig had at least two girls with him, sometimes three, and looked happy as a pig in shit.

Around 4 in the morning, things started to wind down. I helped Richard round everyone up and made sure that only the sober ones were driving, bundling the drunk ones into the back seats to be taken home.

When we realized that Craig was still in the building, Richard gave me the lock-up keys and asked me if I'd mind helping our last straggler so that he (Richard) could get home to his wife. I said sure and headed back into the theater as the last car pulled out of the parking lot.

I found Craig on the raised platform in front of the screen. He was lying on his back, staring at the ceiling and humming some jingle to himself. I recognized the tune—it was from a beer commercial.

"All right, buddy, it's time to go home." I said. He looked at me, surprised, like he didn't know I was there, like he hadn't heard me enter the theater and walk down the aisle.

"Hey, Chris, is that you?" he said, his speech slurred.

"Yeah, it's me, Craig." I answered, putting my hand on his shoulder and gently shaking him a little. "We gotta get you home."

Craig put his hand on mine. I expected him to push it away, but instead he held it there, like he wanted my hand to stay there.

"Wait a second." he said. "Just hold on a second here."

"What?" I said, a little exasperated. I didn't have time for this, not at 4:30 in the morning.

"Chris…are you really, like, gay?"

I rolled my eyes at him.

"Of course I'm gay." I said. "I came out to you in junior high school." He laughed drunkenly.

"You came out to everyone in junior high school."

I had to laugh too, savoring the memory. "Well, I figured it wasn't anything to be ashamed of."

Craig let go of my hand and sat up, dangling his legs over the edge of the stage. He was a little wobbly and almost lost his balance.

"Do you think I'm good-looking?" he said suddenly. "I mean, am I…attractive to you?"

That took me by surprise. What was this all about? He'd never talked like this to me before. But then I guessed I'd never seen him this drunk, either. I figured the best way to deal with him was to be calm and not let anything distract me.

"Craig, you're drunk." I said.

"No, I'm not." he said defensively. "Are you attracted to me? Please tell me."

*Please?*—I didn't think I'd ever hear him say "please" for anything either.

"Give me a break, man," I said. "I've gotta get some sleep—I have to be back here by 11 A.M." But I knew he wouldn't care; he didn't work on Saturdays so he could play his damn baseball.

Craig grabbed my shirt and yanked me close. Before I could react, he'd kissed me, his hot hungry mouth devouring my own. I broke his grip and pulled away, even as I felt my cock harden in my jeans.

"What the hell are you doing?" I said as Craig jumped down from the stage and walked toward me, weaving a little back and forth.

He said nothing but kissed me again. It was bizarre (he was straight!) and wonderful (so that's what his sexy mouth tastes like!) at the same time. He tried to hug me, but I put my hands up between us, trying to keep us separated. I wanted to resist him, but men are men; he'd gotten my libido started, and now my cock and balls were in charge and my brain was on the back burner. With every second it was harder and harder to push him away.

He tried harder to hug me, and this time he succeeded. Even though we were the same size, we both knew I was the stronger one. I could've punched him, I could've ran away from him, later I thought of a hundred things I could've done…but what I actually did was wrap my arms around him and squeeze him tight.

"Craig!" I shouted into his ear. "I know we're good buddies and everything, and I love you as a friend, but we can't do this!"

"Why not?" he said, slurring.

"Because you're straight! And you're drunk! You wouldn't be doing this if you weren't wasted out of your mind!"

His only answer was an unintelligible grunt. Before I could figure out what he meant, he was kissing me again, more passionately this time. As I gave in to my animal desires, I wondered who was taking advantage of whom in this situation.

I returned his kiss, sticking my tongue into his mouth, slobbering all over him. When I squeezed him he did the same to me, and we crushed our bodies together, rubbing our crotches against each other through the denim of our jeans. I loved the feel of his body against mine.

My mind was going a mile a minute; this was incredible, amazing, to finally get it on with this man I'd known almost my whole life, this man I'd lusted after hundreds of times—Craig in my arms after all this time! But it was wrong! Wasn't it?

*You can't do this,* I thought. But look at him; he sure seems to know what he wants. It wouldn't be like I was forcing myself on him—he wants it and wants it badly. *Now shut up and enjoy yourself!*

Was it wrong?

*Who gives a shit,* I realized, pushing Craig back down on his back, devouring his mouth with mine. I broke the kiss just long enough to yank his shirt off while he did the same to me. The sight of his chiseled physique was breathtaking, but there was no time for sight-seeing. I had to take my chance while it was there!

Then our chests were grinding together, and I could feel our bodies heat up and start to sweat. We slithered out of our pants and underwear, discarding them as if they were garbage. My coworker's dick was beautiful, long and hard and dripping with pre-cum.

"Suck my dick." I ordered him, and he obeyed. He took my pole into his mouth and started slurping it obscenely. Feeling his mouth on me was fantastic, and I let my head roll back in sensual abandon. Soon enough my penis was wet and slippery, ready for the main event. I knew Craig was ready from the way his eyes were pleading with me.

*Please fuck me,* his eyes said to me. *Please fuck me now!*

I needed more consent than that, so I asked him, "You want me to fuck you, Craig?" I didn't want there to be any doubt.

"You want me to screw that tight little baseball ass of yours?"

"Please!" he shouted to the ceiling. Lucky for both of us, I knew about safe sex—even back then in the late '80s, I always had a condom and a tiny container of lube on me. With Craig's help I slid the latex sheath over my hard rod, then slicked it up with lube so I wouldn't hurt him more than necessary. My buddy kept moaning beneath me.

"Do me now! You're driving me fucking nuts! Do it, now! Please, Chris!"

"Tonight I'm pitcher and you're catcher." I said, and rammed my cock into the magic inverted "V" shape of his spread-eagled legs and into his asshole. He grimaced in pain as I entered him, but a second his exhale was one of bliss.

Craig was loving every minute of this, I realized. I wondered if he'd been fucked before…but as with all my questions that night, the answer was: *Who cares?* All that mattered was the present, the eternal now in which I was living a dream, doing the unthinkable, taking what was forbidden and devouring it like ripe, bursting fruit.

I started fucking him, shoving myself into him and then pulling almost all the way out before going back in. He grunted with each thrust, punctuating every move I made. Whether they were grunts of pleasure or pain I don't know, but what I do know is that my stud buddy's dick was hard as rock, leaking lube of his own onto his flawless chest.

Besides that, there was one other thing I knew for sure.

Craig was smiling, grinning like a pig in shit.

I breathed in deeply. The theater was thick with the delicious smells of the night's business, the smells of "the movies": popping popcorn, sizzling hot dogs, ice-cold soda and sweet, sweet candy.

Craig and I were having a sizzling candy fantasy of our own, there on the stage. I wondered what the audience that had been there earlier would've thought of the little show we were putting on. I wondered if they would have liked it better than the movie they'd seen.

So there I was, fucking my drunk buddy in an empty theater. The absurdity of the situation almost made me laugh, and then I found myself laughing again from the sheer carnal joy of it. Well, no matter what he said, Craig was definitely "batting for both teams."

Our young bodies tensed and pulled each other back and forth in a tug-of-war of passion and sensuality as we fucked our brains out.

Suddenly, I couldn't hold back any longer. It was lucky for us it was the middle of the night; my yell of ecstasy would've brought people running if there had been anyone else in the theater. I shot my load into the condom where it was safely caught and held harmless. As I shot, Craig grabbed his own stiff rod and pumped it hard. A second later his yell joined mine, and he shot all over himself.

All our muscles relaxed as we fell into each other's arms. I slowly pulled my dick out of Craig's asshole and took off the condom. After a few minutes of just holding each other, I returned from dreamland and realized what we'd been doing—And what time it probably was. I looked at my watch and groaned.

"Five in the morning?" I said. "We've got to go. I have to be back here at 11!"

After I pulled on my clothes I helped Craig get cleaned up (with some paper towels from a quick run I took to the restroom) and back into his own clothes. He wasn't much help, apparently still wasted.

"C'mon, we're going." I told him as I headed up the aisle for the exits. "Gotta get you home." Looking back, I saw my friend weaving and wobbling drunkenly, trying to follow me without much success. Then he collapsed to his knees.

"Fuckin' hell." I said as I went back and pulled him to his feet. "Looks like I gotta do everything tonight." I picked Craig up and slung him over one shoulder. He didn't resist, so I knew he was wasted out of his mind, probably in a blackout. I'd be lucky if he didn't puke all over me.

I carried my buddy out of there, figuring all the lugging of heavy boxes and big sacks at the theater had been good practice for this. After I turned off the main power switch in the control booth, I locked the place up, closing the doors behind me. Then I shifted Craig's body, trying to balance his weight as well as possible before the long walk through the parking lot. My car was all the way at the opposite end. When I finally reached it, I unlocked it and put my buddy down in the back seat as gently as I could.

Needless to say, Craig's older brother was not happy when I knocked on their front door in the wee hours of the morning.

"What the fucking time is it?" he snarled.

"Five-thirty," I said.

"What the hell is this?" he asked, gesturing at the unconscious man over my shoulder.

"Your little brother. He partied a little too hard last night."

"Oh, God, come in," he said. "Dump him on the floor, on the couch, out the window. I don't give a shit." So I left Craig in the "loving" care of his brother, wondering how tough he'd be on my friend that I'd shared this amazing experience with. I didn't want to leave him, but I still lived with my parents for God's sake! There was nothing more I could do. I hoped his brother would go easy on him for waking him up so early.

I was back at the theater on time, after grabbing a few hours of sleep. One of my coworkers asked if I had a good time at the party, and we compared notes. I didn't tell him what Craig and I had done after everyone had left, but I did tell him how drunk he (Craig) had gotten. My coworker looked at me blankly.

"Drunk?" he asked.

"Yeah. Shitfaced. I had to carry him home."

"But Craig wasn't drunk last night. He couldn't be. He didn't drink anything."

As I was about to deny what I was hearing, I realized something: Craig had been behaving like he was wasted, but I never actually saw him with a can or bottle in his hand, and I definitely didn't see him drink anything.

What was going on?

"Are you absolutely positive?"

"Yes," my friend said seriously. "Craig wasn't drunk last night."

Without another word, I left the snack counter and went back to the break room. I sat down in shock, trying to absorb what I'd just learned. So just who had been taken advantage of the night before? Numbly, I decided to stop by Craig's house after work, late enough that he'd be home from baseball. I'd take him somewhere private and we'd have a talk about fucking your buddies over, figuratively and literally.

A long, sweaty, sticky talk.

And this time, I'd be the one taking advantage.

# ORLANDO BOUND

## ALEXANDER WELCH

I t was almost midnight when I stepped outside the crowded
bus terminal in Jacksonville, Florida, for my three-hour lay-
over. I stood against the imitation brick siding of the bus station
restaurant, wondering where all the palm trees and sand had gone.
I was about to voice my complaint to no one in particular, when
he spoke.

"Got a cigarette?"

I wished I'd had one because he was cute. Cute enough for me
to be curious about the bulge in his jeans and pray that his mother
had taught him to share. He was around 20 years old and 6 foot 2,
with green eyes and dark-red shoulder-length hair. The beginnings
of a beard shadow toughened up his otherwise angelic freckled
face. A tight swimmer's body was apparent beneath his thin knit
shirt, and his worn blue jeans were worn in just the right places.
A huge copper belt buckle and scuffed boots gave him the look of
a cowboy running away from home.

"Sorry, no. I don't smoke," I said. "Unfortunately," I added,
allowing sufficient time—if he had a brain to go with that cock

print—for him to notice I was talking to his package and not his equally interesting face.

"You from around here?"

"Just passing through," I answered. "Why? Is this a city worth being from?"

"Hell, no! It sucks!" He didn't seem to have any difficulty putting his feelings into words, despite how brief or lacking in substance. He was straight and I wasn't, and we didn't really have any difficulty figuring that part out.

But something about his manner told me that life wasn't treating him the way he felt he deserved. There may have been some sound reasons for that, but I wasn't into psychoanalysis. At least not tonight. He didn't have money for cigarettes, and I began to wonder what he'd be willing to do to get some. Nothing ventured, nothing gained. So I stuck my pole out over the water and let the hook dangle.

"Not everything that sucks is bad," I shared casually, smiling slightly.

He smiled back, but not really. I was silent for a short while, hoping for a sign. He didn't oblige. Some may have tossed in the towel, but I wasn't one. I like straight trade. The tougher the nut, the sweeter the meat.

"So where are you headed?" I asked.

"Nowhere at the moment. My ol' lady was suppose to drive up from Orlando and meet me here." The disappointment in his voice was extreme. Not sadness, not really anger any longer, just disappointment.

"And?" I prodded.

"She didn't fucking show," he continued. "I called her fucking house, and first she said she didn't have enough fucking gas, then she said the car was running funny."

"Why don't you just catch a bus down to Orlando?" I asked. I knew the answer, but it was important that he knew I knew. The straight-boy game has certain rules. Even if he wasn't aware of them, or wasn't a willing participant, we were still honor-bound to play by the rules.

"With what?" he responded as if I were the dumbest Cajun who ever left New Orleans. "My fucking looks?"

"Yes," I said, so calmly that it even surprised me.

He didn't answer, probably beginning to catch on but not quite sure. I could tell he wasn't interested. That glowing little light in his eyes shifted; I could practically see the hairs rise up on his back.

The ball was now in my court. Shoot or pass?

"Are you broke completely?" I asked, ignoring the danger signs.

"Pretty much," he answered, but guardedly. He didn't take his emerald eyes off me.

"Are you hungry?"

"Yeah," he said. No raised excitement, but a slight more awareness flashed in his eyes. "I haven't eaten since yesterday."

Since it was well past midnight, I imagined he had a nice rumble going on in that beautiful washboard stomach. I hoped he wasn't expecting me to offer him a free meal. Hell, no! His hungry stomach was a selling point. Without missing a step, I began my play, slow and steady.

"Well, here's what I see…" I looked him directly in the eyes. "You need a bus ticket. Am I correct?

He nodded.

"How much is it?

"To Orlando it's $27 one-way."

"OK," I went on. "And you need a few bucks for a meal and cigarettes."

Again he nodded.

"So 40 or 50 bucks should do it."

Another nod.

Time for the bomb.

"Well, I'm hungry too, but not for a hamburger. I'll slip you 50 bucks for a chance to eat at *your* restaurant." My eyes shifted to his crotch. It was possible I'd have a fight on my hands, but I didn't think so. He was tired and hungry, and that was my ace in the hole.

"Are you saying what I think you're saying?"

"Yes," I said, quietly and confidently.

"Sorry, buddy." He shrugged his shoulders slightly. "But you've got me wrong." He was much more controlled than I'd expected. "I'm not like that."

My heart thumped a bit faster. He was truly virgin territory. By his expression, I'd bet the farm no guy had ever dared approached him before.

"I know you're not," I said.

His face said he was torn between being relieved at my statement and confused about why I'd make such a proposition.

"I'm not interested in changing you," I said, almost in a whisper. I smiled slightly, but he didn't return it. "You're a good-looking guy, and I'm willing to pay you for your personal time. That's all. It's simply business." I lifted my hands and moved them as if presenting our surroundings to him on a silver platter. "It's just life in the big city," I announced quietly. The torture in his eyes seemed to disappear, but it was obvious he was still uncomfortable. "You don't need to do anything," I said. "Except relax. I'll do all the work."

He paused a moment to ponder it over but then said, "Sorry, I don't think so." Then he turned and walked back inside the terminal. Five minutes later I looked inside to see him sitting on a bench, his body slumped forward, his head in his hands.

I took off and roamed a block or two around the terminal. I had more than two hours left in Jacksonville and wanted to get a general lay of the land and its potential. Just because I'd struck out on the first try didn't mean other opportunities weren't around the corner.

But nothing turned up, so I made my way back to the station. As I rounded the edge of the building, I spotted my Orlando-bound lad once again standing outside. I found a spot of my own, giving him plenty of distance, and made no attempt to contact him. But suddenly he turned and walked toward me as if he'd changed his mind and wanted to fight. He didn't seem resigned or defeated. He seemed mad as hell.

"Do you know a place we can go?"

"I imagine two intelligent people like us should have no problem finding some privacy," I said. "Especially at this time of the night."

I stashed my bag in one of the bus station lockers, including my valuables, and shoved the key to the bottom of a pocket in my blue jeans. I was horny but not stupid. Well, not completely stupid. After a little exploration we found a jumping area called Jacksonville Landing, complete with a sidewalk café, bars, and waterfront ambience. The sidewalk along the river's edge seemed to extend the length of the entire bank, so we walked it until we were secretly lost among the shadows of waterfront shrubbery.

I sat down on a concrete bench and directed him to stand next to me.

"You mean right here?" he asked nervously.

I didn't pause to answer; I simply reached up and found the knot pushing its way against his pant leg. If this had been a more secure location, I would have enjoyed the process of making him rock-hard underneath the layer of cotton, but time wasn't a luxury here. Before he had a chance to remember he was straight and change his mind, I quickly opened his pants and retrieved what he had been holding securely for me these past 20 years of his life. He stood sentry like a Marine, head up, back straight, feet planted solidly on the ground while watching for passersby.

It's funny: Words aren't necessary when someone is sucking you off in a public area and the danger of getting caught is just as stimulating as the mouth around your cock. His cock wasn't hard when I pried it from his jeans, but it was full and heavy just the same. A thick patch of fiery red hair filled out the crotch and ascended in a thick trail to his belly button. He was more than nine inches long and just thick enough to cause my eyes to glance upward in thanks. A perfect fit.

I unsnapped his 501s, laid the fabric back, and slid my hands up, lifting his T-shirt to just below his nipples. I ran my fingers up and down his flat stomach muscles and through his thick pubic hair. He began to settle down slightly, making quiet murmuring sounds.

The area was darkened, but small slithers of light streamed in between the heavy foliage. His soft freckled skin glowed with a buttermilk complexion. Nothing tanned, nothing flawed. I pulled his jeans down enough to expose his almost blinding white ass and balls. Shifting him around slightly, I slid off the bench and onto my knees, taking his ball sac into my open mouth and devouring it. I felt him shift on his feet, compensating for the weight difference as he rose on his toes from the sensation, then settle back down, shoving his balls and groin into my face. His scent immediately intoxicated me, as my nose became lost in the tangled mass of cock and hair. There was no trace of body lotion or fragrant deodorants. He smelled of sweat and Ivory soap and cotton briefs.

By now his cock was hard as stone, standing outward from his body like a flagpole. I began at the base, running my tongue through the hairy maze, pulling and nibbling at its foundation. He shifted again; now his balls were free from my throat, free to hang, rubbing gently against my cheek. I was in no hurry to make him love me. But I knew he would.

He responded like a well-trained thoroughbred let out to run. His girlfriend hadn't made him jump like this. She hadn't made his cock quiver from a standing position, like it was doing now. I knew that and so did he. He confirmed it when he reached down and guided the head of his cock between my lips and down my throat. I didn't resist. It was important to him to have a sense of control. It was important to me to suck his cock. We were both happy.

"Gawd damn!" he whispered as his cock took a deep dive over my tongue to rub its head against my tonsils. "Where the fuck did you learn to suck cock like that?"

I didn't stop to give a résumé, and he didn't seem to mind. I slid my hands up and down the back of his upper legs, sliding his jeans below his knees, caressing and kneading the strong muscles beneath my fingers. As I edged up and over his ass cheeks, I gripped them roughly, pulling them apart as I shoved his cock forward and down my throat even farther. I felt his knees go weak as he bent them slightly and quickly regained his stance. His words grew guttural as he grabbed the back of my head.

"Gawd damn!" he repeated in his deep country whisper. "Fuck, yeah! Eat that fuckin' cock!"

I could tell he was close to shooting all he had. He bent his legs slightly while slipping his fingers through my hair and guiding me down on his cock. Soon he was bent down almost to a crouching stance, pulling my head and mouth into his steel cock. Through my eyes, his fire-red crotch and freckled stomach were all a blur. I couldn't focus, and my back and neck were beginning to ache. "Fuck yeah. Fuck yeah. I'm gonna cum," he murmured over and over, shoving his cock into my mouth.

He had gotten down so low now that he was sitting backward,

using his right hand to shove my head down on his cock, while his left hand was planted on the ground to keep his ass suspended a few inches in the air. All ideas of being a lookout for unwanted guests had been abandoned. His jeans were around his ankles now, so I had clear access to his cock; his balls hung freely, smacking against my chin as he maintained his rhythm.

"Fuck, I can't hold it," he chanted softly between breaths, but his onslaught didn't slow the least. His cock seemed to swell too big for my mouth to handle, and I found it hard to catch my breath between strokes. I reached up and supported myself, gripping his muscular thighs as they bounced on either side of my head. Without missing a stroke, he lifted his left hand off the ground and grabbed hold of the stone bench I had abandoned. This extra leverage shoved me even lower into his crotch—so fast that I lost my balance and fell forward off my knees, flat on my stomach. He didn't flinch but adjusted by dropping to his knees as well. Having no further need of the bench for support, place his left hand on my head and grabbed hold of the base of his cock with his right hand.

He continued to feed me his cock as if nursing a newborn. His strokes suddenly became slow and deep, less brutal. My lips grazed across his fingers as they wrapped around his cock each time he slipped my head down on his shaft, burying it so far down my throat I thought I'd gag from the pressure.

"Fuck, yeah. Fuck ,yeah." His voice was soft and gentle, like a whisper on the wind, as he slowly slid my head up and down his cock. His hard thighs closed together; I felt the hair on them brush against my ears as he guided my head back and forth along its appointed path. "Fuck, yeah," he said, and this time I tightened my suction around his cock, racing my tongue around the head.

"Ah, fuck. What the fuck are you doing?!" This time his words were barely audible. "Fuck, yeah," he said again. To my surprise, he pulled my mouth off his cock, leaving only the head resting between my lips and just inside my mouth. His thighs closed in around the side of my head, squeezing me like a vise, covering my ears so tight that I couldn't hear a sound. His cock didn't move; as his thighs tightened, he leaned into my body, pressing his stomach against the top of my head, smothering me with his groin.

I couldn't move. I couldn't breathe. I began to panic and thrash about in an effort to escape. Then he hit me. Hard! And I thought that my life was over. His hot thick cum shot out of his cock so hard, as it hit the back of my throat, that I thought he had smashed me against the head with a rock. My body jerked as my hands pawed at him like those of a drowning man desperately trying to find the surface. My cock began spurting, filling my jeans. He seemed to cum forever as I relished its reward greater than the air around me. His body trembled as he continued depositing his sperm and I continued to suck like an infant, draining him of every drop available.

I had the pleasure of licking and sucking him until his cock slowly receded back to a flaccid state. I had this pleasure not because he had suddenly decided that gay sex was OK, but simply because he was exhausted. He could barely move to object.

In his languid state, he confessed that he'd been locked in city jail for the past three months and had been saving himself for his girl. I silently thanked her for not showing up, presented him the wages he justly deserved, and gave his sweet ass a final pat before he pulled his jeans back up.

To this day I can't remember what his name was, or if I ever asked him what it was. It wasn't an essential element

There were no fond goodbyes. I found my way inside the closest bar. An Irish coffee and a chili burger with fries, and I was good again.

My bus arrived on time.

## ORLANDO BOUND

As with most things in life, timing is everything, or it's a bitch, or it's a bitch about everything. Either way, I made some serious eye contact with a young Hispanic man kissing his girlfriend goodbye who then stepped in line and climbed aboard my waiting coach. I was sitting in the last seat, the three-man seat, all by my lonesome self. He joined me, and I put him next to the window. Less room to escape.

"Welcome to my parlor," said the spider to the fly.

# GO WEST

**SIMON SHEPPARD**

For a while I led a bicoastal existence. Back then my route cross-country was on the ground—not several thousand feet in the air—and that meant, every so often, an unavoidable dose of Highway 70. I didn't own a car, so it also meant depending on the kindness of strangers (with wheels).

One winter I was trying to get back to the West Coast after a failed attempt to fit into New York City. I'd been living on the just-recently-fashionable Bowery. This was long enough ago that John and Yoko were hanging out at the bar down on the corner, or so I'd heard.

But Manhattan in January is never a good place to be when things aren't going well and your boyfriend has just dumped you, so I fled to my parents' house in the suburbs, with plans to escape to the Golden Gate. I'd arrived in New York via Greyhound, short of sleep thanks to the all-night banter of drunken GIs. And, hell, even if I *had* been able to drift off, my pillow had been stolen when I got off the bus to take a piss. This time around, I'd try sharing a ride.

I put up notices at nearby Princeton University, a pillar of the

Ivy League. Sure enough, several days later somebody phoned.

"He sounded very...masculine," said my Mom, relaying the message. I'd recently come out to her, and her dubious tone carried a multiplicity of possible meanings. I studiously ignored them all.

I returned his call—he was living in a frat house—and Mom was right: He *did* sound masculine. Whatever. I needed a ride, not a date. (Well, I needed a date too, but I was unlikely to find that by putting up ads at the Princeton student union.) It was easily arranged. We both needed to get to the Bay Area: We'd share gas money and driving, and he'd come pick me up the following week.

When Mike drove up, he looked less like some hyperbutch jock than the reed-slim business major he in fact was. He was gratifyingly handsome; I hoped he drove as good as he looked. I threw my stuff in the trunk and Mike and I hit the wintry road. My mother, all misty-eyed to see me go, watched forlornly as we pulled away.

Fueled by lousy gas-station coffee, we talked in that strained way strangers in enforced companionship often do. He had a girlfriend, I found out. Of course.

"She gave me this sweater for Christmas," he told me. It was a white knit fisherman's jobbie, which was then very much in vogue. I had one too; my mother had knit it for me.

"Nice," I replied. "Want me to drive for a while?"

I took the wheel for the first few hundred miles, rolling down the icy turnpike toward the setting sun. After a while the conversation stalled. *Oh, well,* I thought. *Just as long as the car keeps running.*

Just before Pittsburgh Mike took over, after fueling up on high-test coffee and low-test gas. A few hours later, somewhere near Columbus, it started to snow, flurries at first, then really dumping down. We pulled over and, in the freezing dark, struggled to put on chains.

"I'm going to get in the back seat and try to nap," I said. My fingers were so cold they hurt. "OK?"

"Sure thing," Mike said in that deep voice of his.

As we resumed hurtling through the dark, I asked, "You sure you're going to be all right driving?"

"Still going strong."

"How about a back rub?" Tired as it might have been, this was a gambit that had successfully gotten me into the pants of several guys, though none of them had been ostensibly straight. But then, as a politically aware gay man, I found the whole idea of chasing after hets faintly objectionable. Who knows? At that moment, maybe I really did have just a back rub in mind.

"That'd be good." Flat, noncommittal.

I sat behind Mike and kneaded his shoulders through the bulky white wool. Then I turned my attention to his neck. His flesh was warm and smooth beneath my still-chilled fingers.

Damn, I was getting a hard-on. My hands moved over his collarbone. Mike didn't respond—he just kept navigating through the snowy night. Either bold or stupid—What was he going to do, throw me out?—I leaned over far enough to move my palms over his sweater-clad chest.

"Mmm," Mike said, barely audible over the metallic song of the tire chains. I began to knead his chest. "Mmm."

I tugged up the bulky sweater. Just a thin T-shirt now covered Mike's straight-boy flesh. I felt his prominent nipples through the soft cloth. This trip was turning out better than I'd planned. I reached down, nearly dislocating my shoulder, and pulled Mike's T-shirt free from his pants. His belly was smooth and lean, rippling with muscle. I couldn't help myself. I slid my fingertips beneath his jeans, under the elastic waistband of his jeans, and felt his heat. So close, so close...

"I'm going to pull off up here."

"Huh?" I said.

"Rest stop. Gotta pee."

"Where are we?"

"Still in Ohio somewhere."

"Ohio, huh?" Horniness had made me stupid.

Mike and I ran out to the cinder-block roadside rest stop. My urge to get out of the freezing cold competed with my hopes not to slip on the icy sidewalks and land embarrassingly on my ass. The rest stop was a tile-lined pit, but it was there and it was warm. I wanted to catch a glimpse of Mike's dick, but he headed right for a stall and shut the door. What a tease.

I heard his piss streaming into the bowl long after I'd shaken off and zipped up. He finally emerged. "Needed that," he said. What kind of a smile *was* that?

When we got back to the car, I abandoned the backseat in favor of a place right beside him. "You're OK to drive some more?" I asked.

He nodded and switched on the radio. Country music. The snow slacked off a bit as we headed for Columbus or Springfield or some damn place.

I tried to make conversation—honest, I did—but Mike was having none of it. So I did the only thing I could think to do under the circumstances. I lay my hand on his knee.

Mike the straight boy didn't react, not so much as a flinch, which was probably just as well, given the slippery road. I watched his profile as I slid my left hand slowly from his knee up his leg. Stoic. That was OK; I didn't want enthusiasm, just acquiescence. I stopped mid-thigh and kneaded his leg. He leaned back just a little and moved his leg toward me. Clearly, that meant: *You have the right of way. Proceed.* So I did. By the time my pinkie brushed his denim-clad crotch, my own hard cock was leaking pre-cum into my underwear. But I didn't want to whip it out and maybe spook him. Tammy Wynette was singing about her D-I-V-O-R-C-E.

I took the giant leap and groped his basket. He was hard. I said a silent thank-you to Jesus and all the saints of Southwest Ohio. My right hand joined my left, and I semi-awkwardly pulled down Mike's zipper. It was tough to fish his hard cock out through the fly of his briefs, but where there's a will, there's a dick. Even in the semi-gloom, his cock looked eminently suckable. Not too big. Not too small. Just right. So, hungry as Goldilocks, I managed to scrunch down on the floor and lay my head on his lap. Obligingly, Mike lifted his right arm to make room, then readjusted his grip on the steering wheel. His forearm rested lightly on my neck. I inhaled the almost-fresh odor of his pubic hair.

"OK," he said in that deep voice of his. Succinct. I gobbled down his cock.

Now, there are probably better places to give head than barreling down the interstate in an Ohio snowstorm, but at that moment I couldn't think of a single one. I sucked hungrily on that straight boy's Ivy League dick in a way I imagined no female ever would. Sure, I'd met women who said they liked to give blow jobs, but not one of them seemed half as obsessed with cock as is your average homo.

We sped along, the car thrumming beneath my knees, my mouth working up and down Mike's hard flesh. Somewhere near Dayton, I'd guess, Mike's cock finally fed me, pumping a big, sweetish load in my mouth. For one giddy moment I thought he might spasm and jam down on the gas pedal, which brought to mind the bootleg European paperback of *Hollywood Babylon* I'd read. It's story of the famous film director who'd died giving head to his chauffeur while the Rolls wove perilously close to the cliffs overlooking the Pacific. Kaboom. But Mike was all business and cum, and after I'd drunk the last drop, he reached down, tucked himself back in, and zipped up.

"I'm going to pull over at the next exit and you can take over, OK?" he said. "I'm going to get in back and get some shut-eye." Shut-eye. Cute.

And so 10 minutes later I was driving toward Indiana, snow swirling in the headlights while Johnny Cash was barking out, "My name is Sue. How do you do?" We hurtled through the interstate in the dark, the almost-stranger and I. That's what we were doing: hurtling. The taste of his cum was still on my lips.

We didn't stop for more than a few minutes until we reached Missouri. We lingered only a few minutes in St. Louis—the place where, several years later, Steve, Kristin, and I would be stranded in a blinding rainstorm. (Steve's old Dodge broke down in the shadow of the Arch.) Steve and Kristin would crash in a house full of hippies, while I'd somehow end up in a dorm at Washington University. My host, a dauntingly hunky lacrosse player, would let me suck him before he drifted off to sleep, his stick leaned up against a wall, his girlfriend's picture on the bedside table. The next day Kristin would go shopping with one of the hippies and get busted for shoplifting when her host tried to make off with a sweater. Kristin would jump bail.

But that was quite another story, far in the future. For now, I sat in a Denny's with Mike eating scrambled eggs in Missouri, and it was as if the blow job in Ohio had never happened, nor the second one when he awoke and I, bored as I was horny, got him off near Terre Haute.

In fact, Mike and I would only make small talk the whole trip, never so much as mentioning the sex all the way to San Francisco, where he dropped me off in the Haight and headed over to Berkeley. Jesus, we even shook hands. Shook hands. We exchanged addresses, but we knew we'd never see each other again. California, after all, is a big place.

Appropriately, I arrived in the land of free love horny as the day is long. During that whole transcontinental odyssey, I'd cum only once. Somewhere in the wilds of Utah I reached over, unbuttoned Mike's pants, got his stiffening just-right cock out, did the same to my own, spit in both my hands, and beat us both off till we shot, fairly messily. I had to wipe the jizz off the upholstery. I mean, hell, if you're going to masturbate with a straight Protestant boy while hurtling down an interstate, you might as well do it in Salt Lake City.

# MY LIFE WITH LEGS

**DEAN DURBER**

I mentioned it just briefly in passing. "You've got really nice legs," I said.

My exact words. That's all. No big deal. Nothing meant by it. But then *he* got obsessed and kept hassling *me*. He harassed me, stalked me, hunted me down, and kept asking me to tell him more. I was just trying to be a good player. That's all I ever wanted out of this: some weekly exercise, a soccer pitch, one ball, and a team of 11 men. I never asked for things to get complicated.

"It's just like when kids do sports real hard from an early age," I tried to explain. "And their bodies start to form into a particular shape, depending on the kind of sport they are doing. Swimmers get broad shoulders and flat stomachs. Gym freaks get big pectorals."

I was trying not to picture these images as I spoke. I was trying really hard.

"And you've got good legs. Just like a soccer player should have. You're the only one on the team who's got them. That's all I meant by it."

He gazed into my eyes, standing there wearing his tight blue shorts. I tried not to look.

"You been looking?"

"What?"

"You been checking out all the guys' legs?"

"Nah. Well, yes. But not like that, mate. It's just something I noticed, that's all. I'm a perceptive kind of guy. I didn't mean anything by it, mate."

I felt myself burning up. I left him sitting on the bench in a daze, while I went for a pretend piss and splashed cold water onto my face. The redness in my cheeks started to cool. As I followed him out onto the playing field for the second half, I noticed he had pulled up his socks. His once-bare shins had disappeared, covered now by red and white nylon that stretched right up to and over his knees.

I hated soccer as a kid. I used to run away before kickoff— did that so many times that the school sent me to see some shrink who promised to cure me. It never worked. And now my legs are skinny. They're not nice at all. I was hot and sticky—too tired to be running around this field trying to tackle guys always twice my size. I had this sudden urge to flee, to run home.

I wondered what bruise or injury I would leave with tonight. What sore part of my body would fade into nothing as I revisited in my mind's eye the two of us standing naked in the shower, me rubbing soap up and down the bronzed flesh of his legs?

The shrink had told me soccer was a good thing for normal boys to do and that I should try harder if I wanted to be normal. Fourteen years later, I'm still trying. But I can't help myself. I just imagine what would happen if only the two of us showed up one week, and we had to cancel the match. We'd chat while we stepped out of our tiny, tight shorts. Together we'd bury our cocks deep inside our pants, careful to keep them well away from the pain of the zippers. I'd watch as his hand cupped his bulge and see his pubic hairs sprouting through his fingers. Or maybe he'd take off his shorts and stand talking to me, his limp cock dangling down between his slightly hairy, heavily tanned legs. I'd start to play with my dick, stroking it gently. He'd start doing the same. I'd reach out and—

"For fuck's sake, man!"

The ball flew past me. It headed straight toward our goal. All I could see was a pair of hairy legs chasing behind it.

"What the fuck's wrong with you?"

There were legs panicking all around me.

"You let him get straight past you, you stupid fuckhead!"

Those legs were on my mind as I lay in bed that night revisiting the changing room and the showers. I wanked, came, and spread creamy hot spunk all over my skinny thighs. I reached for a tissue. Why did I have to ruin everything? What was wrong with me that I couldn't just play a game of soccer? I bet the comments had got around. I bet he had told them what I'd said. I hurled the box of tissues at the wall on the other side of the room and left the semen to dry on my body.


"You've made me feel really self-conscious," he told me the next time I saw him. "I'm totally paranoid about my legs now."

"Why? I said they were nice. You shouldn't be—"

I tried to lower my voice, to not sound so excited by the thought of him thinking about me. I wondered whether he lay awake at night looking down at his own naked flesh, rubbing his hands along the length of his thighs, over his knees, and down his calves. Did this make him hard? I thought I saw a patch of white crust splattered across his thigh. Yeah, and—

"Yeah, and now I'm thinking that everyone's watching them all the time. I can't go out in the street without wondering who's checking them out. Do you think all the other guys on the team have noticed them?"

"I doubt it!"

His face dropped.

"I mean, they might have. They could have, sure. It's just, they're probably concentrating more on the game, you know."

"Yeah, I suppose."

I turned my back and readjusted my cock.

"So why weren't you?"

"What?"

"Why weren't you concentrating on the ball?"

"Is this about that goal last week? Look, I didn't see him coming. I was sorta—"

"Nah. Not that."

"What are you talking about then?"

"Why weren't you concentrating on the ball when you noticed my legs?"

"Dude!" I said deeply. "Dude! You walk around in shorts all the time. I didn't notice them. They're just there. It's not as if I am standing around looking at your legs all the time. Jesus man! What do you take me for? What do you think I am? What are you saying, man? I just said you had nice legs. Forget it. Forget I ever mentioned it."

I gasped for breath.

"Oh, right. Sorry then, man. I just thought you were genuinely interested in my legs, that's all."

He slammed the locker door.

"I am. I mean, not like that or anything, but you know, between mates, you've got a nice pair of legs."

He smiled again, and I felt my cock start to rise again. It rose quickly.

"Thanks, mate. That's kewl."

He stepped closer and placed his hand on my shoulder. The hairs on our thighs brushed together.

"I really like that."


We won the game that night. Our first victory in five weeks. The team rushed to the pub to celebrate. I lingered in the changing room, drying myself and rubbing the towel harshly over my body. He stepped out of the steam, his body dripping wet. A small white towel clung tightly to his waist. I could just see the curved base of his ass cheeks.

"Good game tonight."

I froze, wondering how long I had been standing there pretending to dry my cock.

"What?"

"I said, good game tonight."

"Y…" I stuttered. "Yeah. We did well."

There was a silence.

"So, you heading off to the pub now?" I asked.

"Nah, not tonight."

"Why not? Won't the guys be expecting you?"

"Not really into it. Rather just have a quiet drink somewhere on my own."

"Oh, OK."

I shoved my dirty gear into my bag and slung it over my shoulder.

"I'll see you next week then."

I walked toward the door.

"Hey," he said.

He stood staring at me, his chest still covered in droplets of water. I watched them as they slid over the bumps of his nipples, down his flat stomach, disappearing beneath his towel.

"My girlfriend's working early in the morning, so we can't go back to mine. But how about a quiet drink at your place?"

"Sure," I spat enthusiastically. "I mean, yeah, sure, mate, whatever."

"So what is it about legs that you're attracted to?" he asked me as I handed him an ice-cold beer from the fridge.

"Mate!"

I feigned laughter. Our bottles clinked together.

"No, seriously, dude, I'm interested. Really, I am."

"What in?"

I sat down to stop the trembling of my body.

"How is it that you can look at another man's legs and find them attractive? I mean, I'm interested in how a man can do that."

He sat on the other side of the coffee table with his legs spread wide apart. I unfolded mine and then shuffled them open. His left hand started to stroke up and down his thigh.

"I mean, is it because your legs are so skinny?"

"Thanks."

"No offense, but you know, you don't exactly have what they call soccer player's legs, do you?"

He was grinning. I swigged on my beer and watched him as he stroked his own muscular flesh.

"I was thinking that maybe you like my legs because you wish you could have them."

He left a pause, then lifted his face.

"I mean, like maybe you wish you had legs like this."

"It's not something I think about all that often."

"Really? It's just I thought—"

"What?"

"And some of the guys were saying that—"

"What?"

He placed his beer on the table, stretched his arms above his head, and looked up to the ceiling. The tip of the bottle balanced on my bottom lip as I gazed deep into the center of his shorts.

"I mean, if you wanted to touch them, just to know what they feel like…"

He breathed out heavily.

"I'd be kewl with you doing that."

My cock jolted.

"Is this why you noticed them?" he asked, as he started to pound his cock into my ass within minutes of my fingers touching his thighs.

He had thrown me down on top of the table with his full strength. The look in his eyes scared me with pleasure.

"Were you trying to imagine what was between them?"

I couldn't respond. My eyes started to roll. His heavy panting separated his words into unnatural sentences that wanted to flow but couldn't. Droplets of his sweet stinking sweat fell onto my chest.

"Do you run around that field thinking about this dick fucking your ass?"

"No!" I muttered.

"What?"

"I said no. That's not what—"

"Don't you fucking lie to me."

He rammed in his cock as far as it would go and pushed hard against my bruised cheeks. I started to scream, cry, and laugh.

"Think you're some kind of fucking straight guy playing soccer to prove you're a man?"

He pushed my legs right up and over my head. My toes touched the table. I could almost lick my own cock, and my own cum dribbled onto my tongue.

"Think you can play like a man, and nobody will know what you're really after?"

His breath was getting faster. I reached up and grabbed at his chest. I felt his heart beating out of control. He stared down at me.

"Everyone knows you're a faggot on that field."

He spat into my face. Phlegm mingled with cum in my mouth.

"A faggot with my cock up his ass."

I grabbed hold of his sweaty back. My hands slipped down over the smoothness of his ass cheeks, and I felt the light, wispy hairs at the top of his thighs. I groaned. I grabbed hard at his flesh and dug my nails in deep.

"I just love your legs," I whispered. "I just love your fucking legs."

His body spasmed above me. The whites of his eyes spanned into my view. I felt his hot sperm shoot inside me and trickle through the gap between his cock and my hole. He collapsed and spread himself over my naked body. Our sweaty chests stuck together like glue. The table wobbled while I continued to tickle the tops of his legs. I listened to him as he lay there breathing slowly, slightly twitching and moaning.

On the field the following Monday he was wearing tracksuit pants. Every inch of his naked flesh had been removed from my gaze. We lost the match and I didn't care. I had no real interest in soccer. It wasn't my game. I knew that. I wondered how to break the news of my departure. I thought about what the rest of the team might say in the pub that evening. Yeah, soccer's a real man's game. And I couldn't stick it. Because I'm a—

"Shit game, ay?"

His hand touched my shoulder.

"Yeah. Real shit."

I could smell the sweat seeping from the pores of his armpits.

"You coming next week?"

"I don't think so," I said. "I'm not really enjoying it anymore. It's not my scene, you know."

I lowered my face. He sat down beside me on the bench and started to take off his boots.

"That's a real shame."

I looked up.

"A real shame."

I watched him as he slowly eased himself out of his tracksuit pants and then shuffled up closer. His legs were parted and shaking.

"I was thinking it's way too hot to be playing in these pants. Guess next week I'll just have to go back to wearing the old shorts."

# DELIVERY

### QUENTZAL Q. OTTAL

I was groggy. Under the intense light of a full moon, I had spent half the night scraping paint off 100-year-old windowpanes in my recently escrowed Craftsman in Hillcrest. With a steaming coffee mug in hand and thong undies barely covering prosecutable bodily exposure, I opened the screen door to look for my morning newspaper, which had become part of my morning ritual. I had already called in two complaints to *The San Diego Union-Tribune* about my newly assigned delivery person. It seemed this bald-headed, body-pierced sadist enjoyed line-driving the morning news from the driver's side of his '89 Chevy truck, while barely screeching the brakes to a half-second stop, in an effort to minimize his time on the road.

The marine layer was thick, an eerie gray cloud lying low over the neighborhood like an eerie theatrical spectacle from *Macbeth*. After some "toil and trouble," I located the newspaper, which was trapped high in the overhanging bougainvillea above the porch. I sprinted and jumped up several times—too damn lazy to retreat into the house for a step-up stool—but came up empty-handed. I heard Dario's voice come from across the street like a plaintive howl. I wondered if he had caught a glimpse of my full moon through the thick, smoky fog cover of the dawn.

" 'Morning!" he shouted in his deep Southern drawl as he crossed the street toward me.

" 'Morning, Dario. That damn paperboy did it again. He's got to go. He's pitched my newspaper into the bougainvillea for the very last time."

As I finished my statement I felt his breath suddenly on my neck like a warm, soothing breeze. There he stood, in the ruffled glory of his baggy boxers. He looked like an archangel, ruddy among the morning vapors.

"Anything I can do?"

"You can help a distressed Hillcrest jungle queen retrieve what's left of his morning paper."

Dario jumped up to get the paper but couldn't reach it. After several failed attempts he looked over to me. "Hey, I need your help," he said, motioning for me to stand in front of him. "Plant your feet directly in front of me and spread your legs real wide."

"Now, Dario, what would your wife think?"

"She'd think I'm being neighborly," he countered matter-of-factly.

Being equally neighborly, I spread my legs as Dario lowered himself, placing his head between my legs. As he lifted up I was able to grab the paper. In the short time that my legs were wrapped around Dario's neck I was hard and my cock pulsated against the back of his neck like a trapped water hose.

"Got it!" I yelled.

Dario bent forward, allowing me release from his muscular shoulders back to ground level and allowing him to snatch a panoramic view of my widened crack as I landed. I lingered for a split second while I tucked—as best I could—my expanded meat into the elastic material of the thong. "Coffee's brewed," I said. "Want some?"

"Sure. Uwe's out of the house for the weekend in Bakersfield, doing a 'mom' run. I was just about ready to walk down to 7-Eleven for some coffee." Dario and his wife Uwe were the only neighbors who had opened up their house to me since my arrival in the neighborhood a few weeks before. They didn't bake me any cakes, but they did offer a few sensible joints and a glass of wine or two: a nice straight couple living comfortably in this predominantly gay neighborhood. Uwe was a very attractive woman (tight African butt, mountain-peak titties, and a SlenderElla waistline) who was self-employed as an engraving artist with a limited but exclusive clientele. She found it safer to live among queens than be hit upon constantly in other areas of the city. Dario had a business degree and wore well-tailored suits to work five days a week (very *GQ*) but was anxious to strip down to jockey boxers in the evening. He didn't mind the ogling from the gays; he actually felt a genuine compliment and usually responded with a broad smile that melted the ogler on the spot until he said, "My wife thinks so too."

While pouring Dario his coffee I noticed a new visitor peaking out between the airy spaces of his buttoned-down fly. "Cream?" I said as casually as possible while looking at his fly pattern. Caught off guard for a second, Dario responded, "And sugar, if you don't mind." He took his seat at the kitchen table and stirred his coffee. I noticed one of the buttons on his boxers had popped open, allowing for a better view of his ample crotch. We sipped our coffee as I hummed a "come hither" ditty.

"The place is shaping up real nice," Dario said as his flesh peeked out once again. I slowly got out of my chair and filled up my mug, allowing Dario to feast his eyes upon my muscled and taut rear cheeks. "I have to tell you," he went on, "your ass cheeks are right up there with Uwe's."

"Really? Oh, Dario, looks like we have a visitor. Is he thinking of Uwe's ass or mine?" I joked as Dario's member jumped Olympic fashion through the cotton fabric of his boxers, almost claiming another button casualty. I knelt before him, looked up into those blue-gray eyes of his, and covered his growing flesh tool with my famished lips while calmly pulling the chair out from the table for easier access. Neither of us objected to the chair legs scraping against the tile as we both positioned ourselves for a probable café con leche.

I moved my tongue up and down his member with the slow-ness of a snail, lingering upon the manly scent of his flesh. Dario placed his hand on my head but didn't direct or force a direction. Instead, he simply sighed in a hushed baritone. "Oh, man…" he softly cried out. I pushed deeper into the widening slit of the boxers and found ample-sized balls covered in a red-blond layer of baby-fine hair. I placed his legs over my shoulders as I attacked the fleshy sacs that pushed his ass to the edge of the chair shelf. I smelled the fragrance of his ass tissue and allowed my hands free reign over his taut thighs. I felt his hands reach out around my back. We established a slow rhythm, and both of us appeared in no hurry to get anywhere fast. As I climbed his ever-growing tool with my moistened lips, I played with the lips of his butt and felt no discernable resistance. I stopped to catch my breath and lowered his legs from my shoulders, removing his drawers and my pre-cum-stained thong.

Dario got up from the chair and positioned me out and over the kitchen table. He allowed his cock to settle in the valley between my cheeks, just moving through the mounds like a complacent snake. He walked his cock up and down my back, returning into the folds between my ass-cheeks. He reached for the soft butter spread on the table. "The condoms are in the sugar bowl behind the packets of Sweet'n Low," I told him. He sorted through the packets and pulled out a condom. He covered his cock with the butter and applied more directly into the bud of my ass. I felt his thick fingers probing for entrance and I pushed against his warmed digits.

Dario had slowly worked in four fingers, and my rhythm had increased. He covered his cock with the condom and placed the wide mushroom-capped head on my butter-moistened rosebud. "Go on and get inside, Dario," I told him. "You're a welcome visitor." He grabbed my muscled tits and pinched them hard while increasing his thrusting action, pushing the table forward with each thrust. His hands followed the line from my chest through torso country and cupped my engorged cock. My blood-filled member met his hands as his blood-thickened member grew inside me. He covered my ear cavity with his hungry mouth and ran his tongue over the entire area like a cleanup crew after a natural disaster. The groans deep within him traveled up and increased in volume as we both shot our jism at the same time, like sun rays breaking through dense fog. I felt his warmth travel through the condom inside me, while my own juices flowed out through his cupped hand onto the kitchen table, allowing for a stream of cum that marked the table in pearl rivulets until it ran from the table and dripped onto the floor. Dario's body remained splayed over mine and we stayed still for a time, listening to the sounds of each other's breathing.

As Dario slowly raised himself and pulled his cock from my flesh tunnel, I listened to his repeated postcoital sighs of passion. From my spread-eagled and winged position on the table, I looked back at him and noticed that the fog had lifted and the light of the day was filtering through the panes of glass I had scraped throughout the previous night.

"Allow me," I said as I lifted his legs, one at a time, to put his boxer shorts back on his now butter-flavored body.

"Wow," he muttered with glazed eyes. "Thanks for the coffee."

"And thanks for being such a concerned neighbor," I told him.

I walked to the gate entrance and gave Dario the "all clear" signal. As I watched him return to his home across the street—a dazzling portrait in crumpled cotton boxers—I made a mental note to call up the newspaper and offer a kind thank-you for the bang-up job the paperboy was doing.

# ONE-TIME DEAL

**JOHN SCOTT DARIGAN**

"**S**o, my parents left town this morning." My next-door neighbor, Rob, was making small talk for reasons I couldn't immediately discern after he'd overthrown his yellow and blue Nerf football into my backyard.

It was the summer of 1985, and I was truly minding my own business, working on my tan, reclining on a lounge chair, and reading a book from my assigned summer reading list: something lesser known by Salinger.

Rob wore a pair of tight athletic shorts and no shirt, and his darkly tanned body gleamed with sweat. He was speaking, but I wasn't completely with him. I could see the bulge of his dick, which was somehow impossibly and wonderfully at eye level. I had to remind myself to stay focused on his face: *Don't look at his dick, don't look at his dick, DON'T look at his dick...* It was like a mantra in my head.

"So, wanna spend the night?"

Now this was an interesting segue.

"You mean tonight?"

"Yeah, why not? It'll give us a chance to catch up." He flashed a quizzical look. "Why did we stop talking to each other, anyway?"

"You said you couldn't hang out with a sophomore."

"Oh, yeah." Then he gave a look like he was trying to figure out a challenging math problem and said, "Well, since, I'm no longer a senior, guess we're good to go."

I told him I'd be over at 5 o'clock.


I'd had a crush on Rob for more than a few years. We were fast friends when he first moved into the house next to mine years ago, when our sprawling development was just getting started. I would watch the construction guys build his place, then sneak in once they'd all gone home (before the doors with locks were hung). I'd walk from room to room, wondering who would inhabit the place, hoping there would be a boy my age.

Rob was two years older. We got along fine until he entered middle school. I was still in elementary school, and it was like there was suddenly an ocean between us. We'd see each other around the neighborhood, but we didn't ride on the same school bus or eat in the same cafeteria, and our age groups were so noticeably different. Soon, we barely acknowledged each other at all.

I'd be in my room, studying or reading from stacks of library books, and the sound of his laughter would snake in through the second-floor open window. I'd crouch down and steal a glance at him from in between the branches of the oak on the front lawn. He was always with a good-looking football jock. I'd watch until they stopped doing whatever it was they were doing and disappeared into the house. Then I'd jack-off to a wrestling fantasy— the kind that would start innocently and turn into a steamy, unexpected, male-on-male sex romp—using the crusty T-shirt (hidden under my bed) to clean up.

Early in my freshman year, I decided that playing a sport would make my college applications seem more attractive, so I joined the lacrosse team. I made junior varsity, and Rob took notice. I'd be out in the front yard running and throwing the ball back and forth with Bryan Fulmer from up the street. I took to maneuvering the stick quite well and was an impressive runner, which helped in my position as midfielder.

Once, Rob strolled over and, having never played lacrosse, asked to try Bryan's stick. He worked it like an expert. We ran and threw the ball back and forth for over an hour while Bryan looked glum on the sidelines.

Rob was one of those guys—an expert at everything he tried.

After that day Rob would arrive at the bus stop a little early (instead of running out the door like he usually did), and although he wouldn't engage in conversation with me, I'd catch him looking in my direction, only to look away when our eyes locked. I started to get a *vibe.*

Rob never had girlfriends. He wasn't the type to make out or cop a feel at the lockers. And he let Sue Provost, a bulky field hockey player, wear his football jersey on game days. He was always wrestling with his buddies in the backyard.

And now this.

My mind raced as he walked off, his perfect back rippling under the sun. I put my paperback down, raced into the house, and locked myself in the bathroom. I looked in the mirror, messed with my hair, spiking it. There was my body. I'd been using the weight set that had sat in our damp basement untouched for years, and my physique was starting to see some good definition. All that time on the lacrosse field in summer league hadn't hurt either. For the first time in my life I saw myself and noticed that I was turning out OK. I flexed my biceps and did my best Incredible Hulk pose.

Then I went downstairs and worked out for an hour.

Just before 5 o'clock, I jumped from the shower and changed my clothes at least 10 times. I finally decided on OP corduroy shorts and a recently purchased Newport Blue T-shirt. I had my own money from a newspaper route and was just starting my obsession with clothes. I ran from the house yelling to my Mom that I'd be back in the morning. She stopped me on the way out and told me to be careful. She knew Rob had his driver's license and didn't like that I was being vague about the evening's agenda.

I rang the doorbell. Rob had central air conditioning, so all doors and windows were shut tight. I could hear Led Zeppelin blaring on the stereo. Rob came to the door looking like something out of Greek mythology. He was sweating—which seemed strange since the place was about 60 degrees inside—and confessed that he was working out in the basement where there was no air conditioning.

"I'm just finishing up. Could you give me a spot?"

"Sure."

I followed him, but I remembered the lay of the land from the days we used to play together, not to mention our houses were exact duplicates in blueprint. He had a nicer set of weights than I did and a bench with the letters "DP" on its movable back. He was bench-pressing more weight than I'd ever seen anyone lift.

"Are you sure you want that much on the bar?"

He laughed. "I just did the 180 without you, I'm adding."

"What do you weigh?" I asked.

"160."

"Wow. You bench over your own weight."

"Sweet, isn't it?" He flexed for me.

"I wouldn't know." I walked around to the area behind the bench with a sulk of inadequacy.

"What do you bench?" The question I dreaded.

"Let's stay focused on you and your gargantuan feat."

"Leave my feet out of it—how much?" He playfully punched me in the stomach. I blushed. He sat down on the bench and began to let out big breaths of air. I took my place behind him.

"Let me know if you want a lot or a little help."

"I want no help," he said. "Only help me if I need it."

Now I was sweating. I felt as if the pressure was all on *me* to perform. He lifted the bar up and brought it down to his chest. I stared at the bulge that was like a mountain range protruding from the middle of his shorts. Three reps—then I assisted with two more. He was very pleased.

"Thanks, bud. I'm gonna shower. You need one?"

"Now? With you?" I was confused, flustered.

"No, fag." He smiled. "We have two showers."

"I was just joking."

"It's cool, we shower with guys all the time, right?"

He turned from me and walked up the stairs. I followed, wanting to reach out and caress the hair on his legs, but the idea that he was interested now seemed too impossible to fathom.

"Fix a drink. My Dad's JD is at the bar in the living room. I need a shot."

"JD?"

"Jack Daniels. Never mind, I'll get it after the shower."

I was watching HBO (another luxury Rob had that was lacking in my household). He carried two small glasses and a large rectangular bottle with a black label and white writing.

"Do you drink much, Drew?"

"Yeah," I stammered, "at those bonfires, sometimes."

"That's just beer, right?"

"Uh-huh."

"Time for the real thing. One shot now then we'll grab some pizza at the hut, bring it back and hang out. Sound all right?"

I followed his lead and downed the entire shot. He laughed when my face got all contorted. I couldn't help it—the stuff was nasty.

"What's in that stuff? People drink this for pleasure?"

"You'll see. It makes you feel good after awhile."

"I'll take your word for it."

We decided to eat in at the restaurant once we got there. The place was empty and the waitress was a cute and perky blond Rob knew from school. He said she'd slip us all kinds of extra food (which she did). I listened and contributed nothing as they talked about their plans for fall now that they were free from high school. I was envious. I wanted to go to college. I still had two more years of Shanendehowa hell.

Thoroughly stuffed, we ambled back to Rob's tiny Toyota Tercel and drove home.

I had a hard-on for the whole ride.

There weren't any streetlights or electrical wires strung from pole to pole in our development. It was underground. So the place always seemed deserted after a certain hour at night when most people had gone to bed.

It was at this hour—somewhere around 11 o'clock, that I had my sixth or seventh shot of JD and was laughing hysterically like a crazy man. I kept telling Rob how great he was and how I idolized him, how much fun I was having, how I would do anything for him—*anything*.

And then I passed out.

I woke up, probably not much later, and found myself on my back looking up at a ceiling fan that oscillated wildly. It was making me sick, so I turned my head to the side. The couch that we were sitting on had been transformed into a bed. The room was dark—just the golden light of HBO: Meryl Streep in *Out of Africa*.

I looked down at myself and saw that I was in my underwear. I panicked. *Did he take my shorts off?*

Rob was nowhere in sight. I heard the toilet flush and he came out from the bathroom just off the family room. I groaned, pretending I was asleep and turned my head to his direction when he sat down. He was also in his underwear.

"What did I miss?" I asked innocently.

He chuckled. "You don't remember?"

"No. Where are my shorts?"

"You took them off—after you asked if I ever messed around with a guy."

"I did?"

"Yeah. Then you touched my back, got undressed. And I went to the bathroom."

"What happened to your clothes?"

"I left them in the bathroom." He leaned in close and, like it was the most natural, expected behavior in the world, touched the area around my nipple. It sent chills down my spine. I couldn't stop shaking.

We rolled around the bed until we were more comfortable. I kept thinking: *This is actually happening.* I tried to kiss him, but he wouldn't allow it, so I stayed focused on his furry legs and his cock. I took it in my mouth and he went crazy. He held on to my head and shoved it deep, pushing it into my throat and making me choke. He got off on it. I told him to go slower, but he wouldn't listen. My mouth was open wide to accommodate his size.

He wanted to sixty-nine, so we gave that a try for a while. He definitely had a few inches on me, and his cock was nearly twice the thickness of mine. I wondered if my dick was small, at a mere six inches. Over time and through experience, I discovered that my first experience had been with a monster.

He rolled me over and rubbed his dick in the crack of my ass.

He made animalistic grunts, and I knew he wanted to put it inside. He seemed like an expert.

I asked: "Have you done this stuff before?"

"No way, man. This is the first."

Then he said he'd be back in a second, and he disappeared into the bathroom. He returned, carrying a plastic jar of Vaseline in one hand. He slapped some on my dick and told me to hold it in my hand and stroke it. I did what he said, and loved the way it felt. Then he rolled me onto my stomach and announced that he was going to "tease" me with the head of his cock.

I said OK, but told him not to put it all the way in.

I was scared. Rob held me down and kept moving his cock in the crack of my ass.

"Can you cum like this?"

"It needs to go inside for me to cum," he said. "Can we try it? It'll just take me a minute, I promise."

"Well, I want to, but I'm afraid it's too big."

"Come on, man. Women can take it. I wanna pretend you're Sue while I fuck you. You'll like it, and I'll let you do it to me."

I didn't say yes, but I also didn't say no when he started to work it into my hole. When the head disappeared, I felt a white-hot sensation and swear I saw a flash of white once it was all the way in. I just knelt there, on my hands and knees, trying to adjust to this "thing" that was now in me. He started working it in and out and eventually asked how I was doing. I could barely speak. I asked him to hurry—and eventually he had to give up—confessing that it took him a really long time to cum.

So he rolled over and I did him.

My ass hurt and I wanted him to feel the same discomfort, so I really let him have it. At one point he asked me to stop, and I wouldn't. I kept saying, "I'm close, I'm really close." And he let me continue until I blew the biggest load of my adolescent life all over his back. It just kept cumming, and eventually we both laughed to ease the tension.

He never came.

We cleaned up. He put his underwear back on, and we settled in to our respective sides of the bed.

"Wow." I couldn't hide the fact that I was deeply in love.

"That was strange."

"You didn't like it?"

"I don't know. I feel weird. Never done a guy."

"I liked it. I really like you, Rob." I leaned in and tried to kiss him. The proximity of my face seemed to revolt him. Not what I was expecting.

"Yeah, well, this is a one-time deal, OK?"

I touched the bulge in his underwear and he rolled over, away from me.

"Good night." Two words with the finality of a death sentence.

I lay there on my back, looked up at the fan that now turned at a slower speed. About an hour went by and I was still wide-awake, my heart beating fast. Shortly after, Rob rose quietly and climbed the stairs to the kitchen, took a glass of water, and walked up a few more to his bedroom. I heard his door close somewhere above me.

I finished getting dressed and closed the front door behind me. Daybreak was still two hours away, and it was already sweltering.

As I walked the short distance between Rob's home and my own, I heard the sound of a speeding vehicle and watched as the *Times Union* delivery van stopped at my driveway.

"Hey, Jackson."

"Why are you up so early this beautiful morning, Drew?" The old driver, who'd been delivering my newspapers every morning for two years, wiped the sweat from his brow with a red handkerchief.

"Couldn't sleep."

"Knock out the route, then get some."

"Not a bad idea."

*Today's a day just like any other,* I thought as I took the bundle from the man and shot a wave as he drove away. I walked to the garage where the orange and white canvas news-carrier bag hung on a nail. I climbed onto my 10-speed and rode the bike up the hill.

# THROUGH
# THE COMPUTER SCREEN

**KARL BARRY**

I've never been a big fan of online porn or chat rooms. Oh, yeah, occasionally I flip through some sites. When I'm at work in my lonely little office cubicle, with the sound of the droning air conditioner, I follow an endless chain of links with bright flashing windows that pop up to announce BIG HORNY WOMEN NOW! XXX HOT PUSSY EXTRA. Eventually, I arrive at a group of photos that lead me to a quick climax. Then I get on with my work and don't think any more about it.

But I was going through a dry season last summer. Usually, I'm able to get off with a girl at least every two weeks by going to a club and picking someone up, or hanging around a bar until I see a lonely-looking, long-haired something who appears to have been stood up. However, for three months I'd found nothing. My luck appeared to be waning, and I was starting to get nervous that it had to do with how I looked.

The gym has become too much of a hassle for me, and there is a daily special at my favorite fast-food Chinese restaurant that I can never resist. My belly has inched out until I can barely see my dick looking straight down without bending. This is a cause for concern.

So I found myself desiring a more prolonged session with my PC. I was working late—making sure my PowerPoint presentation would be perfect for the meeting the next day—when I got an anxious urge. I wasn't able to find any porn Web sites by browsing through search engines that didn't require you to pay before loading hot fucking scenes inch by glorious inch. I was feeling bad about myself for not having finished this report sooner. I wished some mean-looking women manager would come in and discipline me, so I was particularly interested in finding some sites focused on female domination.

What I came up with fairly quickly was a chat room that focused on a hot new subject called femdom. There were hundreds of members. The site promised photo albums, so I signed up quickly. There was a short registration process, then I received a big welcome message with a picture of a woman dressed like Xena with a whip. I quickly clicked on the folders of pictures and was treated to a series of delights, including women pinching, biting, prodding, kicking, scratching, and whipping men in various states of undress. Photos of men being driven into the dirt outdoors and being soiled particularly appealed to me.

In no time at all, I had worked up a quick pace of circulating the photos: click, stroke, click, stroke. I worked myself into a feverish pace. And when I landed upon a photo of a woman with a devilish look on her face as she rammed a flower up a man's tight pink asshole, I came all over the edge of my desk. I wheeled back my chair quickly so none of it would land on my PC or my suit pants. I breathed harshly as my cock went limp in my hand. Then I used tissues from the box next to a photo of my parents to clean up the mess.

I felt incredibly relieved after that. But I wasn't ready to go back to work quite yet. So I settled down into my cushioned chair again and clicked on a button that said MESSAGES. There were a whole series of posts with links advertising different sites and some messages where an individual had just attached a photo for public consumption. Then I found some messages that were more in-depth. A whole slew of posts were from men describing what they would like women to do to them and various kinds of degradation to which they would like to be subjected.

Some of their ideas sparked my imagination, and I started to feel stimulated again. Then I hit upon a few messages by dirty women who discussed stories about ways they have dominated, humiliated, and tortured men. The stories ranged from light tales of spanking to hard-core physical punishment with permanent damage inflicted to skin and organs. I gravitated toward the medium-spiced stories: a little dirty talk, a bit of playful slapping, and then a harsh session of whipping until the poor guy came. I liked a couple of the stories so much I typed in a couple of responses complimenting them on their form and begging for more saucy tales. I looked at my watch and sighed. I thought it was late and I might as well head home.

I didn't go to the site again for a few days. My presentation had been a great success, and I was running on a bit of a high. But sure enough, I found myself at work late again with a tingling feeling in my gut and a desire for a fistful of fun. I found the chat room by doing the same search I'd conducted during my first cyber-roam and this time bookmarked it in my drop-down list of favorites. To my surprise a couple people had responded to my messages, and one of the women I liked had posted another lengthy story about her trip to a farm to hog-tie a naughty field hand.

In the following days I found myself logging on to the site during my lunch hour and staying a couple hours extra in the evening to read and post messages. There were several people with whom I had regular conversations. We discussed the range of our sexual desires. I discovered aspects of myself I hadn't realized existed before. Such as I found myself incredibly aroused by the thought of being forced naked into the ocean with a woman dressed as a mermaid spanking me with her plastic tail and the idea of being tied to a tree while a group of women threw mud at me. These aren't things I was able to find out on my dates with women normally.

One of the stories I read that excited me the most was of a girl who invited men over to her apartment for jerk-off contests. The woman stood above them ordering them to go faster, degrading them, and judging who was the winner. I masturbated to this story several times over the course of the next few days. And then, to my immense joy, some people began posting messages to arrange another session of this circle-jerk contest.

"Another?" I furiously typed in. "You mean some of you have actually met together physically to do this?" The next day I checked back eagerly to see they had responded to my post.

**From:** harryhenry43
**Date:** 10/7/2001 11:32:30 A.M.
**Subject:** Meetings

Absolutely! Three months ago we met in a camping section of a national park. Those of us who lived in the area, that is. LOL! It was a big success! Three girls and nine guys showed up for it! The girls ran the contest commanding us all to get down on our knees and jerk off as fast as we could. They ran all sorts of contests: penis length, distance for cum shots, amount of times you could cum in an hour. It was a full day's workout and I was sure glad that "miss-muffet" brought a picnic basket with sandwiches and chips to refuel with! LOL!

**From:** krugerfunguy
**Date:** 10/7/2001 12:41 P.M.
**Subject:** Meetings

I was VERY privileged to be at the last meeting in the park. It was AMAZING. Juliecool is a wicked woman! Really tough. She had me on my knees screaming for mercy with a whip around my neck. I must have milked more that day than I had since I was a teenager! :) It's a shame she hasn't posted on here in a while. Where are you, Juliecool?

I was extremely heartened by these posts. They filled me with hope because I knew that a few of the people who mentioned they had attended the last event lived in my state. I was afraid at first. What if they did organize another meeting? Would I have the balls to show up? What if they were all ugly freaks? You always hear stories about disastrous Internet meetings that end with some psycho ruining a poor lonely explorer's life.

But I was tired of the bar and club scene. It wasn't getting me anywhere anymore, and it wasn't exciting enough. If I did agree to show up and no one else turned up, all I would have wasted was an afternoon. So when one of the guys who attended the first meeting suggested a Saturday two weeks away at a public park, I replied quickly, agreeing to attend.

Over the next week and a half, a total of 11 men and four women agreed to show up. There were specific directions given to indicate where to find each other in the park. All who planned to attend were instructed to wear an article of red clothing. The person who chose the spot assured everyone it was very secluded. I wrote a message suggesting it might be easier for someone to just host the event at their home. This was met with the answer that everyone would probably prefer to keep all this anonymous.

Over the entire time I fretted about whether to attend or not.

What if the pressure of the strange situation meant I couldn't get an erection? At the same time I berated myself for having so little faith. I thought it would be pathetic to just sit in front of my computer screen silently stroking myself to the midnight hour. Why not break out of the virtual world and into the real one?

The evening before the big day I went out to a bar with a couple of my colleagues. I had a few beers with my friends. There were some girls at a table we tried to pick up. I chatted for some time with a nice girl named Sarah who was a Web site designer. I hinted at taking her home that evening, but she shrugged off any such suggestions. However, I was successful in obtaining her phone number. At home I stared at the receipt with her number written on the back. I thought, *You have to be an idiot to meet up with complete strangers. Just call this girl next week and see if she warms up.* I collapsed in my bed and sank into a deep, dark slumber.

I was woken up in the morning early by some noisy construction work in the apartment next door. My head ached a bit, but I felt something else aching lower on my body. I pulled up my sheet to see my pecker sticking straight up, red and ready to go. I idly stroked it and looked at the clock. It was 9 A.M. A burst of energy struck me. All my resolve from the earlier night melted away as I dashed to the bathroom to shower and shave. I soaped myself in the shower, imaging what it would be like to have a woman standing over me, commanding me, owning me! It would be thrilling to feel myself in a group of other men bending to the will of powerful women, as if we were trained cattle. I had to stop rubbing myself or I would cum. It would be necessary to save all I had for the big meeting.

I dressed up in simple clothing and was about to leave the apartment when I remembered that I had to wear something red. So I stripped off my T-shirt and ran to my closet, uncertain of whether

I did have anything red. The first thing I found was a red and black plaid shirt. I decided it would have to do, pulled it on and dashed out the door.

I drove quickly and arrived at the meeting point in the park a bit late. It was a good size clearing by a pond, but there were clusters of large trees and bushes surrounding it. Casually, I walked to the pond. There were five men standing in a cluster near it. Each was wearing a piece of red clothing: two red hats, two red shirts, and one with ridiculous-looking bright-red sneakers. They saw me. One of them waved. This was my last chance: I could run away or face up to the desire I'd never admitted. But it would be ridiculous to leave now. I steadied the muscle shaking with fear inside me and walked over as calmly as I could. They spoke in low voices as I approached.

"Well, it's fucking pathetic!" one the men in a red hat said.

I looked around, then said quietly, "Are you the guys from the…?"

"No women have showed up yet," the same man said. "You know it's fucking typical. People bitch about their fantasies, and when there's a chance to actually do something about it—nothing, zilch, zero." He was a short, excitable man who bounced from one foot to the other as he impatiently stuffed his hands in his pockets. He pulled up his hat and scratched angrily at his scalp. No one seemed to know what to say in response to all of this. They just kicked at the dirt or smoked a cigarette quietly.

"Well, I'm giving them another 10 minutes to get here, and then I'm outta here," he concluded.

No one spoke or made eye contact until one of the men in a red shirt finally cleared his throat and said, "So, any of you fellas catch the football game last night?" We looked quizzically at one another. A couple of us shook our heads, and everyone else stayed silent for several minutes. I wanted to get off so badly I figured I'd have to jerk off in the car if the women didn't show.

Whether the 10 minutes was up or not, the irritable man in the red hat had obviously had enough. He looked at his watch and said, "That's it. I'm off. Fuck this." He turned and shuffled to the path kicking up dirt and leaves along the way.

The rest of us stared in wonder. I looked down at my feet and contemplated leaving. Maybe I could call up Sarah and see if she wanted to meet for a date tonight. She might not be as frigid as I first thought her to be.

Then one of the guys said, "So, what should we do if the girls don't show?"

"I think it's already obvious they're not going to," the guy with the red shoes replied. He was thin and handsome and had quick, darting eyes.

The other man in the red hat sighed loudly. "This sucks," he observed. "I've been carrying around this boner since Wednesday." He casually rubbed at the crotch of his pants. There was indeed a noticeable bulge that rested there. He was a thickset man with a tattoo of rose on his arm.

The second man wearing a red shirt, who also had long black hair, crossed his arms. "I was hoping one of the girls would talk dirty to me," he said. "I fucking love it when they do that."

I swallowed hard. "I woke this morning so horny, I thought I'd explode," I said. They looked at me and nodded. Then there was a quiet, tense moment. A bird in the distance called loudly, and we all looked toward it.

The other man in a red shirt said, "I guess we could start out. Build up a bit of a circle jerk, and once the ladies get here we'll be all ready for them to come at us." He rubbed his crotch as well and looked around nervously. There was another tense stretch of silence. Despite myself, I felt my dick growing hard in my pants. I suddenly felt very warm, like I was wrapped in an insufferably hot blanket.

The man in the red hat said, "Uh, I don't know. Seems kind of weird."

"We might as well," the guy in the red shoes said. "Not much other action around here." He looked at the water of the pond like he didn't care and rubbed his chest. "I guess I could be the dominatrix and tell you guys what to do."

All the other men shuffled around uncertain about this suggestion. It was unforeseen and bizarre. But by now all of us had our hand in our pockets or were blatantly stroking an erection through our pants. I was doing it unconsciously. The animal need in me came racing before any thought I had.

The man with the long black hair and red shirt shrugged and said, "Whatever. As long as I get my load off."

"Fine," Red Shoes said. He walked around us and said, "Line up against the pond with your backs to me. It'll be easier to imagine like that." We hesitated for a moment and then all moved at once. We lined up and stood tensely. The pond's surface was calm, and there were several patches of green algae. My feet and palms felt hot and itchy.

"First things first," he continued. "Get your dicks out and make sure they're stiff as a board." I glanced to the side at my three anonymous pals. Red Shoes paced behind us. No one wanted to be first. "Now," he shouted. I was afraid someone out on the trails might hear, but I instantly forgot this when the men in the red shirts unzipped their flies and exposed their already hard penises to the air.

The man in the red hat was frightened and obviously trembling. I swallowed the sour saliva in my mouth and unzipped my own fly. My penis softened a bit from the tension. I rooted around in my pants for a second and then pulled it into the open to taste the cool breeze. I stroked it as the red-shirted men were. Both their penises were rather large and meaty. My own meat looked small in comparison.

Finally, the man in the red hat sighed, cleared his throat, and pulled out his own cock. It was a stubby bit of flesh, noticeably much small than any of ours. The man with the long black hair had the thickest cock with the largest head.

Red Shoes walked around to the side of us so he could look at the cock lineup in profile. He bitingly asked, "Call that hard? The fucking ground is harder than that." He kicked up a pile of the soft dirt at us. It landed mostly on the leg of my jeans. "Stroke those cocks. Make them point to the sky." The air of sexual excitement was infectious. I couldn't help being aroused. What if someone happened by while walking the trails? The buzzing worry over the present dangerous situation slowly melted into my sexual pleasure, which stimulated me to rub my cock shaft harder. It grew and I felt a fine film of pre-cum emerge from the tip of the head. I used this to rub over the head, which excited me more.

Red Shoes caught me doing this and said, "Very good. Mr. Plaid has the right idea. Why don't the rest of you lubricate your cocks with some spit?" The two red-shirted men did as he said, but the man in the red hat continued to work his semi-engorged stub while he stared at the water. Red Shoes walked around to him.

"I said, spit," he grumbled in the man's ear. He didn't respond, but his face grew increasingly tense. "All right," Red Shoes commanded, "hold up your hand." He punched the man's ass when he didn't respond and repeated, "hold up your dirty hand!" The man released his cock and raised his hand. Red Shoes opened the man's hand and spit a large wad into it. We all stopped and looked at them in amazement.

"Keep stroking!" Red Shoes yelled at us. The man in the red hat closed his eyes and rubbed the saliva all over his cock. He seemed to enjoy it immensely. Red Shoes was so brisk and professional about this. I would have sworn he had done it before.

We were now all obviously very hard. I even had to slow my

strokes or I would've cum. I didn't know if it was allowed yet. My testicles were aching.

Almost telepathically, Red Shoes said, "All right, drop your drawers so your nuts can feel the wind too!" We each pulled our pants down. There wasn't any more hesitation. This was the real thing and we were all enjoying it. We stood in a line of hairy, bare thighs.

I couldn't help watching the other guys jerk off in a bewildered fascination. The guy with the largest dick was pumping his cock the hardest. His right hand yanked away at it while the left clutched his balls.

Red Shoes had found a stick somewhere. He poked this guy in the ass with it and said, "OK, big fella. Looks like you're ready to go. Milk it to the finish." The man's breathing grew harsh as he worked even harder. The arm of his red shirt blurred as he moved it furiously. He stepped forward right to the water's edge as he did so, pumping that thick red meat for all he was worth.

Red Shoes commanded, "Finish it off." We watched him as if we were hypnotized. He arched his head back and groaned loudly. We expected him to cum then, but he didn't. His strokes became faster until they reached an inhuman speed. Then, without warning, long pellets of cum shot from the head of his cock. They flew out free and landed on top of the water with a soft plunk. We stood still in amazement as reams of white fluid shot into the little pond. Finally, his testicles were empty and he stopped stroking his cock shaft. But he continued breathing harshly and looked as if he were about to collapse from the force of his explosion.

"I didn't tell anyone to stop," Red Shoes shouted at us. I wondered if maybe this was going too far. It was a very weird situation, and I felt uncertain about what it meant. But at the same it was exhilarating—even if it was wrong. I didn't know these men and would never see them again. They would vanish back into the obscure realm of the computer screen as soon as I walked back down that dirt path. To hell with it! Why not enjoy what was offered?

I began stroking my cock again with the other two men who were still hard. The red-shirted man turned around and gave us a satisfied smile. He reached down to pull up his pants, but Red Shoes stopped him. "Oh, no, big boy. You're not done."

He looked at Red Shoes in confusion. "What do you mean?"

"First one to spill his load becomes the bitch. Those are the rules and now you have to give us a cunt." Red Shoes's look was hard. His face was coloring red in anger.

"I don't have any idea what you mean," the man replied.

"OK," Red Shoes said in a flat, stern tone. "Here it is simple. Turn around. Bend over. And spread that pink cunt for the other fellas to cum into."

"You must be out of your—" he started to talk back, but Red Shoes grabbed his wilting cock and balls hard. The big man let out a shriek of surprise. Red Shoes pulled him forward and toward the ground. He fell down on his knees cursing under his breath.

"Shut your mouth," Red Shoes said. "This is what you like, don't ya?"

The big man breathed hard and hung his head down and shrugged.

"Sure it is," Red Shoes assured him. Then he pushed him forward so the big guy was leaning on the ground doggy-style. He seized the man's ass and pulled it up so it was fully in view. Then he took a cheek in each hand and pulled them apart so the pink of the anus was visible through a tuft of dark hair. "Now who's going to cum on him first."

The man in the red hat backed away, "No way, man. I'm not fucking any ass."

Red Shoes scowled, "I don't want you to fuck it. Just cum on it. Pretend it's the hairy cunt of some tough broad. Shoot it over her and drench her 'cause she's horny."

He backed away farther and looked uncertain.

"Now," Red Shoes said. "You first. Don't be scared. It's just a pussy."

The other fellow in the red shirt said, "I want to have a go."

"No, you wait your turn," Red Shoes said. "First, Stubby Cock."

The guy in the red hat blushed at this. He looked angry like he was going to shout at Red Shoes. Then he said, "OK. I'll shower that pussy."

"Good boy," Red Shoes said. He opened up the big guy's ass wider. The guy with the red hat shuffled up to it stroking his little prick. He bent forward and stared straight at the guy's asshole, tugging harder and harder at his cock. It seemed his method was to stroke it quickly several times and then rub around the head sensuously for a second or two.

Red Shoes watched him and said, "Yeah, pump it for that bad pussy! Come on, man. Give it to her!" The man's grip tightened on his cock shaft as he worked it harder. His breathing quickened almost to the point of hysteria. At last, pearly cum shot straight out at the big guy's asshole. It landed along the ridge of the anus and stuck to the hairs. Stubby Cock stumbled backward in exhaustion.

"Next!" Red Shoes didn't waste any time. The other guy in the red shirt walked straight up to our surrogate cunt. It hardly took any time for him to cum; he was so fired up. Before we knew it a thick stream of white was flooding the big guy's ass to mix with the other man's spunk. "Good boys!" Red shoes said. "Now you, Mr. Plaid."

I walked up to the big guy's backside. All the tension I'd been feeling over the entire day shed from my body. I suddenly felt totally free and ready for anything. I looked down at the pink, messy piece of ass and felt my cock draw toward it. I didn't feel the movement of my hand. All my focus was directed at that pink hole. It seemed hungry and ready for me.

My balls tightened. Red Shoes mumbled words in the background, but they were drowned out by crackle of electricity that heralded the orgasm building inside me. And then I came. It rose up out of my shaft gloriously, but failed to leap through the air. Instead, it kind of dribbled out to the ground. I didn't want to miss my mark so I thrust forward and touched the man's hairy pink asshole with the tip of my cock as it was still spurting forth globs of jizz. I worked at it like a painter with his brush. "Oh, yeah!" I bellowed. It was incredibly satisfying.

Red Shoes laughed and said, "Work it in, bad boy!"

After I finished, I noticed the other guys had already zipped up. They were obviously uncertain of what would come next and looked eager to leave. The guy in the red hat looked especially nervous. We all looked at each other quickly and then down at the ground. Our desire had spilled over into a new territory from which we couldn't return. But we could. It was simple: Just escape.

The guys who were zipped up left first, offering a hasty "See you." Then they rushed off into the shady woods. Red Shoes let go of the big guy and let him stand up. For a moment, the big guy looked around for something to clean himself with, but nothing was available. He just pulled up his pants over the sticky mess. I had tucked myself back in and was scared out of my wits. Red Shoes was about to say something when I said "Later" and rushed away to the path. I wondered if those two guys said anything to each other after I left, or if they scurried away separately, utterly ashamed liked the rest of us.

I didn't return to the discussion forum for another two weeks. When I did, I noticed there weren't any messages about our meeting. One user who lived on the opposite coast and hadn't been able to attend asked how it went, but he was met with silence.

Things now carry on much as they did before. Occasionally, when working late and the urge calls, I look over some pictures on the forum and relieve my growling balls. Whenever I feel in a more engaging mood, I post a message or two. There's just been some talk of organizing another meeting in the southern part of the state. I don't think I'll go. I've been dating Sarah off and on for several months. She hasn't put out yet, but I know it'll happen some weekend soon.

No. I don't think I will go, but I have printed out the directions. Just in case.

# HOT WINGS/HOT SEX

**DOUG ROBERTS**

For a German restaurant, the place had the best hot wings outside of Buffalo. My Saturday afternoon wanderings often brought me there, to savor wings so spicy they made my mouth pucker as I washed them down with a tall, chilled Guinness on draft while I read the newspaper or watched a game on television.

I looked up from my paper and noticed a guy at the bar staring in my direction. He didn't look away when our eyes met. I nodded and returned to the crossword puzzle.

This half-empty restaurant would never be considered a pick-up joint, especially not on a Saturday afternoon. Couples and families dined nearby. Six large monitors displayed the same football game.

My fingers tinted orange with hot sauce, I wiped my hands and tossed the napkin onto the growing pile beside a plate littered with chicken bones. After savoring the tingling sensation in my lips and tongue for a few seconds, I reached for my glass, but it was empty.

When I turned to signal the bartender for a refill, the guy from the bar was standing beside me, his jeans-clad crotch mere inches from my face. Caught off-guard, I stared at his zipper for several seconds, imagining what lay beneath.

"Mind if I join you?" he asked, setting a Guinness beside my plate.

"Nope," I said, gathering up my newspaper to make room. I looked the guy over. About my age, which meant early 30s. Dark-brown hair, almost black. Clean-shaven, except he might have skipped this morning—his face looked dark and rough. Casually dressed, like me. Jeans and a button-front shirt, his sleeves rolled up at the elbows.

I felt my heart accelerate slightly. Was I reading the situation correctly? Was the guy checking me out and now making his move? I'd never had this happen before, though I'd occasionally lain in my bed in the morning before I got ready for work and fantasized about situations like this.

After a long dry spell, I'd only recently started dating again. The woman I was seeing interested me, but I didn't think the feeling was reciprocal. So far, she'd allowed me to kiss her on the cheek after dinner, or to drape my arm around her shoulder while we strolled through the Contemporary Arts Museum, but she never offered much affection in return. A relationship probably destined to end up as a good friendship and little more.

Frustrated, I'd flirted with the idea of dating a man, something I'd never done before. Since high school I'd considered myself gay-curious, but I'd never had the courage to act on my curiosity. During a school trip to London, my roommate—my best friend's younger brother—had offered one night, after several drinks, to blow me if I came to his bed and did him first.

He flicked the light beside his bed quickly on and off. In that brief instant I was treated to the sight of his naked body and long, sleek, hard cock. I asked him to meet me midway. Neither of us wanted to make the first move and couldn't come to terms.

Concerned that news might leak back to his brother, I resisted, masturbating silently in bed while he did the same only a few feet away. When he was done, he flicked cum across the room, some of it landing on my face and chest.

In the dozen or so years since then, I'd never had another opportunity present itself. I'd bought some gay videos and was immensely turned on by blow-job scenes and money shots, but I felt I could never form a romantic attachment to a man in the same way I did with women. So I stuck to women.

"Neal," the guy sitting across from me said.

"Bob," I replied, wiping my hand before I reached out to shake his. "Thanks for the beer."

"My pleasure. Though I don't know how you can drink that stuff. Liquid bread, a friend of mine calls it."

I took a sip and noticed that my hand shook slightly as I raised the glass to my lips. I didn't know what to say next. When Neal drank from his own glass, I noticed his wedding ring and I wondered if I'd read the situation wrong. Confusion addled my thoughts. He licked his lips as he set his glass down. A come-on gesture or just licking his lips? My mouth felt dry, so I took another drink.

"I've been watching you," he said at last. He leaned forward and spoke softly.

I felt his leg nudge against mine under the table. I didn't move away from the contact. "I noticed."

"Is there some place we could go to talk?"

I felt the heat of his leg, even through two layers of denim. My cock had grown hard and throbbed inside my jeans. I felt moistness forming at its tip. Not trusting my voice, I nodded and fumbled for my wallet, tossed a twenty on the table, and gulped down another healthy draught of beer. My newspaper provided convenient cover for the bulge in my pants.

Outside, the midafternoon sun seemed blindingly white. "We could go for a drive in my car," I offered.

Neal nodded, and I led him to my Honda. As I started up the engine, my mind reeled. Where could we go? I didn't want to have to be driving as we talked—I wanted to be able to concentrate on what was happening, to savor this developing experience in its fullest.

"Do you want to go to my place?" I asked, my heart pounding in my throat. My words seemed a faint whisper. I didn't know where I'd found the courage for such a question. I glanced at Neal, who stared back at me, slight amusement registering on his face.

"Wow, that's fast. That's not what I had in mind when I approached you."

I wondered if that was true, but I played along. "We can just drive, if you want. Have you ever done this before?"

"Picked up a guy, you mean? Not really. Once, I guess, several years ago, but not like this. A guy I worked with. We worked late a few nights, and we ended up doing it in the photocopying room."

I nodded. "And today, did you—"

"I didn't set out planning this," he told me. "Not at all. I was just going to have a drink and go home. When I saw you sitting there, though, I suddenly felt like I had to meet you and see what would happen."

Knowing I risked ruining the situation, but unable to resist, I said, "You're married."

He sighed. "Yeah. Five years. Got a kid too. But part of me wants to be with another man. A big part. I'm trying to figure it all out, you know?"

I nodded again. The urgency of the situation had eased slightly. The pressure inside my crotch had abated, though I definitely felt dampness from the pre-cum that had oozed from my cock when Neal first joined me at the table.

Suddenly, he reached over and put his hand on my right thigh. "Still want to go to your place?"

My heart leaped. So did my cock, mere inches from his hand. "Yes!"

"OK. Let's go."

During the 10-minute drive I didn't see another vehicle. They were there—I just didn't notice them. I stopped at lights and intersections, but I was in a trance. Neal didn't move his hand from my thigh. Every time I moved my leg from the gas pedal to the brake, I felt its weight. It seemed comfortable and natural, but I wanted to feel his hand on my crotch. I'd already had enough distractions, though, and an accident would put a serious damper on the rest of our afternoon.

We didn't speak the rest of the way to my apartment. I led him up the staircase to my front door, thinking, *This is it!* Inside, I ushered him to the couch. *What now?* I wondered. "Want to watch a video?" I asked.

"Porn?"

I nodded.

"Sure."

I found the tape and popped it into the VCR. Not bothering to rewind it to the beginning, I simply pressed the play button. A young blond stud leaned against an outside railing while a strapping hunk with dark hair and a tattoo on his right biceps pumped his cock into the guy's ass. The blond stroked himself. As a rule, I wasn't overly turned on by men fucking as a rule—the oral scenes were what did it for me—but I didn't hit fast-forward, as I usually did. Besides, I remembered the end of this scene, and it had two great cum shots.

Neal sat next to me on the couch, and we watched in silence for several minutes, our arms gently touching.

"Have you ever kissed a guy?" Neal asked when the blond guy

on the screen blew his wad all over the railing. Thick, ropy jets of cum spewed from his impressive cock in stream after stream.

I shook my head absently, transfixed, waiting for the upcoming shot. The dark-haired stud withdrew from the blond's ass. The blond, jizz still oozing from his softening dick, whirled around and positioned his mouth to receive his partner's ejaculation. He held his mouth wide open, his tongue protruding slightly. The first blast missed his mouth and streaked across his face. The next three bursts hit their target, though. The blond licked his lips, wiped the cum from his face, and licked his hand. Then he stood up, and the two men kissed passionately. Tongues danced, and I imagined the dark haired man tasting his own cum in the blond's mouth.

I turned to Neal. He leaned toward me and kissed me directly on the lips. My mouth opened to admit his tongue. He probed inside my mouth. A few seconds later my tongue returned the favor. In many ways it was just like kissing a woman, but his face felt rough against my cheek.

My heart was still pounding forcefully in my chest. My cock felt like it would rip through my jeans. Neal had made the first move, and I was determined to make the next. While we continued kissing, I dropped my hand to his crotch and massaged his impressive bulge. I imagined how much better it would feel if I could touch his throbbing organ without the stiff denim in between.

Suddenly, he withdrew. Was I moving too quickly?

"I'll be right back," he said and went to the bathroom.

What was he doing? Women often excuse themselves before things get hot and heavy, but I didn't know guys did too. Although I didn't find out that day, I later learned that the moment I started stroking his cock through his pants, Neal suffered a premature ejaculation. He went to the bathroom to clean up the mess.

When he came back, I was standing, casually watching the video, wondering what was would happen next with Neal. He came toward me and took me into his arms and we kissed again. He was slightly shorter than me, but our crotches pressed greedily against each other. We took turns opening each other's jeans. I fumbled with his complicated buttons, but finally his pants fell open. His dick protruded firmly through his underwear.

When he unfastened my pants, it was like a huge raging power had been set free. A wet spot adorned my dark gray briefs. I'd been oozing pre-cum for the past half-hour. I let my jeans fall to the floor and stepped out of them, then dropped my shorts while he did the same.

And there it was, his raging hard-on in all its glory. The first time I'd ever seen one this close up, and with the imminent promise of getting to experience it much, much more closely. Playfully, I thrust my hips slightly so our cocks touched. He grabbed both in one hand and pressed them together, shaft against shaft. At about seven inches, he was slightly longer than me, but I had him beat in girth. I noticed these details through some detached part of my mind. Most of my focus was on the fact that another man had my cock in his hand. It seemed like every other nerve in my body had gone to sleep so that I could fully experience the sensations in my dick.

More than anything else, I wanted to taste Neal's cock, to slather it with my tongue and feel it between my lips. I wanted to take it into my mouth as deeply as possible and torment him with my tongue until he came. What to do when he ejaculated was still an open question. I was conflicted between wanting to feel his orgasm inside my mouth and wanting to watch delicious cum spurt from that magnificent organ.

Without a word I dropped to my knees and took him in my hand. I savored the sensation of his hardness. I let my fingers graze against his cock and watched it react. Though a hard cock felt familiar and comfortable in my hand—I'd been masturbating for nearly two decades by then—his erection felt just enough different from my own to make it a unique experience. The angle was different too. Plus the fact that as I stroked, nothing was happening to my cock, which continued to leak clear fluid from its bulbous head.

I couldn't hold back any longer. Leaning forward slightly, I brought my mouth to Neal's cock. As I'd learn later, the taste and smell that greeted me came primarily from his earlier accident. I didn't mind in the least. I attacked his cock with zeal. Something I had fantasized about for most of my adult life was finally coming to pass. The analytical part of my mind kept repeating, *You're sucking cock!* The rest of me fell into enjoying the experience and worked at making it as pleasurable as possible for both of us.

Even though he'd cum in his pants just a few minutes earlier—which I still didn't know—I felt him tense up. Clearly, I was doing something right!

"Ah, ah," he said: Words that brought pleasure and pride to my ears. Not only was I a cocksucker, I was good at it!

"I'm gonna…" He trailed off as ecstasy took over. In that split second, I elected to take him in my mouth. He thrust gently against me as my head bobbed up and down, swallowing him almost to the base.

And then it happened.

Without warning, slightly bitter liquid filled my mouth. It's hard to describe the impact of that event. The liquid seemed to appear, like magic. It didn't spurt into my throat or choke me. I just became suddenly aware of its presence all around his fleshy, warm organ. I kept licking and sucking, feeling overwhelmingly connected to this cock, as if it had become a new part of me.

He started to withdraw as my ministrations became too much for his now-sensitive cock. I wrapped my lips closely around him as he pulled out so that I could capture every drop of his precious cum. Then I swallowed. Licked my lips and swallowed again. Not bad at all. I'd tasted my own cum on numerous occasions in the past, but his tasted different. Again, it was subtle, but definitely different.

Awareness returned to the rest of my body. Rough carpet pressed against my knees. The hair on his legs tickled my palms. I scrambled to my feet. His eyes were slightly glazed, but he drew me close and kissed me again, not shy about sticking his tongue into my mouth. I remembered the video scene we'd just watched and realized he probably tasted himself.

Things didn't go as well when it was my turn to receive. I sat on the couch, and Neal dropped to his knees between my legs. His lips and mouth felt warm and moist against my raging organ, but he occasionally brushed against my cock with his stubbly face. This happened, usually, as I got very close to precious orgasm, and it pushed me repeatedly away from the brink.

He tried jacking me off, and I spent long periods near that apex, a millimeter, a millisecond away from emptying my balls, but it didn't happen. In fact, his labors were starting to chafe me. I sympathized with his frustration, but I finally forced him to give up. If he didn't stop, my cock was going to be sore and tender for days.

"I have to get back home," Neal said, uncomfortable and embarrassed that he'd gotten off and I hadn't.

"It's all right," I told him. "This was amazing."

"I wanted to taste you."

"We can try again," I said, thinking that I couldn't wait to get my lips wrapped around his cock.

"I can come over on Wednesday night. Around 7?"

"OK."

Four days—such torture to wait that long. At least by then any slight injuries to my cock would have healed. I drove him back to the restaurant where he'd left his car. We exchanged E-mail addresses.

I went straight back to my apartment and wrote Neal a long message describing the wonderful time I'd had and how much I looked forward to our next meeting. Much of my letter was devoted to the wonderful sensation of savoring his cum as it had materialized in my mouth.

He wrote back the next day and confessed what had happened on the couch, how he'd spurted in his pants at my first intimate touch.

The next four days dragged by. I could hardly concentrate on anything except my anticipation. Finally, Wednesday afternoon came, and then Wednesday evening. Seven o'clock came and went. I sat on the couch, my cock wilting in my shorts, sure he'd chickened out.

He drove up at 7:15. The railing on the concrete steps leading to my apartment rattled as he ascended. He didn't have a chance to knock on the door—I had it open by the time he reached the landing. I ushered him in and closed the door behind him.

"Made a wrong turn," he said.

I nodded and we kissed in the entranceway, then I led him to the couch.

"What happened last time...it might happen again," he said.

"You recovered quickly—I was amazed. When you came out of the bathroom, you were rock-hard and you came again not long after."

He smiled, and I saw relief in his eyes.

"Let's get it out of the way," I told him. "Then we can relax and enjoy ourselves."

I unbuckled his pants and pushed his jeans and shorts down around his ankles. Without wasting any time, I knelt and went straight to work on his cock. The first time hadn't been a fluke—the wondrous sensation was still there. Maybe it had to do with having something living and responsive in my mouth. With a woman you can get some of this by sucking on nipples or clits, but a cock is so enormous, so tantalizing it's almost like a living entity of its very own that just happens to have a man attached to it.

There's an old joke that dogs lick their balls just because they can and the addendum to that is that if a man could suck his own cock he'd never leave the house. At that instant I firmly believed in the truth of that witticism. When I was younger and more limber, I'd desperately tried to suck my own dick and had on one memorable occasion gotten the tip of my cock head pressed briefly against my lips. Shortly after, I'd somehow miraculously gotten my tongue to dance against the sensitive knot of flesh on the shaft just below the crown. I'd never been able to repeat that and had strained my back trying, though I told the doctor I'd injured myself lifting boxes of books.

True to his prediction, Neal didn't last long. This time his orgasm was prodigious, filling my mouth to the brim with energetic spurts of semen. I swallowed as quickly as I could to get it all down. I didn't want to miss a single drop. His cum tasted wonderful, and I loved the sensation of it spurting into my throat, feeling it ripple through the length of his erection to leap onto my waiting tongue.

This time I led him into my bedroom. A picture of the Starship Enterprise decorated the wall over my bed, and in later years when the woman who would eventually become my wife joked about the poster, I'd recite the line "where no man has gone before," knowing full well that wasn't quite true. When I eventually told my wife about my experimentation, the phrase became a standing joke between us, though the poster had been retired to the attic of our new house.

I was determined to have a good time, even if the previous weekend's events repeated themselves. We reclined on the bed and kissed, then Neal crawled around to find my cock with his mouth. His flaccid penis was only inches away from my own head, so I toyed with it, licking away a stray drop of jism, bringing it back to life. When he was hard again, I caressed and teased his shaft with my tongue.

"I want you to cum," he told me, lifting his head briefly from my cock. I nodded but didn't stop sucking on his tasty dick. I tried to let his ministrations carry me away, but his rhythm was off, and whenever I got close and my back began to arch, he did something different that pushed me away from the edge again.

In the meantime, my attentions to his cock were having the desired effect, and soon he was spewing into my mouth again. Not as much as before, but I still enjoyed every last drop.

He swung away from me then and devoted his entire attention to my penis for what seemed like half an hour. Long enough that he had yet another erection. His resiliency amazed me!

Eventually, he crouched with my right leg between his legs and he laid on me, our cocks pressing frantically together. He kissed me, then pushed himself upright. Our cocks were only inches apart. I reached down and took him in my hand. He did the same to me, and we jerked and rubbed each other.

Finally—finally—I felt that irresistible tingling pressure build deep within me and rush toward my groin. It took a while to get there, but I knew I was close, so close, and if he would just keep on rubbing me like he was doing, I'd cum.

What finally pushed me over the edge was his third orgasm of the evening, an impressive performance. When I saw cum spurt from the tip of his cock and land on my own cock and belly, that amazing sight gave me the kick I needed, and a few seconds later I was gushing and spouting jizz all over the place. The first burst was so intense I could actually hear it squirt from my cock. My cum hit the pillow beside my head. The second blast hit me on the chin, barely missing my mouth. Stream after stream splattered across my chest, smearing my nipples and blending in with my chest hair.

Neal's cock was still in my hand, and I felt his semen trickle across my thumb. I released him and raised my hand to my mouth, licking his thick drips. Neal fell upon me and licked my belly clean. My cock felt like it was on fire—battered and tender from his prolonged and occasionally rough attention, but burning from within at the long awaited release. Cum continued to ooze from my tip. Neal descended to my waiting organ and sucked me into his mouth. I had hoped for the sensation of cumming inside him, but that wasn't to be. This was the next best thing, though.

We showered together and cleaned each other off, and then Neal got ready to go. He'd told his wife he was going to a meeting, and he had to get back home.

After he left, mild postcoital guilt gripped me. I had no regrets about having sex with a man, and I would willingly have continued to see Neal and experiment with him but for one thing: his wife. And kid. Without much soul-searching I realized how unfair this was to his family. I wasn't looking for a long-term romantic relationship with a guy, and I didn't believe he was either. What would happen if his wife found out? What if she read my E-mail where I described how much I loved feeling his cum spurt into my mouth?

I couldn't be a part of that. If the tables were turned and I'd found out my partner was screwing someone else—male or female—I'd have been devastated. So, I decided that night—with the taste of his cum lingering in my mouth and my belly still sticky from my own ejaculation—not to see Neal again.

He was understanding, though disappointed.

Only a couple of months later, I met a wonderful woman. We started dating, and by the end of that year we were married. As our marriage enters its eighth year, I know I'll never have the opportunity again to experience sex with another man.

So, Neal, wherever you are, you were my one and only, and I remember our times together fondly whenever my thoughts turn in that direction.

# THE BACHELOR'S FIRST PIECE OF ASS

### EMIR

It was damned near midnight, and the bachelor party was still in full swing—titties and asses everywhere. As the five girls danced around the hotel room in various stages of undress, it seemed that no matter where I looked, I couldn't help catching another eyeful of female flesh. The nine of us, Mike, Maurice, Jason, Scott, Walt, Bob, Daemon, me, and the soon-to-be-married Darryl, just sat back laughing, watching the entertainment, and enjoying the drinks and snacks as well as the chance to hang out with the fellas. We hadn't really gotten the chance to hang out much since graduating from the University of Pittsburgh, but our boy Darryl was about to get married, and we had to send him off right.

Once the last drink had been knocked to the floor, the last bra had been tossed across the room, and the final lap had been danced on, the girls got dressed and packed up to leave. We'd hired them for a five-hour evening, but they gave us a free hour for being such big tippers. As the girls filed out, the usual seven got their shit together and left with them. Those guys never know how to just let go and chill the fuck out. The party had to go on till they all lost consciousness.

"Hey, Darryl…Mir…we gotta run. We goin' take the girls out to the Metro for a drink. We'll catch ya'll at the wedding. Peace out!"

The door slammed, and as the air settled, Darryl and I realized they'd left us to clean up the hotel room by ourselves. We didn't jump right up and start working, but chilled on the couch for a minute as our buzz slowly faded.

"That party was the bomb," Darryl said, laughing.

I nodded and smiled. There was a long silence, then Darryl stood and began picking up half-empty cups. I looked at him.

"What are you doing?"

"What's it look like?"

"OK, Mr. Smart Ass!" I lunged forward, grabbing his shirt.

We always used to wrestle and fight in the dorms—our little male-bonding brotherly-love ritual, I guess. Darryl won most of the time. He'd wrestled in high school and remained in more than excellent shape. Locked tightly now, we rolled around on the floor bumping shit and splashing through puddles of booze. The match was much shorter than usual, thanks to the booze. Huffing and puffing, we both let go after only a few minutes and fell on our backs onto the floor.

There was another long moment of silence.

"Darryl, you awake?"

"Yeah."

"I thought you fell asleep."

"Not yet, I'm still amped up!"

"You nervous?"

"A little…"

"This is a big step. You think you're ready?"

"Yeah, I love her and she loves me. We want kids and the whole picket-fence dream. Yeah, I'm ready."

"So you think you can burn your little black book? No more booty calls?"

He chuckled. "Yeah, I can. I don't need no other pussy but hers."

There was pause.

"Hey, Mir, you know, you should be looking to settle down too."

"For what?"

"I know you get lonely and I know you'd like someone in your life full time, right? Tell me if I'm wrong."

"Naw, you're right...but..."

"But what?"

"Nothing..."

I was the first to stand. The subject was getting too personal. I wanted to tell Darryl about myself, but I knew from many campus discussions that he could never understand his best friend being gay. I'd done a hell of a good job hiding it, and to tell him now might kill him or, worse yet, get me killed.

"But what...?" he insisted.

"Later, man. Get up and help me clean."

"Let's just leave it for housekeeping."

"So are *you* willing to pay that fee the manager mentioned?"

"Yes, Emir, I'll pay it since it was *my* party thrown by my *friends* and they are too cheap to cover the charges." He used the annoying sarcastic voice he knew grated on my nerves, then laughed at having pushed my buttons—which he did all too well.

I stopped cleaning and plopped back onto the couch as he walked toward the bedroom.

"I'm taking a shower, watch some TV, and chill..."

I nodded as he disappeared down the short hall into the bedroom.

After about three minutes I heard the shower turn on. I lay back, closed my eyes, and—as I had always done in college each time Darryl took to the shower—fantasized about his fine 5-foot-11 swimmer's build lathered with soap, his hands washing those tennis ball-sized nuts before travelling the length of that pendulous donkey dick. I was aroused and needed satisfaction quick. This was probably the last time I would see Darryl naked. I stopped massaging my cock through my jeans, then I stood and slowly crept down the hall into the bedroom. There was no door to the bathroom. It was like being in the dorms again. Nothing could have been easier. As I approached the doorway, I could hear him humming a tune. Once my eyes adjusted to the light, I just stared.

Darryl stood in the glass-enclosed shower. The water cascaded across his broad chest—through the muscular valley of his pecs—washing the suds down his torso. Small drops fell from his erect dark-brown nipples. The suds and water trickled over his hard, tight six-pack and ran down his legs to the drain. As he turned, letting the water hit different parts of his body; his cock bounced and swayed, giving clear measure of its size and heftiness. I had seen it exposed, bouncing and swaying on many occasions during our time as roommates. Each time, my own cock would stir uncontrollably—so much so, in fact, that just the sight of Darryl unclothed would damn near make me bust a nut. Now was no different, as I spied his fine muscular bod. My pole expanded in length and girth, pulling the blood from the rest of my body. So much blood surged through my member, I was becoming light-headed. This was my last chance to see homeboy's elephant dick and coconuts flopping freely.

I couldn't take it any longer. I unzipped my pants to unleash my eight-and-a-half-inch serpent and began to beat off right then and there. But once Darryl had turned the water off and was opening the glass shower door, I darted out of the room and scrambled to force my iron-hard Johnson back into my pants.

As I reached the sofa, Darryl called, "Yo, man, I'm finished. You can take a shower now!"

"Naw, that's cool. I'll shower at home."

Darryl walked into the room, a white towel loosely wrapped low around his waist. His damp body glistened in the dim lamplight.

"Come on, man, I thought you was my boy."

"I am. What are you talking about?"

"Why you goin' home? I thought you was gonna stay here and chill. This shit is paid for. I'm staying and getting my money's worth."

"Your money's worth? You ain't paid for nothing."

"OK, then, I'm staying to get *your* money's worth!"

We laughed, but he had a good point. The guys and I *did* chip in a walletful, and we really didn't have to leave until 2 the next day.

"All right, I'll stay."

As he walked back into the bedroom, I walked past him into the bathroom, stripped off my alcohol-reeking clothes, and began to shower. Then it hit me.

"Darryl."

"What?"

"I have got any clean clothes to wear once I get out of the shower."

"Calm the fuck down—neither do I," he said as he entered the bathroom. I turned around fast to conceal my hard-on. "I was going to send mine down with room service to have them washed. So, by the time we wake up and get ready to leave, they'll be back."

"Oh, OK. That's cool. Thanks." I had to answer over my shoulder because I definitely did not want to let him see what his fine-ass body did to me.

I continued to look over my shoulder as he left the room. Since my opportunity to watch Darryl and jack off had been disrupted, I decided not to even bother. So I pushed the desire out of my mind, completed my shower, turned the water off, and, after drying off, wrapped the towel around my waist and walked into the bedroom.

There was Darryl, lying there with the blanket loosely draped over part of his torso and one leg. He was so into watching one of the porn films we'd bought him that he didn't even notice when I came in.

If he had noticed me, he would never have continued to run his hand up and down the length of his cock under the bedsheet. Seeing him beat off sent my now-flaccid dong, like a Mustang going from zero to 80 in 10 seconds, back to its previous iron-hard state. I stood there, hard and motionless, just staring. His hand continued to extend the length of his tower, making the sheet shift and slide. It was only a matter of physics that his cover would eventually slide off. When it did, his hard-as-hell cock was in plain sight. Something like lightning hit me at the base of my nut sac, and I formulated a goal, a mission: Darryl and I were going to have sex.

I stepped back out of the room as quietly as I'd stepped in, but this time before entering I made a bit of noise to announce myself. As I had hoped or expected, he stopped stroking and recovered himself with the sheet. I approached the bed sideways, since I was still brick-hard under my towel. I looked over at the television where some white girl was deep-throating Jake Steed, my favorite straight porn star. Darryl did not even acknowledge me as I undid the knot in my towel and let it drop to the floor. I stood there, ass-naked with my cock pointing straight ahead, and just as I lifted the sheet to slide in, Darryl looked over at me and laughed his ass off.

"Damn, nigga, you gonna put somebody's eye out with that thing."

"Ha, ha, ha. Shut the hell up!"

"Just making an observation. You horny, huh?"

"Hell, yeah!" Little did he know it was for him. "But I ain't alone, am I?"

"Nope." He pulled the sheet back to reveal that gorgeous mammoth cock resting against his hard abs.

I licked my lips, taking one edge of the sheet and covering myself once I lay down. I could feel Darryl's body heat as he lay less than two feet away. We continued watching TV as Jake sprayed his thick, hot cream on the woman's face.

"Must've felt good," I slyly commented.

"Yeah, that shit was off the hook!"

"When was the last time you had head?"

"Damn. It's been a while."

"Why?"

"Stacy don't like giving head."

"What? But you about to marry her—and she don't suck dick?"

"I know that's one of my two complaints."

"You have another one?"

"Yeah. She ain't into anal sex either. She's scared it will hurt."

"Well, I've seen your dick and I'd be scared too. I mean, come on, Darryl, how many of those honeys you used to mess with could really handle you?"

"I'm feelin' you. You got a point 'cause the ones that tried got as far as letting the head in but then started complaining and shit, so I pulled out."

"So you ain't never fucked no one in the ass?"

He thought for a moment before answering, "In all honesty? No."

"Damn—and it's the bomb, dude!"

"How you know? You ain't never fucked no one in their ass!"

"Think what you want. All I'm saying is I feel for you. You 'bout to get married and ain't never had it and sure as hell won't once you get married. That's fucked up. See, if you wasn't slinging damn near a foot-long cock, maybe some ho would have let you get more than just the head in."

"OK, you can shut up now."

"I'm just sayin'…"

"And I'm just saying you keep running your mouth and I got a foot long to shut you up!"

"All I'm saying is if I could take you, I don't see why she can't. But that's your girl."

Darryl's laughter rapidly slowed. I could tell he had no idea how to take my comment, but he managed to form his lips to ask, "What do you mean?"

"I'm saying, I'm a guy, your boy, and if I could handle you, I don't see why…never mind."

I know he was wondering if I was serious or just fucking with him. He turned his full attention on me. "What the fuck…there's no way."

I sat up. "No way, what?"

"That you could take me!"

He was calling my bluff and playing right into my hands.

"Whatever, fool!"

"You can't—"

"You think what you want. I know what I can and can't do."

"Prove it." His voice shook with anticipation.

"Prove it? How?"

"How else, mothafucka? Let's go!"

I threw the covers back to expose our muscular naked bodies. I stood and walked over to the dresser where a gift basket of rubbers, lube, and a wide array of other sexual paraphernalia had been placed as a decoration for the party. Darryl licked his lips and repositioned his body, moving closer to the center of the bed. Magnum condom and a bottle of lube in hand, I walked back over to the bed, tore open the condom wrapper, and took hold of his red-hot, brick-hard cock. When my thumb brushed gently over the head, a droplet of pre-cum appeared. As I brushed it away, Darryl's body shook with pleasure, and he let out a soft moan.

I slowly rolled the condom over his nine-inch torpedo, then, picking up the lube, straddled myself over him. I popped open the shiny, plastic bottle and applied a generous amount of slick stuff to the crack of my ass. After massaging the area for a moment, I inserted my right index finger, which was accompanied by my middle finger in an attempt to make this entry a bit easier. Who the hell was I trying to fool? This was going to be difficult and painful, no matter how many fingers I stuffed up there. During my preparation, Darryl had closed his eyes and relaxed, leaving everything to me. With all his gay talk over the years, I expected him to put up more resistance. But I sure as hell wasn't going to complain.

I directed his cock to my tight, moist hole, and lowered my weight. The pressure and the burning sensation was almost unbearable but I, being a man on a mission, endured. After nearly 20 seconds, I felt the bulbous helmet enter.

I froze.

"Take your time," Darryl advised.

I took his advice and after about two minutes of deep breathing exercises, resumed my descent. From there, it was simple. I relaxed and lowered my weight more and more until all nine-and-a-half fucking inches of his dick were buried to the pubes in my virgin ass.

"Ooh, fuck…" His moans increased.

"I told you I could take it."

Darryl opened his eyes and looked up at me as I began to pull off. No matter how ridiculous it seemed at this point, I was determined to play the role.

"Mir..?" He reached for my waist. "I…uh…shit, I can't explain this, but please don't."

"Don't what?"

"Don't pull off."

"But we're done. I proven my point."

"Please."

"Why?"

"You feel good…and I want to finish, uh…to finish—"

"You wanna fuck me?" I was playing this game to the max.

Darryl had this very odd look—shame?—as he responded, "Yeah."

We stayed motionless for a second, then I allowed him to pull me back down until my full weight rested on his groin and his throbbing meat pulsed inside my guts. Looking at him for the go-ahead, I started to ride him. Up and down, up and down…

"Ahh, fuck, Mir, that feels so damn good. Ohh."

My pace quickened. His chest heaved. His hips rocked with mine, and very faintly I could hear him chanting my name. I slowed down. There was no way I was going to let him blow his load yet. I'd rise just to the point that his cock was about to plop out, and then I'd allow it to fully reenter.

Darryl began to pump upward, fighting against my slowed pace. I pulled off him suddenly. His eyes widened as he prepared to speak, but I placed a finger on his lips and uttered a barely perceptible "Shhhhh…"

I then lay on my back and pulled at him till he got the hint. My legs in the air gave him an easy target as his cock aggressively pushed the walls of my hungry hole apart to find that spot I had only read about in the gay magazines. That place they called the male G-spot.

"Aahh!" I groaned as his thrusts intensified.

Darryl pounded my ass. I reached up, grabbed his hips, and pulled him deeper.

"Darryl, fuck me, boy, FUCK ME!" I blurted out before I realized what I was saying.

He was also shouting without thinking. "Take it! Take my dick! Take it, aaaaahhhhh!"

Having him buried deep within me—the feeling of his balls slapping the underside of my ass—put me on cloud nine. I could not hold off any longer. A gallon of semen welled up in the pits of my balls. Our moans linked together like some religious chant.

"Aoooo, aaawwwww, ummmmmm…."

Darryl leaned forward, locked his arms around my back, and with our faces now suddenly less than an inch apart, he kissed me. A small peck turned into a full-on, openmouthed tongue-duel. My muscles locked. "Darryl, I'm gonna cum…ohh, *fuckkkkkk!*"

Darryl pulled back to watch me bust my nut. Hot juice blasted onto my stomach and chest as he continued to pound me in the ass with his sledgehammer. As I shot out three long streams of jizz, Darryl also began to unload.

"Damn, boy! Yo ass feels so fuckin' good. Oh, *fuck!*"

I felt the heat of his milk being released into the condom's tip. His spasms slowed after a while. The quivering waves of sensitivity died down. He lay on top of me, motionless, as I stroked his back. Then he pulled out, removed the condom, and tossed it into the trash. I halfway expected him to leave the room and not return but he lay back down beside me, and for the rest of the night we slept in each other's arms.

We slept for nearly five hours and awoke when room service knocked on the door to return our clothes. As we yawned, stretched, and looked into each other's eyes we gently kissed. Hand in hand, we entered the shower together.

Afterward, as we dried each other off and applied lotion to our bodies other, I asked Darryl a question that up till then had remained silent.

"Can I suck your dick?"

He smiled, nodded, and as I dropped to my knees to take his

stiffening pole into my mouth, he let out a low hum. As my tongue tickled around the head, I felt it swell within the cavern of my jaws. It was sexy as hell. I bobbed my head up and down the length of his staff, sucking and slurping crazily as Darryl placed his hands on the back of my head. It didn't take long.

"Damn, son, you suck a mean dick…*shit!*" were his last words as a hot river of cum coated my throat.

I took my cock in hand and, in four quick strokes, unloaded my nut, hitting his leg three times. After I wiped him off, we laughed and got dressed. Seeing the room in the daylight, we realized it was not all that bad, and so we left.

Days went by and we did not speak. Even at the wedding our greeting was brief, eye contact more or less avoided. When the minister asked the traditional question—if there was anyone present who thought these two should not be wed, they should "speak now"—Darryl glanced over at me for a deeply passionate split-second. I don't know if he was expecting me to say something or what, but I just smiled and nodded to him.

For months there was nothing and then one night a phone call.

"Mir, can I come over?"

Needless to say, I told him yes.

# GARDEN PARTY: A LONDON FAIRYTALE

**ALPHA HIPKISS**

The house was beginning to buzz with that peak-arrivals feel. There always seems to come a point at a party (one that doesn't fall flat on its face, anyway) at which the sober, jittery feeling of the first couple of hours is replaced with an appealing uncertainty. The noise builds, voices crescendo, and some weird stranger takes over the music. There's the slightest prospect of social danger or a loss of control. Or perhaps that's just me. I've never felt entirely happy in crowded places.

It was my friend's house and my friend's party. He was a minor player at an independent record company, as he insisted on calling it. In fact it was just a subsidiary of one of the majors. He was only a lackey, and I got the impression when I spoke to him the next day that he was as shocked as I was that any celebs deigned to turn up, no matter how minor they might be.

But I'm jumping ahead of myself. I wouldn't have known the minor celebs in question from anyone else in the place. Well, I might have guessed right, put on the spot—but that didn't happen, so I'll never know. As it was, I didn't know anyone at all, apart from Julian, and he was too busy to bother with me. I was just an old school friend who'd been called in to help with preparation—not so exciting as his friends who had friends who knew people.

I walked into the kitchen at some point to get a refill. It was like running the gauntlet: so many faces and voices, and smoke filling the air between the heads and the ceiling. Then I saw this precious thing who looked like a '20s flapper on first glance: neat, thick bob framing an exquisite little face with perfectly applied black makeup around his eyes. Lips—already full beyond temptation—made into a voluptuous sex organ with the plum gloss that covered them. I noticed that the dress I'd taken for a '20s number was, in fact, more of a '70s gym slip: gray cotton and sleeveless, falling plain straight to groin level, save for a zip down the front and ending six inches later in tight pleats. It was just about decent.

There was something odd about the "femininity" of this person. My eyes kept on travelling. Below the dress were thin thighs covered alluringly in glossy stockings (you could see the tops and the clasps of the belt), smooth knees, and slender calves. On the slightly bigger than expected feet there were chunky boots. This was a guy, yet it barely registered.

And I was staring. I only realized when someone else—who'd clearly been watching my gaze as it travelled—broke into a knowing grin. On a reflex, I raised my eyes back to the beautiful creature's face. As I knew by then, he had his gaze on me. But instead of the expression of disdain and dismissal I'd expected, the lips parted and bared his perfect teeth in a smile that was halfway between lascivious and conspiratorial. I almost melted.

There was no doubt that the look was meant for me alone, despite the distance and the crowd between us. I held eye contact for a beat too long before heading to the drinks table. The girl who'd caught on to my wonderment started to make conversation, diplomatically omitting mention of my fascination. She was pretty—no, make that beautiful. Long golden hair and a low-cut top that showed exactly how generously she'd been endowed in the one way in which the boy was lacking. But my mouth was dry with desire, and it wasn't for her. Ali, she was called. I don't know how I remember that. But as she chatted me up, my eyes kept drifting back to Jamie.

Silly to keep on as if I don't know, now, who he was—after I've listened to every album, every single, every interview so many times that I could recite them by heart. It would be an awful disservice not to mention also that I'm really, really happy now with my partner, Sam. She knows all about Jamie and about the magic of that night for me. Sometimes she takes the piss and plays hurt. But she knows it was never in the same universe as what we have. Sometimes you just get the chance to touch light; it doesn't mean you don't want the cozy long-term places. There's something to be said for sanity.

So, back to the party: I couldn't help but notice this enormously tall skinny guy standing next to the vision. He was Steve, the bassist, of course. At the time, I thought it was his boyfriend; they were so touchy-feely with each other, stealing sweet glances into one another's eyes. Every so often Jamie would slip a glance my way. I guess I was pretty cute back then with my long hair and my shyness. It sounds sick even to say that, but you realize these things later on.

Ali certainly fell for me: In a last-ditch attempt to steal my heart, she moved into the path of my eye line and stood on tiptoe to place her lips onto mine. She tasted sweet—of the mixer she'd been drinking. But I pulled away, suddenly panicked.

"Sorry," I said, "I need to be somewhere else." I walked purposefully out of the kitchen, away from Ali, away from Jamie's burning eyes. I don't blame Ali for not attempting to follow. She must have felt slain. Whether he'd follow wasn't something, surprisingly, that dominated my thoughts right then. I just needed to escape his gaze and her lips, if only long enough to catch my breath.

I stepped out of the familiar back door of Julian's flat, the ground floor of a typical huge Edwardian terrace in Camden. The garden was longer than you might expect, stretching narrowly around mature trees and shrubs to a high fence about 25 yards away. It was a rare hot August evening, and I was surprised at how few of the guests had left the claustrophobic confines of the flat. I walked beyond the little chattering mass and breathed deep. The warm air soothed my nose. I felt a bit drunk and unsteady.

Beyond a huge old beech I hid myself, sliding my back down its cool bark and slipping open the buttons of my thin shirt as I landed on the spongy grass beneath. I remember looking down at the contours of my chest—just gently there, the result of recent attempts at fitness. The full moonlight complemented the ambient street lighting from the road. I touched my left nipple and watched it harden. Somehow it got lost in a world that just contained my body. I snapped my head up and remembered why I'd really come out. I had a small joint and I didn't want to share it, especially with some female I didn't want to fuck. I skinned up quickly, vaguely recalling that I had a beer out here with me too. As I toked and gulped, some serenity returned. I contemplated gender and the fluidity of emotions.

Then my little spark of magic happened. He appeared very suddenly, my vision in a gym slip. There was that smile again, only this time it was five feet away. I know now that he was only 23 and that he'd only just finished recording his first album. He and his band mates were still high on their very existence and

Jamie, especially, felt invincible. But right then all I knew was that, come what may, this guy could do exactly as he pleased with me. Strange, considering I'd never touched another man's cock before.

He let out a little cackle of delight as he placed a heavy boot on either side of my thighs. With the most dainty of actions, he flipped the pleats of his skirt upward, showing me a silky pouch whose contents could only be masculine. Not that I hadn't worked it out, of course, but I think he was being polite—and trying to avoid having his face smashed in. Holding up his stockings was the lacy suspender belt whose ends I'd glimpsed earlier. My mum used to have one, but I've a feeling it didn't look so good on her. When I smiled at him (probably for the first time) he stepped level with my hips and, leaning lightly against the tree, let his skirt fall on top of my head. My face was buried, suddenly, in a delightful place. My nose and lips savored the youthful eroticism of his silk-encased flesh. I dampened, then drenched, the fabric and his balls, licking like an animal, suddenly desperate for him. Slipping a hand behind his thighs to press his tender round lobe farther into my mouth, I realized that the pouch was just a pouch. This darling had the gall to brave London nightlife with almost no knickers under a mini dress. I was impressed.

As I continued with my low-calorie happy meal, the silk rose up with his engorging cock. He slid down my body then, trailing his moist package over my bare chest and stomach, coming to rest, uncomfortably, on my hips. I met his eyes—close, for the first time. He leaned into me and caught my lips with his. I nearly passed out, so intense had my desire for those lips become over the past half-hour or so. I thrust my tongue between them and, coming to my senses, realized that it was now or never. He moaned the moan of a whore who means it (or so I imagine) as I pressed ever farther inside his welcoming mouth, my fingers playing around the smooth luxury of his bared buttocks.

As he pulled away, there was a part of me that regretted it. But very soon those swollen lips began to kiss down my chest, over my abdomen, into my navel, and down beyond. My jeans were unzipped, and the warmth of his mouth enveloped me without warning. I let out a cry of some long-lost pure carnal craving. He was here for a reason, I knew.

He shifted around, never shirking his mouth's task, so that his naked ass faced the dark perimeter of the garden and was within my arm's reach. I licked my fingers and followed his urgent lead, spending only a few moments caressing him open before driving inside with one, two, then three digits. With the third, his little whimpers became more frantic. I probed and explored, finding quickly the place that made him whimper the most and relishing, at the same time, a more expert blow job than I'd known before.

There was an unspoken need for haste. His lips left the tip of me with an affectionate suck to finish, my fingers pulled free, and he twisted so that his skirt covered our action. He was sitting in my lap again. I pulled the large tag at the top of his zipper, yanking it down in one swoop to expose his pink nipples. With one smooth action, he pulled a condom and a couple of lube sachets from the dainty little pocket of his dress. He looked down for the briefest possible time to roll the rubber very seductively over my rock-hard cock and to daub the prong with gel. As his eyes met mine again (I remember every time it happened) it was as though he wasn't quite looking at me. He was probably completely out of it. Yet it didn't seem so.

There were voices approaching. Damn. Someone fancied a walk. He put a finger across his lips, pursed them, and made me shudder inside. In a flash, with his head thrown back, he planted himself onto me. By the time the couple drew level with us, all was still and decent. Jamie flashed the sweetest of smiles at them as he clenched his muscles around me. I winced. The couple, after smiling back, turned away. Maybe they were seeking privacy themselves.

Jamie raised himself up and eased back down, smiling wickedly at me. His brazen look was as welcoming as his beautiful opening down there. It was my turn to whimper as he pumped me into him—so slow at first that it was sheer torture. I bent forward to take a hard nipple between my lips and grazed it with my teeth. He tilted his head upward to exposing his exquisitely feminine neck as he cooed into space. Those plump lips shaped into an "O" as he pleasured himself on me. I just watched, dumbstruck and on the edge.

Then came barely perceptible footsteps on the lawn. He heard them first and ceased the action. I was about to protest when he put his finger, once again, across those lips.

"*There* you are!" said the tall one. He stood alone, towering over our little scene. The merest of glances was spared for me. "We've got to go, Jamie. We said we'd go to Sarah's bash." Jamie rolled his eyes theatrically as my cock twitched inside him. He twitched back. Steve cast a longer glance my way, slightly accusing. I shrugged as best I could.

"Five minutes, OK?" It was the first time I'd heard Jamie speak; the metallic male sound was a shock. The tall blond rolled his eyes in turn and disappeared, and the naughty smile returned to Jamie's lips. He said no more—speech would only waste time. He grabbed the other lube sachet from the grass next to us, ripped the corner with his teeth, and flipped his pleats up one deft action. He grasped his erection and shifted the skirt so that I could see what he was up to. His lips parted slightly as he started to pump. I couldn't decide which I wanted to watch more—his mouth or his hand. In the end I opted for alternation. His attention was elsewhere.

In those scant minutes, and despite not being equipped to appreciate it at the time, I came to understand stardom and all that it entails. He knew how to tilt his head back just enough to suggest ecstasy, yet without compromising the view I had of his beauty. I realized how very incidental I really was, as an individual, to this pleasure of his. I could've been anyone with reasonable looks and a certain demeanor; I was just his audience. Yet I didn't mind, didn't take it as an insult. I was a groupie touching the tail of the comet.

As I watched him bring himself—and, incidentally, me—to very intense climax, I watched his love of himself. A part of me knew that the way he was driven wouldn't make a happy person of him. Not that I wished him badly; I just saw.

And I saw his eyes raised skyward, his nostrils slightly flared. His lips puckered like the place I pillaged with my hot cock. And it was heaven, in exactly the same way a good drug or an excellent film is heavenly. His narrow chest thrust forward and his nipples grazed the zip's teeth. I wanted to suck them, but time was short. Prompted by his rising whimpers, I looked down to his frenzied hand, which accelerated along with his pumping. His silken balls crashed down onto my body with increasing urgency. I pumped back. I pumped and shot into him—into the rubber—as he showered my belly with viscous juice.

For a few precious moments, he collapsed against my chest, laying grateful little kisses on my sensitized flesh. "Thank you," he murmured, his breaths becoming less ragged.

He noticed the discarded joint on the ground next to me and picked it up, pulled away, and placed it between his lips. I lit it and we smoked the rest, toke for toke, in silence. His eyes never left mine. They were the palest eyes I'd ever seen, deep yet meaningless. And then he zipped his dress, replaced his "underwear," and straightened his hair.

I stroked the side of his face and let my fingers linger under his perfect chin. He leaned forward and kissed me, tenderly this time, his tongue saying things inside my mouth that would never be said aloud, but nothing personal all the same. Then he was gone.

I think the party went on for a few more hours. No one else seemed to have as good a time as I did, but I didn't give a shit. I sat under the beech tree, smoked fags, and quietly waited for the dawn.

# RIM MATES

## TOM G. TONGUE

"Lick lower! Get under my balls!" I begged, almost whimpering. My hard-on was killing me. After much pleading on my part, my wife of three months was *actually* giving me head—or a making weak attempt at it.

Pulling away, Nancy yelled at me, her eyes wet with tears. "NO! You are so disgusting, Tom! I love you with all my heart, but I'm not putting my mouth down there ever again!"

She pulled herself up, stumbled, as if drunk, off the bed, and ran into our bathroom slamming and locking the door loudly— the sounds of retching and running water filling my ears.

Damn that Paul Douglas! He was the reason for all my problems...

My name is Tom Gould. I'm 23 years old, with brown hair and blue eyes. I'm a muscular 185 pounds, and my body is smooth except for my pubes and my pits. Nancy is always going on to her friends about how lucky she is to have married such a good-looking guy.

I, on the other hand, could *never* complain to my friends about how unlucky I was. Nancy and I began dating our freshman year of college, but because of her fanatical Bible-beating upbringing, she wouldn't put out until we were married. I love her like crazy and was willing to wait (and *yes,* as guilty as I felt about it, I fucked around with other girls behind her back).

The honeymoon, however, held some horrid surprises for both of us. Her mother actually told her on our wedding day that it was her responsibility to "lay there and endure it for her husband." It had taken all my cajoling to get to the point where she would consider oral sex—*but*... And that brings me back to Paul Douglas!

He and I had been assigned as roommates by the campus housing authority. I was worried I'd be fixed up with some dweeb, but figured I could always make friends and find someone else to bunk with if he was really bad. When I walked through the door, loaded down with all my worldly possessions, I found a very muscular guy facedown on one of the beds. He was wearing a black football jersey and nothing else!

Somehow, the noise I'd made didn't wake him, and I was treated to a very intimate view of my assigned partner. His left leg was dangling off the edge of the mattress, and his right leg was bent and pulled up spreading his large but muscular cheeks wide open to my surprisingly curious gaze. He was a dirty blonde and the hairs around his hole were there but seemed translucent. His pucker was obviously tight and moist with sweat. Even though I stood there for only a moment, the image of his hole and his big testicles below was—and is still—etched in my brain.

To the present for a moment—I hate to admit it, but sometimes while making love to my beautiful but nonresponsive wife, that mental picture alone is enough to drive me to heights of ecstasy. A few weeks ago I almost screamed out Paul's name as I reached climax, but I managed to turn the *p* sound into "P-p-pussy, swe-e-et pussy!" Of course, *that* was a big no-no, and I was apologizing for my vile language for days.

Back to Paul. Did I tell you that while I stood in the doorway, my cock reared its head and grew fully erect within seconds? Luckily, I was wearing a baggy T-shirt that hid my nine-inch bulge. Turning toward the door, I took a deep breath and composed myself before slamming it a bit harder than I probably should have.

Paul awoke with a start, and still reclining, turned back to face me. "With a sheepish grin, but no embarrassment, he said, "Hey, you must be Tom! Practice was a killer this afternoon, and I just had to take a nap before I showered." He reached back and scratched his right ass cheek, causing me to follow his motion with my eyes. I forced myself to look away so he wouldn't see me staring at his silky smooth ass.

Grunting, he pushed himself up until he was standing in front of me, with a 10-inch erection pointing right at me. He caught me looking and smiled. "He gets that way all the time. You'll get used to it." With that he lifted off his the jersey, revealing a perfect chest and abs, lightly dusted with blond hairs.

I was too embarrassed to respond to him. Over the next few days, I discovered that my roomie, Paul, was the most sexually uninhibited person I'd ever meet. He was naked whenever he was in the room, and he was right: His dick was hard almost all the time. He just didn't give a damn. He was jerking off one time about three days later when I entered the room, and he didn't stop, despite my presence, until he'd deposited a huge load across his chin, neck, and chest. Looking me right in the eye with "that look" again, he dragged his finger through the cum and licked it off his dripping finger.

"I love the way my cum tastes! Ever try your own?" Again, I

was straight and didn't feel right talking about these things to someone I'd only known such a short time—especially another guy! It was too weird. And, yes, I'd tasted my cum, and it wasn't bad, not bad at all. I felt myself blushing, and busied myself at my desk, with Paul laughing behind me.

As time passed, Paul and I became the best friends. We shared most things easily and comfortably. I wasn't up to talking about sex with him at first, but he did loosen me up. One evening he was lounging around, naked with a hard-on as usual, and I was just returning from the shower with my towel wrapped tightly around my waist. As I moved to put on my tighty-whities (with the towel still on, of course), he jumped up, tackled me across my bed, and stripped me bare, saying, "Dude, you are too much. I know what you look like, and it's silly to put clean underwear on before you go to bed." The fact that my dick was hard wasn't discussed by either of us, but over time I became almost as relaxed in my nudity as he was. I even jerked off a couple of times with him, licking myself clean at the same time he did. I was amazed that I let myself do these things with him. We didn't touch each other, but we both knew our nakedness and hard dicks turned each other on. We just didn't talk about it.

It was with Paul, not long after our mutual jack-offs began, that I scored my first pussy. We picked up a pair of sorority sisters at a local, and after we brought them back to the room, we spent the whole night fucking their brains out. I loved it, and whenever I started to lose my arousal, one look at Paul's big, hard butt pounding away at his "date" was all it took to get my prick throbbing again.

Life progressed nicely, and Paul and I moved into a one-bedroom apartment together after our first year in the dorms. Our two full-size beds almost filled the bedroom, set up in opposite corners, and Paul had a parade of girls, the likes of which I couldn't believe. As much as I hate to admit it, I loved watching him, feigning sleep, of course. He was a great lover, and the women who visited him all left happy. I often got very intimate views of his puckering hole as he pummeled the dripping slit in front of him. I was getting my share of pussy as well but was still too shy to do anything in front of Paul very often. I also shoved any thoughts of his beautiful man ass to the back of my brain—unsuccessfully, most of the time.

During our college years, we became inseparable, and people grew used to seeing us together, and even Nancy liked Paul—although she was jealous as hell of him at the same time. As he and I grew closer, though, Nancy began to demand more of my time. It was unspoken that she wanted all my attention. She had no idea what my attraction was for him, beyond friendship (and I wouldn't even admit it to myself), but she still didn't like his "influence" on me. I sensed that Paul wasn't too crazy about her either, but they reached a silent truce of sorts—I guess to keep me happy.

Paul grew even more handsome as he crossed the line to full adulthood, and he was a babe magnet. He oozed sex and was always ready whenever a beautiful coed threw herself in his path. I guess I developed nicely as well, but that's not for me to say…

Things took a dramatic turn four years later, about a week before graduation. I'd had a fight with Nancy about sex—or the lack thereof—and was horny and in a foul mood. Paul and I went out to drink a few and look for pussy. We managed the first very well but had no luck with the second. For some reason every female I pointed out wasn't good enough for Paul. By the end of the night we were drunk and dateless.

We staggered back to our apartment with our arms around each other's shoulders for support. Once or twice his hand drifted down my back and landed on/squeezed my ass cheek. I was drunker than hell and couldn't wait to crash, but Paul had other ideas. After getting undressed, I fell across my mattress, naked and surprisingly awake, thinking how good Paul's hand had felt on my butt.

Turning my head, I watched and laughed as Paul undressed. He nearly fell three times trying to get out of his shoes, socks, and jeans. Finally, he was dressed as he was when I first met him, naked except for his black football jersey. And, yes, his John Henry was hard and throbbing.

I closed my eyes to keep from being too obvious with my stares. I didn't heard any noise from Paul's bed as his weight hit it. I sensed he was still in the room but couldn't figure out what he was up to. After a few minutes I settled into steady breathing but was wide awake. I thought I'd hear Paul jerking off, and the thought made its way to my balls.

I had turned my face toward the wall and could see Paul's shadow clearly against the wall above me. He was standing over me, and I could see his head was moving and that he was bent forward. Softly, so low I could barely hear him, he whispered, "Tom, you awake, man?"

I didn't react. I wanted to see what he was up to. Was I ever in for a shock! Louder, he said, "Tom!" Again I didn't move. From my vantage point I could see his shadow bend over me, and I felt his warm breath on my neck. I heard him inhaling, breathing through his nose. I heard him make a small grunt as I felt his breath move lower down my back, approaching my wide-open ass. With me being in a position similar to the one I'd first seen him in, my knee bent upward, I felt him blow warm air on my exposed pucker.

"I know you're awake, Tom," he said. "But don't worry, pal, you can pretend you're asleep. Tonight I'm gonna do something I've wanted to do for nearly four years! You've been shakin' that thing at me too long, and you ain't gonna make a move to stop me!" I could tell by the sound of his voice that he was kneeling beside my bed.

He grabbed my ass cheeks and pulled them apart just before he dropped his face and drove his tongue directly into my anal ring. I was disgusted and amazed at the same time. I'd never felt anything that good! As he dug deeper and wiggled his long snakelike taster, I was feeling better and better. I had to turn my face into my pillow and bite it to keep from moaning out loud. Small grunts from deep inside me did escape, but Paul didn't notice a thing; he was making his own noises, much louder than my own—growling, grunting, and slurping.

"Oh, yeah, Tom!" Lick. Slurp. "You've got a tasty butt here! I've been wanting to chew on it for a long time!" Tongue-stab. Lick. "And tonight I'm gonna get all I want!" He didn't yell, exactly; it was more like a husky whisper. He was speaking directly into my hole, and his hot breath almost burned my tender anal skin.

For the next 20 or 30 minutes he ate my ass. With my hard cock throbbing between my belly and the bed, his continuous filthy monologue and his talented tongue were driving me closer and closer to orgasm. I heard him pounding away on his own weapon. Groaning into my by-then-gaping sloppy-wet hole, Paul sent a vibration up and down my spine that went directly to my balls. Then, quickly, he pulled away, stood up, and climbed onto the bed. He knelt between my now widely spread thighs and blasted a white-hot load of cum onto my ass, aiming until the tip of his dick was touching my hole, shooting its seed deep into my guts.

Feeling that molten-hot liquid inside me took me over the edge, and biting my pillow again but making little noise, I shot directly onto my bedspread, not giving a shit, only loving the way my eruption felt and the pleasure Paul's attention to my asshole gave me.

But he wasn't done yet. He pulled back, not leaving the bed, and proceeded to lick up every drop of cum that dripped from my cheeks, down my crack, and out of my hole toward my balls. I never lost my erection, my cum providing a nice lubrication on the poly-cotton fabric.

To my regret, giving a final suck-kiss to my hole, and with a slurpy voice, Paul spoke, "Pretend this didn't happen, Tom, good buddy, but be ready for more tomorrow night. I ain't had enough of that sweet-tastin' hole." He backed away, and I heard him collapse onto his bed. Moments later I heard his deep breathing and knew he was asleep.

I was torn. I wanted more. I wanted to go over to Paul's bed and return the favor, but I just couldn't. The thought of sticking my tongue up a guy's hole...well, it made me sick. I was such a prude, or I was too shy. Moving quietly, I grabbed my wet bath towel off the end of my footboard and wiped my body and the bedspread clean, then fell asleep with the towel somewhere—OK, directly under my nose.

The next evening, I came home late from my finals-study session at the school library to find Paul alone—a rare event. I'd avoided him in the morning by getting up earlier than usual, flipping my stained spread, showering, and dressing in the living room—basically, I was sneaking away.

Tom was in his normal naked state, lying on his bed on his side, his free hand slowly stroking his big dick. He smiled at me in that knowing way, and instantly, the electricity in the room was palpable. Neither of us spoke as I undressed for bed. After brushing my teeth, I climbed on top of my bed, pulling back the comforter and sheet but not climbing under them. I lay on my stomach and made sure my ass was pointed directly at Paul. I spread my legs wide apart.

I didn't have to wait long for Paul's visit. Within seconds he had placed his tongue flat against the sole of my foot and dragged its wet surface upward with lapping licks. I nearly giggled when he reached the back of my knee, but the pleasure he was giving me and the anticipation of his mouth on my hole kept me from making any noise.

As much as I loved what he was doing, I still had doubts. I wondered if I could just go with it. He seemed to like it. OK, he loved it, and since he said I didn't have to discuss it, I became determined to let him do what he wanted, as his tongue grazed across my ass cheek one last time before he began his oral excavating.

Just like the night before, he ate away, grunting and groaning, until we both reached climax, he on/in my ass, me on the towel under my crotch. (Did I mention I'd put a towel there?) This time, however, he used his fingers to push his cum deep into my gaping hole, and his digit kept brushing up against something inside me that had me turned on like I'd never been turned on before.

I heard him sucking his finger as he pulled it free. He was so nasty, but as with anything sexual, he had no inhibitions whatsoever. He gave me one more suck-kiss before lightly slapping my ass and saying, "Night, bro." He was asleep within seconds again.

I lay there, breathing heavily, still horny as hell but not knowing what to do. I wanted him to play with my ass even more! And I realized the only way to do that was just to get up and crawl over into his bed...but again I just couldn't. It was a step I wasn't prepared to take.

Again I snuck out each of the following two mornings, returning late to find Paul naked, hard, and waiting. The night before graduation, my family and Nancy's parents were in town, but Paul was again waiting for me. I'd been out to eat with the families and was on edge. I couldn't concentrate or make polite dinner conversation. I was thinking about the wonderful feelings

Paul had been giving me. My hole was tender and a little sore, but pleasantly so, and I wanted my best bud's kisses and licks to make it all better.

But he was waiting for me in a different way—he was lying on his stomach, again wearing only that same black football jersey, legs widespread exposing his beautiful ass to me completely. As big a tease as ever, Paul was actually winking his pucker at me. I stood in the doorway wanting more than anything to climb between his massive thighs and bury my entire head into his hole.

But I didn't. I regretted it, but I had practically proposed to Nancy and didn't want to complicate things by taking what Tom and I had done any further. I know: My thinking was totally fucked up. Instead, I quietly undressed and climbed onto my bed in exactly the same position I'd assumed the previous four nights.

Paul was up and on my bed surprisingly fast, laughing lightly as he quickly latched his sucking, licking mouth to my eager anal opening. I nearly screamed in pleasure. My best bud and roomie had some new thought on his mind that particular night. He began to push one, then two, spit-slick fingers into my dripping hole, sucking on them and rewetting them a few times on the outstroke.

Suddenly, I felt something—he shifted his position, and an altogether new sensation met my saliva-filled pucker. I felt the blunt head of Paul's huge penis as he used it to rim my hole. With a twist of his hips, half of his huge missile entered me, and I was amazed! I experienced no pain, only a wonderful, full feeling. As he pushed himself completely into me, I pushed back to meet his thrust, until I felt his pubes tickling my ass lips. His huge glans touched that spot deep inside me, and I let a groan escape.

"Yeah, you love that, don't you, Tommy? You've wanted this ever since you first saw me!" Paul was panting and groaning as he slowly began to fuck my ass for real. His swiveling hips widened my hole, causing him to brush my prostate more thoroughly on every stroke. I buried my face in my pillow, whimpering in pleasure as Paul fucked the hell out of my ass—he was a master cocksman and used every trick in the book on me.

Every time either of us approached orgasm, Paul stopped his strokes and completely impaled my ass on his dick, letting me feel his massive organ throb deep inside me. Speaking with a growl directly into my ear, Paul said, "Tom, I've wanted it too, and I'm gonna fuck that sweet hole of yours all night long!"

And he did just that. With me lying there, totally passive, Paul shot six loads of steaming hot splooge into me, only to pull away and suck it back out again.

OK, I wasn't exactly passive; I pushed back with my ass to meet his thrusts over and over again. The more he fucked me, the more responsive I became. I learned to milk his weapon as it slammed in and out of me. I rotated my hips from side to side, as did he, to create new points of contact for each of us. I shot at least six loads into my cum towel, which I had to throw away the next morning. My ass was sore for two weeks, but every ache made my balls tingle.

As Paul ground his pubes into my gaping, dripping hole during our last fuck, he whispered into my ear, "Tom, I wish you'd given in completely…but I understand. You asked Nancy to marry you, or you're gonna. We'll be leaving here in a few hours and go our separate ways, and if you want, you don't have to have anything to do with me anymore." He sort of sighed as he gave me a somewhat vicious thrust. "But I'll tell you this…if you want to do this again, I'll be there. But you've gotta be awake!"

Back to the present: With Nancy crying and retching in the bathroom, I slipped on some gym shorts and a T-shirt, grabbed my keys, and headed for my car. I didn't know where I was going, but I had a good idea. As I pulled into the parking lot, I thought of how easy it had been to comply with my fiancée's wishes and drop Paul like a hot potato. He called several times, but I always made excuses and gradually I grew to miss him less and less...but my brain couldn't put aside the thoughts about what we had done.

I never looked at other men—well, maybe a little—but Paul was always my fantasy. As I parked the car and moved toward the apartment door, I thought of how great a friend Paul had been. He and I had enjoyed our encounters, and he asked for nothing else from me. I realized how selfish I'd been with him. Well, I planned to change that.

I knocked on the door, and heard a familiar voice shout, "It's open! Come on in!" I turned the knob and entered. There, lying before me, was Paul, looking almost identical to when I'd seen him for the first time. He was wearing a black football jersey and nothing else, except this time he was on his black leather couch. I'd called five minutes earlier and had the quickest of phone conversations with him.

"Hello."

"Hi."

"Tom?"

"Yeah, we need to talk..."

"Come on over."

"Bye."

Click.

I hadn't seen him in almost two years, and he looked better than ever. Again he was winking his asshole at me, but he was smiling too. "Tom," he said. "I think I need to take a nap here. Excuse me..." And he turned his head toward the pillow and couldn't stop himself from laughing. I was laughing too, as I threw off my clothes and crawled between his wide-open thighs...

Paul is getting married next month, and I'm his best man. His bride-to-be is a real beauty, and she has a good brain too. She and my now-happily-sex-deprived wife are becoming friends, which is fine with me and my "rim mate." Nancy—who allowed Paul back into our lives surprisingly easily—and I had them over for dinner, and while the ladies went to the living room to discuss wedding plans, Paul and I went to the basement for some ass-licking butt-fucking fun. Life is good.

# BAG BOY

**H.L. GINSBERG**

I have a problem. I'm making dinner myself tonight. I like to cook, but I don't love it. It's my night, though. Daddy's night. And I only use the freshest of vegetables. Nothing canned.

At 34, I have a respectable bank balance, a wife, and a 2-year-old daughter. We've had her tested, the daughter. She's gifted, which makes her eligible to attend the Maria Brandt Academy when she is, you know, of age.

This evening as I sit here on the toilet—dick in hand—I can still see him. I see him as he was just 30 minutes ago. He's slipping the arugula into my paper (not plastic) grocery bag. Carefully.

Our dog, Miggsy, placed fourth in the American Kennel Club's Best of Breed competition. She's a weimaraner. We taught her to lift her paws for us so we can wipe her feet before she enters the house.

Chad, the bag boy at Wonder Mart, places my fresh loaf of pesto bread atop the rest of my groceries.

And I want to suck his cock.

I don't know how it happened: This, the undoing of Herbert Leland Ginsberg. I was never a choirboy. I saw *Cats* on Broadway only once, and I hated it. I've never liked pastel dress shirts or avocado sandwiches or Barbra Streisand. But it has happened, regardless. "It" is the feeling that my dick will explode like Old Faithful at the sight of Chad's biceps sliding and swelling, as he lifts my sack of goods into the cart.

"Herbert!"

I've found that stroking my balls is always the best way to start. If I close my eyes, I can almost see the green Wonder Mart smock stretched across Chad's permanent boner.

"Herbert!"

"In a minute!" I do up my pants. I'm still hard and frustrated. Why Lois won't use the bathroom upstairs, I'll never know.

After eight weeks, I've had enough nights of unsuccessful masturbation. The Wonder Mart is on my way home from work. This Friday evening I make an unscheduled stop. And it isn't for arugula.

As top Midwest sales rep for Kurtz Copiers, I'm a man who knows opportunity when he sees it. I'm also a man who isn't afraid to take a risk, or so I tell myself as I pull my Honda Accord into a parking space alongside the smoking blue Cavalier with the hood propped up.

Is it fate?

"Fuck!" Chad stands in his worn jeans and a white T-shirt with his hands balled into fists at his sides. He's tall, with a V-shaped torso: wide chest, slim at the waist. Sweat and damp heat from the Cavalier's angry radiator have curled his blond hair. What is he—18, 19? A college boy, I decide. Oh, God.

"You need a ride?" I try not to smile as I lower the car window. He nods.

On the way to Chad's house, I uncap a bottle of sweet whiskey, and—as if we'd agreed on this long ago—I pull off the road and park the Accord in a field behind a small grove. We sit there and look at each other for a moment. Then, terrified, I put my head in his lap. I nuzzle his crotch and inhale the raunchy, beautiful smell of him through his threadbare jeans.

Chad grabs me by the hair and pulls my head back. He looks into my eyes, arches his back, and pops open the buttons of his jeans, like it's some kind of magic trick. Pop, pop, pop and presto! Out comes his cock. I roll my tongue around its full, firm head, taking it in as deeply as I can manage. I let it slide sloppily from my mouth, and I kiss his balls.

"Suck it!" Chad moans. He repositions my mouth over his dripping dick and pushes down on the back my head. And I do, I suck him like I love him, and I weep as I swallow his hot cum, which coats my throat and tames the taste of the whiskey. *The essence of Chad,* I think. Mmmm.

I'm a slender fellow. I run, work out occasionally, and generally try to keep in shape. But I have never felt so tender and trim as I do right now—as I clutch the Honda's dash and slide his slick rod into my ass. The pain! So sharp I wonder if I missed his johnson and shimmied onto the gearshift knob instead. Chad's meaty ex–high school football hands clench my waist and my muscles relax. At last, my ass accepts this novel challenge, its destiny, and I start into the rock-and-fuck mode. *So this is what it's like to break your cherry. Not bad.*

"I have a girlfriend. At school," says Chad, singing the first postcoital verse of the ballad of the part-time queer.

"And I have a wife. At home," I counter with a verse of my own.

# UNMASKING THE DELEGATE

**S. JAMES WEGG**

Nothing ever happens to me at conferences. Still, a weekend away from married life was nothing to be sneezed at.

This time, Vancouver was the host city for our annual performing arts organization's get-together. My direct flight from the nation's capital had been uneventful except for a few turbulent moments on the descent. As always, the view of the Canadian Rockies was spectacular. Nothing could match that sight, or so I thought as we taxied to the gate.

The four-star hotel overlooking the harbor had screwed up my reservation, but I was upgraded to a two-bedroom suite at the same discounted rate, so I decided not to complain. After unpacking, I showered thoroughly, ignoring the upward thrust of my long-neglected tool (after my wife gave birth to our first child, our sex life diminished; following the second, my right hand and a vivid imagination had to suffice—cheating was out of the question.) I threw on my conservative blue blazer, khaki pants, and turtle neck, then sauntered off to the opening reception in my gleaming penny loafers.

As I entered the opulent ballroom, the roar of the 200 dele-gates indicated that this event was in full swing. I decided to save the hors d'oeuvres for later and headed straight for the open bar.

Two double scotches and five spring rolls later, I had pretty much completed the required rounds and brown-nose greetings, I decided to gulp down just one more libation, then call it a night. Even a three-hour time difference wreaked havoc on my body's biorhythms.

"Excuse me, aren't you from the National Philharmonic?"

I spun around in response to the unknown voice whose owner had also tapped my shoulder. The inquirer beamed mis-chievously as he proffered his hand and shook mine vigorously. "Marlin Thomas, Thunder Bay," he announced warmly.

"Why, er—yes." I introduced myself to him. "Did we meet last year?" I asked, feeling strangely awkward. There was cer-tainly no reason to be. He was roughly my age and smartly dressed, although I could never wear an open-neck shirt to a for-mal reception, much less pants that were so close-fitting that I could tell he wore boxers. Furthermore, his name tag indicated junior management whereas mine read "artistic director."

"Gosh, I don't think so. I only started work a few weeks ago —but I've heard so much about your accomplishments I was hoping you'd let me pick your brains, especially about program-ming contemporary music. You drinking the Chivas too? Great, I'll get the refills."

And so we began a lively conversation that never paused. We laughed, groaned, and sighed our way through the difficulties of marketing music not promoted on MTV, until the scotch bottle became as empty as the room.

"Wow. Guess we scared everyone off!" he said. "Thanks for your time. And you've been so helpful—I hate to ask another favor, but you see, by the time I got around to registering, the hotel was booked solid. Any chance I could bunk with you tonight?"

It was as if my bump-up to deluxe had been preordained.

"Of course. Thanks to those fools at the front desk, I've got more space than one person could ever use. Let's get your bag."

Ten minutes later, after having raided the minibar for nightcaps, we sat on the couch and dissed the lame monologues of the Comedy Channel's stand-up wanna-bes.

And so when Marlin's sinewy hand landed firmly on my thigh, I thought, at first, he was just getting my attention prior to delivering his next sarcastic line. But he remained silent as his fingers pressed harder into the fabric of my wrinkle-free trousers.

Uncharacteristically at a loss for words, I stared straight ahead and drank deeply from my glass. Marlin's hand moved steadily toward the center of my personal universe. Much to my astonishment, I made no attempt to hinder his progress even as my neglected meat engorged itself trying to meet his fingers halfway.

*What's going on down there?* I wondered. *Men don't turn me on.*

I slowly shifted my gaze from the electronic chatter and looked directly into the eyes of my companion. He held my stare, captured his prey, and abruptly cut off whatever words had started to sputter from my throat by locking his mouth onto mine. Within seconds his slippery tongue slid by my teeth and explored my gums. Our saliva merged deliciously. I was in such a state of shock that I failed to realize that his nimble fingers had released my aching boner from its confinement. It was now encircled by his unrelenting grip. My eyes bulged to the brim of their sockets as his other hand scooped up my balls and milked them gently, intent on liberating their cargo.

The insistent bristling of his late-in-the-day whiskers against my cheeks was the most incredible tactile sensation I'd ever felt. My self-amazement increased exponentially as I found one of my hands gently massaging his lightly haired left nipple after I slipped my wayward fingers under his silk shirt.

Then I started down a road I'd no business taking. It began on a path of short, coarse hair just below his navel and, aided by the timely deflation of his otherwise smooth stomach, continued past his belt, then underneath the elastic guardian of his clearly outlined pole. The forbidden journey ended with his uncut, tantalizingly slick dick-head pumping out a small but steady stream of homemade lubricant into my virgin palm.

The bad jokes kept coming over the Comedy Channel, though our turgid state rendered us oblivious to them. I let the liquor blind my judgment and shot the biggest load of my life all over my now-bare heaving chest. And as he dropped his lips to my trembling skin and hungrily ate my spunk, I squeezed his iron rod with all my might and was rewarded with a shower of thick cream. Its pungent scent filled the air as he screamed his delight. Without hesitation, I inhaled his still-throbbing shaft, savoring every creamy drop until his spent flesh receded.

We lay entwined for an hour, saying nothing, stroking each other's hair and gently nibbling whatever was near.

Finally, scared, exhilarated, and puzzled, I clicked off the TV and spoke. "How did you know?" I blurted at last.

"When I looked into your eyes, and you didn't turn away, there was hope," he said. "But when your crotch jumped after agreeing to let me spend the night, I knew your wedding band was all that was keeping you from an important discovery."

We struggled into bed and slept together, but by the time I got up he was already gone.

The next night he stayed elsewhere, but not before trying to set me up with a "friend" whom I couldn't bring myself to touch.

I hurried home to my family, content with twice-yearly couplings and a renewed respect for the ministrations of my hand. It would be another decade before I'd completely accept what Marlin, magically, had known in a flash.

# ANGELIC SNOT

## CHARLIE VAZQUEZ

With a manic medley of furious punk and metal tunes blaring a beautiful cacophony in the cavern of my skull, I ran down the carpeted stairs of my apartment building and, with a cigarette pinched between lips, headed for the Sex Palace. I'd been drinking a little that night, and some very excellent Ecstasy pumped through my body. It mixed with the kind of adrenaline rush that blossoms from your core as soon as you realize that something you really desire is about to be yours. It was a heightened and heady romantic feeling, except that it was a sustained rush that never went away; in fact, it kept growing. It ebbed and surged like a tide.

Naturally, I was insatiable.

The streets were clear for a Friday night. Other people were on their way home, while I was on my way out. Like a drugged-out and horny vampire, I entered the Sex Palace and purchased a small lubricant bottle and a couple of condoms, just in case I scored something more than my usual blow job from another queer guy. I stalked the aisles like a predator. Wary men avoided eye contact with me.

A guy and his hooker-trick stumbled drunkenly from one of the stalls, so I snagged the space as soon as they left it. I locked the door and thought about the germs on my fingers and how they were beautiful. I sifted through empty drug bags on the floor while trying to avoid the small puddles of fresh cum around them.

The stench in the cubicle was horrendous, so I opted to occupy another one. As I walked past one of the other rooms, I noticed the door was halfway open and peeked inside. There I saw a stunning man—mid 30s, rock-and-roll facial hair, shorts down around his ankles, shirtless. He was sitting on a chair and masturbating like a desperate animal.

I asked, "Mind if I watch?"

He ignored me, probably figuring me for a fag, but he was so horny that he couldn't take his hand off his cock for a second to close the flimsy, cum-stained door. I stepped inside, tested his boundaries. He was heavily tattooed on his arms and had beautiful hair on his body. Just enough. His muscles were firm as well: His biceps were packed, and his chest was wide and welcoming. The Ecstasy was still zooming in me and all I wanted to do was help him out, suck him off, but still he ignored me. I excused myself. He looked up suddenly.

"You coming back?"

"Did you want me to?"

"Yeah, come back in a minute."

I figured he was pee-shy, or something like that, so I honored his request. Some instinct within me told me to go and buy fruit-flavored lubricant. So I did.

Upon my return his door was locked, so I knocked a few times. The door opened and I saw he was still alone. I entered, locking the door behind me. His cock looked even bigger than before. He stroked it maniacally while he watched a woman getting fucked by two men on the TV screen above us. The tiny room was filled with moans but they weren't from him or me. They were the piggish grunts of overweight women getting fucked by big black guy's dicks. *Not too bad,* I thought. I was slightly aroused, I was on drugs, and I was expecting to get a blow job from another fag like me. And suddenly a devilishly handsome cat was asking me to hang out with him while he stroked his nine inches of working-class punk-rock cock. I immediately knew that he was straight. He exuded a certain combination of suspense and confidence.

I asked him, "Why did you want me to come back?" I stood a short distance away from him, fully clothed.

He ignored me a spell, then answered without taking his eyes from the porn flickering on the TV. "Just hang out, man."

His eyes opened wide and he spread his legs wider. Something goosed his excitement. Someone knocked on our door.

He kept his eyes on the screen while I waited for a reaction from him.

He looked over at me. "Open the door, please." Lovely sexy baritone.

"Sure." I clicked open the greasy lock.

A tall and bizarre-looking man walked in without introducing himself. He had lesions on his face and there was a hint of make-up on him: a true nocturne, perhaps a drag queen out of drag, another vampire.

"Here you go, Mitchell." He handed Mitchell a small bag of something. Drugs.

Mitchell looked at it and handed him a twenty.

The man looked over at me and winked. I didn't like his appearance or his vibe.

He asked us, "Mind if I watch?"

"Get out," I told him. He left immediately. I locked the door, double-checking that it was secure. I wasn't in the mood to share at that point. This Mitchell character was treating me like he trusted me. He snorted the drugs off the top of a CD case and shook his head wildly from side to side. He gave me some. I didn't ask him what it was—more Ecstasy or meth, I supposed. My drugged knees shook uncontrollably.

I wanted to touch him and suck him off. The edge of my sexual desperation was sharp as a knife. The prospect of mounting his large, slick cock occupied every corner of my head-space.

I told him my name was Israel. He smiled and told me it was a nice name. My eyes watered, and I sneezed repeatedly and wiped my snot on the cum-stained walls.

"Hey, Israel. Are you a cocksucker?" He gazed maniacally at the TV. I liked the feeling I got from him.

"Of course I'm a cocksucker. Why else would I stand here watching you beat your meat?" He glanced at me and smirked. He had beautiful green eyes and a sleazy mustache. He leaned over and grabbed me by my belt.

"Come suck this dick, man." He offered himself to me. I was excited to perform on him because I could tell he was straight and straight guys are completely in your control when you're gay and you're sucking them off—even if they think the contrary is true. His eyes bulged out of his head when I grabbed his impressive length and slicked it up and down with fruit-flavored lube. I had to handle it manually for a few moments just to get him to want me to suck on it sooner. He was about to get on a ride he would never forget.

I admired his body for a moment as he impatiently wiggled his midsection. He wanted it badly.

By the time I put his throbbing cock in my mouth, he'd waited long enough and let out a puppy-like whimper of relief. I was pleasantly surprised when he began to caress my ears. Solid fingers combed through my hair as I gave him all I had. My own drugs were beginning to take off—for the second time that night—and I was ready to be a whore for him. I sucked him hard and stroked him with my hands while he watched the hetero porn and moaned in a deep sexual gluttony from a place deep within him.

He lit a cigarette and called me "Honey." I continued to suck him like I hadn't sucked a man in years. His cock was perfectly shaped. His balls were like hairy walnuts. As I gave them a good licking, he whined like a little boy and begged me to get back on the pole. His crotch was musky, almost skunky. It drove me wild.

In the background the television blared obscenities. People climaxed, one after another, in a string of moans and gasps. Lots of heavy breathing. In the stall next to us—number 24—a man screamed at the top of his lungs. I imagined he was getting fucked with an oversized dildo or some other random phallic object. I distinctly heard another man try to calm him down.

I wondered what would happen next. This Mitchell character was so handsome that I resolved to relish every lick and every sniff. It's not every day that a gorgeous punk rock fantasy-daddy spreads his legs for me and begs me to suck him like the bitch I am.

I got back on the pole, much to his delight. And mine.

Another bang at the door.

I moved to get up and open the door, but Mitchell grabbed my hair and shoved me back down on his cock. I was turned on by the minor violence and complied eagerly.

"Wrong fucking door!" Mitchell yelled at the unknown knocker: The interloper moved on.

As I sucked him off, I smelled the mystic aroma of a burning joint. Mitchell offered me a drag as I slurped on him. I let go of him and took a deep draw. The smoke got in my eyes and temporarily blinded me. I thought of the music I'd listened to at home and how I wished Mitchell could have heard my own personal soundtrack—the pulsing drums and bass, the wailing guitars, the singer about to lose his mind. The drugs were on. I ignored the benign pain and got back on the meat pole. I sucked his cock until I had his full attention—that is, until his legs started to shake. He removed his shorts and underwear. Now I had him completely nude (except for a pair of beat up Converse sneakers) and completely in my grasp. Glorious.

He said, "oh, baby," over and over again and I felt the Ecstasy I'd forgotten about and I was thrilled because my jaws weren't sore yet. I had the feeling it would be one of those eternal drugged-out blow jobs that ended with a sore and floppy dick with nothing coming out of it.

I buried my head under his balls for a change of scenery and licked him in his hot spots, which he enjoyed while his body jerked in little spasms of pleasure. At that point he became every one of my punk rock fantasies rolled into one. He became the old roommate—the sexy artist punk that I fell in love with. And then he became Simon, the always-wasted British boy with solid hairy legs who would grab me by my shoulders and call me mate while I examined the patterns of his armpit hair.

He morphed into the Latin punks I'd known as a kid in New York, their torsos golden and muscular, their arms smooth and tattooed with their girlfriends' names. They would always twist the hair on their navels while coming on to one of your sisters. He became the rock stars I'd always wanted to blow—every last one of them. Then he was the upstairs neighbor guy who'd bought me beer before I was of legal age. He certainly deserved a good sucking for getting me drunk at least two hundred times.

And after that he was the drummer guy whose name I'd forgotten, who used to go have beers with me before I'd even come out. One time he sat calmly in sweatpants—with no underwear on—and confessed that he thought he might be bisexual. I'd fantasized about him endlessly and now I had him too. On the day we sat outside sipping beers, I allowed my eyes to fall below the surface of the table to catch the shape of his flaccid beauty resting softly behind a cotton curtain. But now he was hard in my mouth.

Next he was the hot skinhead guy I'd met at a club in Seattle. How I wanted to run my hands down that man's chest just to feel the sheet of hair and muscle that jutted out of his nearly unbuttoned shirt on a hot August afternoon. He had an inverted Swastika on his right pectoral. I remember watching a bead of sweat running down past it, only to be absorbed by the fabric of his shirt instead of by my tongue. Yet in my mind, in that cheesy sex booth, I was sucking him off instead and he was begging for more when I'd stop to take a full breath of air for my collapsing lungs.

Then he was one of the Italian thugs who would chat up my dad when I was a kid. With piercing, animalistic eyes they would make a panoramic sweep of the street around them while saying hello to you. They always had their hands in their trouser pockets, and now I was ripping those same hands off their cocks when they would try to stroke themselves. I wanted to do it all for them, and they obeyed me. Luigi would say in his New York Italian accent, "Suck that fucking dick, you fucking faggot." I would get insulted and stop. Apologetically, he would lure me back to it and then behave.

And then Mitchell transformed back into himself—the tattooed stallion from who-knows-where with a hairy barrel chest. The television still emitted guttural moans and the sounds of slimy bodies slapping together. I heard latex and aggravated pink skin making friction. I started to think about what he was thinking about—this tattooed Romeo with Devil and Reaper tattoos. He was a stunning creature with soft eyes and a wet mustache that looked like candy to me as he slicked it with his own tongue and saliva—this man who had allowed me, a complete stranger, unhindered access to his sexual core. As I was sucking, as I went up and down the length of his pride, I thought about what sort of life he might have, what he might do for work. Perhaps he had a wife and children. What I didn't have to wonder about was whether he was gay. I could tell he liked the ladies, but that he also liked something weird and freaky every now and then.

Mitchell was affectionate and appreciative, not abusive and manipulative like the occasional encounters I'd had with other straight men. For most of them, the cocksucker, the engineer of the sex act, is emasculated and rendered subhuman, lower than a cowardly man. Mitchell called me by my name and said things like, "Dude, that feels so good," and, "Hot cock sucking, man."

When he picked up the TV remote and began to surf the channels, I decided to finish him off.

He stood up for a moment to feed the machine more money.

He lifted me up off my knees. "Get up, dude."

"What?" I stood up in front of him. He undid my zipper and squirted fruity lubricant on my cock.

Then he said, "I wanna suck your dick, man." I was surprised and remained silent. I allowed him to, of course.

His cock sucking was loose, not experienced. I told him to suck harder, and he did for a minute. He put my whole cock in his mouth and sucked it gently while I looked at his sideburns and his tattoos. I ran my hands through his hair and encouraged him to suck me even harder, but I got the impression that he was afraid of hurting my cock. He lost interest in sucking my dick, and I noticed that his erection had fallen.

"Suck my dick again, dude." He looked at me with needy eyes and I couldn't resist. He was a sensitive misfit, an angelic mischief-maker. I wanted to suck him while he was soft—that's a huge turn-on for me—and I felt like I was about to explode. He rubbed himself reluctantly and I knew exactly what he wanted. He stood up against the wall this time. I got on the floor. I spied streaks of dried cum on the walls and the door. I kneeled before him and let him have it.

I pounded my face into him like a jackhammer, squeezed him and twisted my hands around his shaft, and kneaded every square inch of his agitated prong. He began to moan, so I slowed down my rhythmic assaults to build him up again. He put his hand on my head to encourage me to resume my attack, and I slowly built to my original speed. Before I knew it, he was whining and grinding his pubic hair against my nose and lips.

"Harder," he begged.

I sucked him harder while the women and men in the porno started to lose their bearings. As they ascended to orgasm my head filled with the sound of people on the brink of a very fleeting insanity. Mitchell's breathing intensified and pre-cum oozed from him like fruit juice. He grabbed my ears, and I was deafened for a few moments. All heard was the sound of my head hitting his midsection like a demolition ball and the sound of my slurping mouth. I pulled on his cock as hard as I could, and suddenly my mouth filled with warm cum.

While he came, I squeezed the base of his cock tightly, and his eyes popped out of his head like cannon balls on tethers. I interrupted the ejection of his sperm with alternating sucks and high-pressure squeezing at his cock's base.

Mitchell hopped on his feet as his orgasm stretched past its usual duration. Semen continued to squirt out of his cock, his legs shook, and he tried to pull his cock out my mouth. But I was adamant about sucking every last drop out of him. He looked down at me in half-horror as I lapped up the last drops of man seed that dangled from his beautifully red and slackening prong.

I stood up and jacked myself off. My spunk shot four or five feet in front of me and onto the wall. It crawled down the wall like angelic snot as we dressed ourselves.

"Thanks, Mitchell." I admired his breathtaking nakedness for the last time.

"Thank *you*." Awkwardly, he stepped forward and stepped back again.

"Where are you going now?" I twisted around to wrap my belt around my waist. I checked the time. It was seven in the morning. A pack's worth of cigarette butts littered the stall floor. We'd been in there for hours.

"What time is it?" Mitchell gazed at me. His friendliness hadn't worn off post-sex.

"Seven."

"Good, the bars just opened. I can't go home yet. I can't deal with her right now." He smirked and we left.

After a few laughs over some beers at a sports bar, I went home. I've never seen him again.

# JOHN A.

## CUAUHTEMOC Q

I moved away from my own regurgitation, repelled by the stench, and looked up into the gray afternoon light filtering into the room. I saw his face looking down on me like a warm storm front, holding back but gathering momentum.

John's pouty lips opened to allow a sotto voce utterance: "Tied one on, didn't you?"

"I guess so. How'd I get here?" I asked, tripping over my words.

"I dragged your tired ass up to your room before bad-ass Sergeant Major had a chance to write you up and drum you out of the service, boy."

"That bad, huh?"

That bad."

I was drifting among devils and angels, assigned to a company in Germany, part of a U.S. Army battalion stationed outside of Munich. John A., as I liked to call him, happened to be one of my assigned angels of the day.

I'd gone off on an assigned morning detail with an old disgruntled black enlisted man, and we somehow happened to buy a few bottles of good German white wine and got pissed—all on government time. When he dropped me off at the barracks after our wine-tasting adventure, I stumbled out of his car and was rescued by John who saw me tripping over my own feet way too early in the day.

I was a punk kid with half a brain, so by default I had become the company's training noncommissioned officer. Actually, nobody else wanted the job, and the vast majority of the brawny assigned men of military cadre could barely spell their own names correctly. Because of my three-striped rank I was given my own room in the barracks, a small room that served as a safe haven for smoking hash with a select group of trusted individuals, including John A. We'd all sit on my mattress on the floor, happily drinking brew and lighting up dark squares of hashish when we were flush with cash from our meager paychecks. We spent our time together laughing, dreaming, and counting the days until we could each return home.

John was the quiet leader of our group, able to accommodate himself to the personalities around him and make each feel like he was their spiritual big brother. On many occasions, long after the others had gone to bed, John and I would talk long into the night. Like a poet he'd recite streams of elegant words from his favorite authors and tell me stories about his friendship with Jack Kerouac and others. I hung onto his every word. I was a young, goo-goo-eyed kid content to imbibe as much as I could from my intellectual mentor, John A.

John just happened to be straight. He was one of those men who carries a disarming stardust smile that immediately captures everyone's attention as soon as he enters a room. He had eyes the color of a young evergreen, which sat calmly below tufted eyebrows resembling wild sagebrush. You could say John was my latest "mental tattoo." I wanted him to be a permanent part of me, though I knew I had to share him with way too many others. His exploits with the women were notorious and envied by his military peers. John's scorecard far outdistanced the others, in part, by the sheer power of his understated magnetic animal attraction. His eyes had something to do with it, but his ample member spoke to that same kind of attraction as well.

And could he drink. After hours drinking and smoking and yakking with the boys, he'd return to the barracks, weave up the steps to my room, and tap lightly on my door. We'd then talk into the night about his demons, about life, about our futures. No matter how tired I was, my door was always open to John, my own poet laureate.

There had been a few nights when John, still fully clothed, passed out next to me on the floor. Nothing ever happened between us sexually; I simply made sure he had enough covers throughout the night. John had to share a room with three other guys, but most nights he visited my room and more often than not spent the night. I think he just couldn't sleep; he seemed to be a military insomniac, haunted by the past and confused about the future.

John and a few of the other guys returned to my room later that evening with a bit of hash to smoke. I had cleaned up the vomit and was feeling much better. Youth has such marvelous recuperative powers. After passing around and finishing the hashish, the group decided to go to the base movie house. I bowed out, knowing it wasn't a movie I would enjoy. Surprisingly, John said he'd stay behind with me. The others left, mumbling under their breath that we were a couple of party poopers and deadbeats.

John looked over to me and just stared.

"What?" I said, feeling swallowed up by those eyes.

"I don't know how to put his, boy, but…"

"Well, you're the one with all the fancy words."

"OK, I'll say it. When you looked up at me this morning from your bed and that pool of green vomit, you didn't exactly keep anything inside." I just looked at him and he went on. "It's not what you said exactly, but it was how those eyes of yours were talking."

"Hey, who was drunk, you or me?" I asked him, even though I knew what he was saying. I didn't know what to do with my feelings for him. And I guess, even though I tried to disguise those feelings, they came through loud and clear. Besides, I knew my feelings were off-limits.

"I think we should shower, come back to your room, and then see what happens," he said. He motioned for me to follow him down to the showers and, like a puppy following his mama's tail, I stayed inside his warm shadow, waiting for the next nudge.

I remember entering the shower stall and I remember lathering up , but I couldn't look at John or the droplets of water falling from his taut body. Somehow I managed to towel off, and somehow we managed to return to my room, and somehow we managed to be in the same bed lying next to each other naked.

"Do whatever you want," John encouraged in a deadpan voice.

Although I wasn't a virgin I hadn't had a lot of experience with men. I was usually the nonaggressive partner, allowing the top to plunge deep within my youthful peaks of tender pink flesh.

John lay back with his hands behind his head as I shut off the light and let my eyes grow accustomed to the darkness. Like most, I was braver in the dark. His skin touched my flesh like a song in the darkness. I felt the notes but somehow didn't know the lyrics. I kissed his torso and moved my tongue within this confined territory of muscle. I felt his hand come forward and touch my back reassuringly. I shook with both fear and delight as I inched my tongue over his naturally developed pecs, and as I pulled on them, teasing them into stiff peaks, I felt his cock jump through my thighs, pushing my cheeks slightly apart. His cock throbbed, a welcome intruder against my round flesh mounds.

I was hesitant of any further movement. I contented myself with John's pectoral region and enjoyed the feel of his flesh against my ass cheeks. I kept thinking of his thick lips and the way they opened when he talked. I wanted to find that tongue, the one that mouthed all that poetry and led our nightly conversations. I lifted myself up and smashed down into his mouth, forcing my tongue in a youthful, clumsy frenzy upon his more mature, experienced tongue. Pre-cum flowed from my cock; I concentrated hard to hold back a premature ejaculation.

John kissed me back while grabbing my ass cheeks and shuttling them back and forth against his cock. My tongue eventually made its way to his throbbing member and tasted his salty pre-cum. I moved down to his ball sac and bathed with my saliva, which caused him to sigh with pleasure.

I had experienced the pain and pleasure of a driving thrust into my butthole without lubricant and sufficient preparation; it always left a bloodstain, as if to mark the juncture of ass and cock, a crimson remembrance of a good time. John, somehow picking up on my thoughts, rolled on top of me and lifted my legs heavenward. He drew down to my hole and allowed his saliva to drip onto my budded orifice. His tongue plunged in and explored my sphincter; he then inserted his fingers up my hole, slowly preparing entrance for his ever-thickening flesh stick, all the while mouthing words as rich as melted chocolate.

He lifted my legs higher, spread them into a V, and inched his crimson cock head into my slick asshole. I pushed toward his cock to greet him, felt the pain, and accepted the ensuing pleasure that followed. Once he was inside, I tightened my muscles around his member and tangled with my soldier-warrior for what seemed hours. We were bathed in sweat when John announced he was cumming; as he pulled out, streams of white jism shot out and I tasted the salty sweetness of his cum. While tasting his river of passion I, too, came and my jism joined the sticky flow on my face and chest.

Throughout the night, John and I tossed our nightmares into the sky while holding on to each other. And although we never repeated this scene together, he did visit me in my room and he continued to recite poetry, until one day he left, separated from the Army after three years with Uncle Sam.

Although this happened many years ago, I can still feel the pain of his departure: He lifted his hands high into a farewell, raised them like an outfielder looking to catch a line drive, and looked toward his small group of friends huddled together in a departing tribute. But as he waived, a trace of a smile passed over his face. John looked at me, and I saw that I still swam in a small, shallow stream within those evergreen eyes of his.

# COMMUNE LUST

### JAY STARRE

It was 1971 and I was just 20. It was the heyday of the hippie era, and I was living with my wife in northern Washington State on a rural commune. We planted potatoes and corn and raised goats with a few hundred other young dropouts who thought they were latter-day native Indians. It was a blast.

It was also when I met Hugh. He was the mellow "leader" of the commune, since it was his parents' sprawling 800 acres of forest and meadows that we commune-dwellers called home. It was love at first sight. I met him on the day my wife and I came to the farm, and his sandy-haired, mild-mannered good looks hit me with the force of a flying arrow, straight to the heart.

Hugh was married as well and had two small children. He lived in an octagonal log cabin and graciously helped me build my own log cabin that first summer. On a commune in those days just about anything was allowed. I worked naked most of the time under the hot northern sun, and often Hugh joined me as we raised the walls of my small cabin. I was delirious with lust from the first time he took off his shirt. Hugh was short and stocky, but his body seemed perfectly proportioned to my desire-filled eyes. He had broad shoulders, big arms, and a hairless well-formed chest. When I first saw him naked, I sprang a hard-on I had difficulty hiding behind the framework of the cabin we were working on. I was sure he saw my boner, and when he showed no sign of disapproval I was heartened. I dared hope he had the hots for me as well.

A few months went by while I kept my gay desires to myself. But eventually I could not take it anymore. The proximity of my new friend and the experience of working with him almost every day had me frustrated and in a constant state of sexual excitement. It was a bright afternoon in August when I confronted Hugh with my hidden desires.

"I want to have sex with you, Hugh." I blurted out. I had been rehearsing that little admission for weeks on end. But in the end, the plain truth just shot out of my mouth.

Hugh and I were all alone. We had traipsed up to the cistern that was the source of water for the northern end of the farm's inhabitants. The large metal container was situated in a tiny, secluded ravine near the mountainside spring that fed it. No one could see us or was likely to interrupt us. I had figured this was a good place to talk over my infatuation with Hugh, and if good fortune was with me, to consummate my raging lust.

I recall how bright it was that day. Hugh's short sandy hair seemed to glow around his head. He was dressed in ragged jean shorts and sandals and was shirtless. He didn't tan well, and his hairless torso was more pink than brown. His smoky-gray eyes were calm and serene. I breathlessly awaited his reply.

"I thought you probably did. You're quite attractive, Jay, you know. You've got the body of an athlete, and you're tanned from head to toe like some wild Indian. If I was going to have sex with a man, it would definitely be you." Hugh spoke quietly and smiled

COMMUNE LUST

pleasantly as he did. He seemed unembarrassed by my admission.

As flattering as his words were, they fell short of what I had hoped for. "But you don't want to have sex with a man?" I had to ask. The plaintiveness in my voice was painfully obvious.

"I didn't say that. You know Sylvia and I have an open marriage, and we can have sex with others if we feel the need. So far I haven't really done much fooling around. But I am willing to experiment."

I felt my entire body tense. Did I dare hope? "With me?"

"If you like. What about your wife?"

"Tessa does as she pleases." Which was the truth. My wife was a real party girl and drank heavily. She ended up in the arms of one man after another on a regular basis. "So do I," I added, which was not the total truth.

I was gay and knew it. I had always known it. But I had not come out, and instead had married because I was determined to raise a family and keep my gay interests separate from my marriage. Tessa did not know this. It was my secret. But I had just blabbed that secret to Hugh. It was a very intense moment.

Hugh was a sensitive man. I am sure that was the reason for a great deal of my attraction to him. He was 28, which seemed much older than my more innocent 20. I looked up to him. I am not certain I could have made the first move past that daring admission. Fortunately, he took things into his own hands.

Hugh didn't say another word. Instead, he dropped to his knees on the grass in front of me. I was wearing a skimpy pair of running shorts, which he reached out and gently tugged down to my knees. My cock sprang out, half-hard already. It instantly leaped to full attention. Hugh's hands rose from my shorts and went to my crotch. One callused hand cupped my fat ball sac, while the other explored my stiff whanger.

I was breathing heavily and biting my lip with trembling

174

anticipation. His palm cupping my balls felt incredible. His fingers running up and down my cock and rubbing the leaking head felt fantastic. I was leaning into him with my hips and panting audibly. I was terrified to speak and possibly destroy the moment. It turned out there was no need for words. Hugh glanced up at me and smiled, his pale eyes half-lidded with what looked like desire. Then he looked back down at my cock bobbing in front of his face and suddenly opened his mouth and swallowed it.

Noisy slurping filled the air as he inexpertly bobbed up and down over the erect shaft. I had been sucked off by a number of women and a few guys. Most did a more proficient job. But Hugh made up for his lack of practice by his enthusiastic performance. His head went up and down like a flying piston. The heat and wet-ness enveloping my cock were nearly overpowering. Hugh's hand cupping my balls was both gentle and insistent. His other hand had reached around and clasped hold of one of my naked ass cheeks. It seared that sensitive mound. He shoved my hips for-ward with that hand and fucked his own mouth with my cock.

It wasn't only the heat of his mouth that had me so excited. It was the fact that it was Hugh, whom I had such an infatuated love for, down on his knees sucking me off. He was straight and good-looking, with a beautiful wife. And he was sucking my cock!

"I'm gonna shoot!" I suddenly gasped. The wet friction bathing my cock drove me over the edge. I barely pulled out of Hugh's mouth before letting fly. Gooey jizz sprayed from my boner all over the grass at our feet. Hugh had pulled back just in time to pre-vent that cream from coating his face and chest.

He laughed. I was dizzy with the intensity of my ejaculation. Hugh rose to his feet and held me with steady hands on my shoulders. "Do you want to return the favor? You don't have to if you don't want to."

I was still dripping cum as I dropped to my knees. Hugh's light chuckle was in my ears as I tore at his fly. His jeans popped open, and his cock bobbed out into the afternoon sunlight. It was fat and hard. I had never seen it hard before. It grew stiffer as I yanked down on his shorts. I shoved them to his ankles and he stepped out of them, now naked in front of me.

I was face to face with his hard meat. It was not that long, but it was very fat and very stiff. It pointed in the air in a rigid arc, throbbing slightly as I stared at it, attempting to catch my breath and slow my pounding heart. I glanced up at his face and saw him looking down at me with a reassuring smile. He was so fucking handsome.

I took his cock in my hands and stroked it. It felt like hot iron. Hugh sighed and leaned into me, his hands on my shoulders gripping more tightly. His stiff meat fascinated me. I rubbed it up and down, testing the silky flesh with both hands at once. Then I moved my mouth down to the head. I stabbed out my tongue and lapped at the slit. Oozing pre-cum slid onto my tongue. It was salty and tangy at once. I shuddered with the emotion of the moment. Hugh was hard for me! This straight handsome dude with the beautiful wife was letting me play with his cock! I lapped at the head with renewed vigour. Then, as I heard his deep sigh from above, I opened wide and swallowed it. The feel of that hard pole in my mouth was incredible. I loved it. I slurped it deep and began sucking and tonguing it enthusiastically.

By then my hands had moved of their own accord, slipping around behind Hugh's waist to the mounds of his ass. As I busily sucked on his boner, my hands began to play with his ass. It was as hard as rock. The twin mounds were hairless and sleek. He had them tensed with the passion he was feeling and they seemed as if they truly were made of solid stone. But then, as my fingers stroked toward the deep cleft of his crack, he inexplicably spread his feet apart and opened up that crevice. My mind was in two places at once. I was feeling every inch of that fat pole between my sucking lips, but I was also feeling Hugh's hot butt and even hotter crack. My fingers dug greedily into the parted butt crack. I found slick, sweaty flesh there, just as hairless as the rest of his butt. And I immediately found a crinkled little butt hole, twitching and convulsing as I began to stroke it in time to my sucking mouth over Hugh's cock.

My head was swimming as the reality of what was occurring hit me. Hugh was letting me suck his cock, and he was obviously enjoying it. And he was letting me play with his butthole, and he seemed to like that as well. The straight dude liked his asshole played with! I went wild. I sucked him right into my throat and gurgled over his fat boner. I spread his butt cheeks apart with my fingers and dug into his sweaty asshole. The tight butt lips spasmed against my teasing fingertips but did not open. I continued to stroke them and tease his tight butt aperture.

"I'm going to shoot too!" Hugh suddenly moaned.

I sucked him in deeper and held his cock between my lips. I was determined to suck the jizz right out of him. His hands on my shoulders gripped with fierce strength. His breathing was loud and fast. I felt his ass tense and his butthole clamp down against my toying fingertips. Then a river of sperm flooded my tonsils. The warm cream ran into my throat. I swallowed and sucked madly. Hugh leaned over my face, and his legs began to shake violently. He was about to collapse.

Gently, I disengaged. The cum boiling out of his balls had subsided, and he was barely standing. I rose to my feet and took him in my arms. We stood there in the warm summer air and held each other.

"That was nice. We can do it again sometime if you want. But maybe we should keep it to ourselves. You know how everyone gossips around here."

I agreed. I was delirious with satisfied lust and an even

stronger infatuation for this gentle, lovely man. But I realized it would be best to let him have some space. I didn't want to push myself on him and ruin our friendship. I bided my time, although whenever we were together, my cock was stiff as a board and I couldn't keep my eyes off his body. And I was fantasizing about that shapely ass of his. I recalled how hard it had felt, and how tight the hole had been.

Eventually my desires became too strong to resist once more. The opportunity for us to be alone had arisen when both of our wives had gone with some of the other women to shop in the nearby city of Spokane. They were intending to spend the night there, after going to the local bars for a "women's night out." *Good riddance,* I mused to myself.

Hugh asked whether I wanted to spend the evening at his cabin playing cards while his two young children slept in their own small cubicle behind a beaded curtain. It grew late as we drank home brew and laughed away the evening. "You may as well sleep here, Jay. The couch is comfortable enough if you don't mind," Hugh offered about midnight.

"Thanks," I replied, feigning tiredness. It was the opposite of my true state. I was wired. I was alone with Hugh, and he would be sleeping across the room in a bed by himself. Now was the time to make a move.

He stripped naked, the sight of which had my cock stiff and aching in my shorts. I stared at his rounded ass, pale as the full moon, as he clambered up into his high and wide bed. I wasn't exactly certain what I wanted to do, but I knew I had to get my hands on that ass again.

I lay down and waited. As I thought of what I should say to Hugh, other than "Let me play with your amazing ass," I realized he was snoring away. I rose and tiptoed to his bed. In the light of the moon streaming in through the windows, I saw his face against the pillows. I was shaking like a leaf as I climbed up beside him. I was fully prepared for his rebuff as I pulled the covers aside and exposed his nude body. His cock was lying across his flat belly, soft and vulnerable. I reached out with a tentative hand and began to stroke it. It rose at once, almost instantly hard.

Then I realized his breathing had altered. It was slow and steady. Either he had fallen into a deeper sleep, or he was awake and letting things proceed as they would. I grew bolder, leaning into him with my own naked body and running my hands softly over his chest and legs. I pumped his cock slowly. Then he moved, and I pulled back, waiting for him to speak.

Instead, he rolled over on his stomach. Facing away from me, he spread his thighs wide apart and lay quietly. I was shaking more than ever. Was that an invitation? The curved mounds of his butt gleamed in the dim moonlight. They beckoned to me. I could not resist. I reached out and began to caress them gently. Hugh's ass rose slightly to meet my hands. And then his thighs opened up as he moved his legs farther apart. There was no mistaking that.

Unable to believe my good fortune, I rolled over on top of him. My cock was planted right there between his heated ass cheeks. He rolled upward to meet my body with a gentle but unmistakable pressure. Without really thinking, I began to rub my cock up and down between his ass cheeks. The sleek skin was hot and sweaty. It felt fantastic. Suddenly, I realized my cock head was poised against his tight butt rim.

Again, almost without thinking, I began to shove into him. The snug little rim became abruptly pliant and malleable. My cock head was suddenly sliding into a clamping, heated hole. I bit my lip and moaned. Then I pressed deeper. The hole parted and allowed me to slide halfway inside. I gasped and arched my back, leaning on my hands. The clamping butt lips and ass channel were like little fingers gripping my cock. Sweat lubed the way as I began to pump in and out, an inch at a time.

Hugh's body rose and pushed back against me. Without speaking, he was telling me all I needed to know. I began to fuck him in earnest. Without going nuts, I shoved my cock in deep and then pulled nearly all the way out. Then I shoved deeper, until I was feeling my balls nestled up into his beautiful, sleek ass crack. I was shaking so hard by then, I could not hold myself up anymore. I lay down over him, feeling his muscular, hot body pressed against the length of mine. It was awesome. As I fucked him, Hugh fucked back. Without uttering a word, we rose and fell in the throes of a harder and harder fuck. We were both gasping as I suddenly found myself reeling under the power of an orgasm. I spewed cum up his tight butthole.

Hugh sensed what was going on as I drilled deep into him and held my cock there. He had to have felt my body tense and then go limp as I unloaded all that pent-up spunk. He took it all and kept on fucking upwards into me. Through the dizziness of my orgasm, I realized his body too had gone tense. He was cumming all over his own sheets, without even touching his own cock. The friction of his bone rubbing against those sheets must have been enough.

I lay over him for some time, neither of us moving. Then I eventually rolled off him and lay beside his unmoving form. He still hadn't spoken. But then he rolled over and held me in his arms. I fell asleep like that.

I awoke by myself. Hugh was up and making breakfast for his kids. As I rose from the bed, he smiled at me briefly but then made no mention of the previous night. I felt a little odd, but was still floating in the joy of that incredible fuck.

The women returned to the farm. Hugh and I did not speak of that fuck, and then abruptly he and his wife left the farm. I only spoke to him one more time before I too left the commune later that year. He was having trouble in his marriage, and he and his wife had agreed it would be best to be away from the commune for some time. He was sorry he hadn't spoken to me about it, but it was a trying time for him.

I sympathized, but was too hurt to say much more. I never saw him again. But I'll never forget the sex we had. It had seemed like a dream, too perfect and too secret to be real. But I knew it had been real.

# I WAS A TEENAGE STRAIGHTFUCKER

**ALEC FURY**

I'd been wanting in my friend Mark's pants for months, and after hours of tequila shots and Truth or Dare in his room, the moment of truth had finally arrived.

I had my dick in my hand and his dick in my mouth when all of a sudden he slumped backwards onto the bed. Passed out cold. For just a second I considered going ahead and fucking him anyway. Not very cool, I know, but I was 18 and horny, and he was such a little hottie I couldn't help it.

An ass is a terrible thing to waste.

Frustrated, I pulled off his shoes and made sure there was a trash can nearby for him to heave into, then I headed out.

In the living room, I was surprised to see Mark's roommate sprawled out on the couch watching TV and wearing nothing but a pair of baggy shorts. On the weekends Josh usually stayed over at his girlfriend Jennifer's house, but here he was, a remote control in one hand and a beer in the other.

We nodded hey to each other, and he asked me if I wanted to have a beer and watch wrestling with him.

"Might as well," I said. "Mark's fucking passed out, again."

"Fucking alcoholic," he sneered, tossing me a room-temperature can of Coors.

Josh was cool. Funny, sarcastic, and just recently 21, he was always willing to buy some beer for an underage friend in need like myself.

Plus, he was really cute.

He was tall, easily over six feet, and on our college's basketball team. He looked like a young Ben Affleck. Everything about him was just huge. Big hands, big feet, I couldn't help but wonder how much cock he was packing.

He kept bringing up Michelle, a girl I'd recently started fucking. She knew I was into guys and chose to deal with it, kind of. Apparently, she thought she was going to change me. It would have taken better blow jobs than hers to do the job—I can tell you that much. I don't know if you could call me bisexual, but I've always been so oversexed that I never turned down any opportunity that came my way. Pussy, dick, or ass: They're all good to me.

"Michelle's hot," he said between swallows. "What do you want with that good pussy anyway? I thought you were supposed to be gay. You think you're hot shit because you got chicks crawling all over you, huh? 'Cause you're such a little pretty boy. And you think you're so tough. Well, fuck you, pretty boy."

Actually, he was right on both counts. Not to brag, but I was definitely one of the hotter teenagers in our little corner of the world, and a lifetime of karate and kickboxing lessons had turned me into a regular little hard-ass. There was a reason they called me the Marky Mark of our sleepy little college town.

"You probably think you could kick my ass, huh?"

Fortunately for him, he was smiling when he said it, because the fact of the matter was, yeah, I could kick his ass. And the way I figured it, it wouldn't have taken very long.

He wadded up some newspaper and chucked it at my head.

"Why don't you kick my ass, then?" he said.

I busted out laughing because all of a sudden I realized where this was heading. I had what I called the five-word rule throughout high school, which basically stated that a guy who knew what I was about and spoke more than five words to me anyway wanted my dick. The five-word rule was in full effect.

"Oh, don't worry. Your ass is mine," I said, swigging my beer and giving him my come-and-get-it stare. This was kind of my sadistic stage. See, I was happy to mess with straight boys, but aside from Mark, I liked to make them beg.

And make no mistake—this was a straight boy.

I looked him up and down for a few seconds, admiring his long, veiny muscles, his superheroic jawline, and the dark trail of hair that sprouted from the waistband of his black Umbros up to his belly button.

He leaped up off the couch and, blocking the TV screen, stood right in front of where I was sitting. His legs were spread and his hands were on his hips, pulling his shorts down just enough to reveal his tan line and even more of his treasure trail.

I started to complain about not being able to see the screen but then noticed that the light of the TV was shining through his shorts, making them practically transparent. He wasn't wearing underwear.

Just as I'd thought, his dick was every bit as huge as his other appendages. For just a moment, I stared transfixed as his tool morphed from a thick hose hanging halfway down his thigh to a semi-hard meat monster that tented out the flimsy material of his shorts just inches from my nose.

Then I sprang up from where I was sitting, wrapped my arms around his thighs and took him to the ground.

We wrestled around for at least 20 minutes, breaking the coffee table, knocking shit over and just basically making a huge mess. Big as he was, he wasn't any stronger or tougher than I'd figured, and I pretty much knocked his ass all over the room. It was fun. If you've never squirmed around on the floor with a half-naked college athlete, you don't know what you're missing.

Finally, with both of us sweating like pigs and breathing hard, I knocked him on his back, straddled him, and pinned his arms over his head. Little rivulets of sweat ran down from the matted patches of hair under his arms and disappeared into the carpet.

"So now what are you gonna do to me?" he panted.

"What do you want me to do to you?" I asked.

He turned his face to the side. Sweat dripped off the tip of his nose.

"Hey, what do you want me to do to you?" I said again.

But he wasn't talking. To break the silence I smacked his pecs with my open-palmed hands, playful but hard enough to sting.

"Don't fucking hit me!" he yelled, bucking underneath me and reaching out to grab my hands.

"What are you gonna do about it?" I taunted, pulling free and smacking him again. He thrashed around between my legs, but I wouldn't let him up. Especially since in the course of all his wiggling I had felt his now fully swollen cock rubbing against my ass.

When he calmed down, I sat up and slipped my shirt over my head. I threw it behind me, not caring where it fell. I reached into his shorts and put my hand on his stiff, dripping dick. I stroked his knob for a few seconds, wetting my fingers with his pre-cum, and then I grabbed him by the chin with my other hand and turned him to look at me.

I put my slimy fingers in his mouth, and he closed his eyes.

"Yeah, suck it," I said, and his lips and tongue started to work hesitantly on my sticky digits.

I leaned down.

"Kiss me," I said and he did. Which was surprising because straight guys usually didn't—never the first time you tell them to and often not at all. Motherfucker must have been as horny as I was. Too bad he was such a shitty kisser. But then, most straight men are.

I stood up and dropped my shorts. My own big boner bounced up to slap against my stomach while Josh stared at me wide-eyed and unblinking. It was probably the first hard dick he'd ever seen aside from his own.

"Take off your shorts," I told him.

He lifted his ass off the ground and slid them down but otherwise remained completely still.

"Don't go anywhere," I commanded. Leaving him sprawled on the living room floor with his dick pointing straight up at the ceiling, I went into Mark's room to grab the lube I had planted earlier.

When I came back he was lying exactly as I had left him. I decided to take things to the next level and kneeled between his legs, spreading them with some difficulty. He resisted just enough to assert his straightness but not enough to bring the encounter to an end.

Realizing I'd have to lick it before I could stick it, I scooted backwards and put my face in his musky crotch, licking the sweat from his inner thighs and tonguing his fat, steamy balls. I continued up the underside of his cock, just barely licking it, and scraped my teeth lightly back and forth on the sensitive skin under his dick head.

When he started groaning and thrusting his hips into the air, I knew it was time to make my move.

I grabbed the lube beside me, squeezed some into my hand and brought my finger to his hole.

He jerked away with a start, squirming off my finger and, realizing I'd have to work it a little bit more, I went down on him for real this time, taking the whole of his stiff dick down my throat as I simultaneously slipped my finger deep into his ass.

He sucked air and I sucked dick faster and faster and began finger-fucking him in earnest.

He was moaning like a mental patient and after a minute I knew he was going to cum any minute and I wasn't going to get my dick up his ass. I took my mouth off his cock, eased my finger out of his tight hole and moved up so that I was kneeling by his head.

Once again he looked away, even going so far as to clamp his eyes shut, but again I grabbed his chin and turned him to face me. My dick loomed large over his handsome face.

I teased my cock slowly over his closed lips, letting him know that if he didn't help me out he wouldn't be getting anymore himself. Eventually, he got the message and opened his mouth somewhat. I rubbed my shaft back and forth lengthwise over his lips for a few minutes so he could get used to it. Then I slipped just the head into his warm, beery mouth.

Behind me, he began flogging his cock furiously. I knew this was it.

"Stick out your tongue," I panted, feeling the pressure building in my nuts as I rubbed the head of my dick along his tongue and stroked faster and faster.

His face scrunched up, and I looked behind me just in time to see the cum geysering out of his dick. I shot my own huge load just as he opened his mouth to grunt. I got jizz all over his face and in his mouth. And he swallowed it.

After a brief moment of stillness, he popped up off the floor and grabbed his half-empty beer can off the coffee table. He walked into the kitchen, big dick swinging, and stood in front of the sink. He took a swig of beer, swished it around his mouth, and then spit. Then he walked into the bathroom and closed the door.

I pulled on my boxers, went upstairs, and climbed into bed with Mark. I fell asleep to the sound of the shower running.

In the morning, I was awakened by Mark's morning wood pressing insistently against my leg. He tried to get me to suck him off, but I was so hung over I could only manage a halfhearted hand job for him. Nonetheless, he came buckets and it excited me so much that I was even able to jerk off in spite of my pounding headache.

Mark and I have remained good friends over the last few years, and we continue to mess around on an infrequent basis—usually when he's between girlfriends and always when we're totally wasted.

As for Josh, not long after we fucked around, he and Jennifer got engaged and came up with a long list of *j*-names for their future children. We never really hung out again—oh, except for the night of his bachelor party, when he pretended to be asleep on my couch while I fucked his wife-to-be's brother on my living room floor.

# HOCKEY FUCK

**DARREN MAXWELL**

I was living in a Vancouver suburb when I met Grant. I worked at an ice rink and played drop-in hockey regularly on Wednesday and Thursday mornings. I was a goalie, and Grant was a defenseman, so we ended up playing closely together on the ice. Immediately, I was attracted to his easygoing manner. He was good-looking in an understated way, with short sandy hair and soft brown eyes set in a broad face. The first time we changed in the locker room, I found his lean muscularity and fat, juicy dick very appealing.

"You've got a killer body, Darren," Grant said as we exited the showers.

"Careful what you say to that boy. He's gay, you know!" Ted, one of the other players teased. "He might ask you to suck his dick or fuck his ass!"

A few of the other players snickered at Ted's crude remark, but they all liked me and didn't seem to care that I was a fag. It was hard to find good goalies, and they appreciated my skill.

"I'm sure I can trust him not to grab my butt or anything." Grant smiled pleasantly as he toweled off beside me.

He had a nice butt, and I wouldn't have minded groping it. But he'd made his position clear. Too bad. Still, he seemed to like me quite a bit and began to invite me out to lunch after our morning hockey games. He chattered away about his bad luck with women and how his last girlfriend had cheated on him and made him wary of relationships.

"I'd like to just get my rocks off and forget the relationship crap, if you know what I mean," Grant announced one late evening in the locker room. We had played on a Friday night with some friends of his, instead of at our regular time in the morning. The other players had changed and disappeared while we dawdled as we undressed. We were all alone.

By then, I had developed a major lust for the soft-spoken guy. I'd always liked the shyer types, and his being straight gave him a luster of unavailability that made him all the more appealing. I had no intention of following up on any of my fantasies, though. "I find that works for me a lot of the time. Just fuck 'em and forget 'em!" I laughed.

"I'm really horny, Darren. I wouldn't mind fucking right now."

I wasn't sure I'd heard him right. "You need a wet pussy to fuck?" I teased as I rose naked to head for the showers.

"How about a tight ass? I'd like to fuck yours."

I halted in my tracks and swiveled around to stare at him. He had shed the last of his hockey gear, except for his jockstrap, which I immediately noticed was tented with his stiff bulge. I looked up into his eyes. He was grinning. Was he joking? Then he stood, and with his eyes still on mine, he slid down his jockstrap, revealing a raging boner throbbing at his waist.

"I'm not gay, as you know. But I could fuck just about anything right now," Grant said, his voice trembling. He had moved toward me as he took his cock in hand and stroked it brazenly.

"Well, doesn't that make me feel good! You'd fuck just about anything, so my ass will do." I shook my head and chuckled at his suggestion. But my cock was rising fast, and he noticed that immediately.

His smile was apologetic, but he had gone too far to back down. "I like you, Darren. And you have a great body. You know I'm not in love with you or anything like that. But I would like to fuck your ass. I think it would feel awesome. How about it?"

I was still chuckling as I bent down and rummaged through my hockey bag. I found the package of condoms I kept for emergencies. I rose and held them out in my hand for him to see. Then without saying another word, I turned and headed for the showers.

"I'll bar the locker-room door," I heard Grant saying breathlessly behind me.

Well, well, well. Was he really going to fuck me? I was wondering if a straight guy could keep his hard-on without a pussy involved. But he had said he would fuck anything, so my ass was probably good enough for him right then.

"Soap it up and bend over. I'll put on a condom."

"How romantic!" I smirked as I stood under the shower and got soaped up.

"Sorry, Darren! But if you don't want to do it, I'll understand."

"Fuck my butt. I'm sure I'll love that big juicy cock up there," I laughed as I reached out and flicked his hard boner with my fingers.

Grant winced and shivered at the feel of my fingers grazing his hard-on. But he didn't back away. His cock was big and very stiff. I obliged him by turning around and leaning into the shower wall with my hands braced against the steamy tiles. My own shaft was bobbing up against my stomach. I hoped he would go through with it.

Then I felt his hands on my butt, tentatively grasping each

cheek. He pulled them apart and I heard a low gasp. He must have been looking at my shaved butthole. It was wet and soapy, and I used my considerable expertise to expand the rim into a gaping maw. He gasped again, and I felt the head of his cock slide up against my hole.

I didn't wait for him. I reared backward with my hips and swallowed his flared cock head whole. The rim of my asshole spasmed around the fat bulb while he groaned from behind and gripped my butt with shaking fingers.

"It's so fucking tight!"

Tight? I've been fucked countless times. I stopped being tight some years ago. But in comparison to a pussy, I suppose I was tight. Besides, I was clamping over his cock with my anal muscles at that point, not entirely relaxed yet. And he was big too.

"Go ahead—it's all yours. Fuck my ass!"

Grant held my ass as his hard cock shoved into my ass, impaling me on half the thing in one hard thrust. I snorted and spread my feet wider apart. He was very big—very, very big! And his cock was long too, I quickly found out. Grant barely paused before pulling out an inch and then shoving right back in, this time all the way to the balls.

"Fuck! The whole thing is up my ass! What do you have there, a baseball bat?" I grunted.

"Yeah, I got a baseball bat up your tight pussy," Grant muttered from behind.

"Fuck my snug, soapy pussy with that bat! Fuck it good!" I mimicked his choice of words, figuring whatever got him off was fine with me. I'd give him good pussy, if that was what he wanted. I was certainly getting good cock. He was leaning into my back with his cock buried to the hilt, his hairy ball sac nestled up against my crack. His hard body was slick and hot against mine. His cock throbbed perceptively inside my asshole as he held it deep in my guts. He was shaking all over, which made me feel pretty good. He was loving my ass, no question about it.

I took the opportunity to wiggle my ass in circles, squeezing the length of his cock with my inner butt muscles and sphincter. Grant trembled against me and hissed in my ear. Then he responded by pulling halfway out, my butt rim expanding and following his shaft with clinging friction. He held it there for a moment and then rammed back into me, so hard his hips smacked loudly against my wet ass.

"Yeah, fuck that pussy!" I growled encouragingly. By that time my asshole had grown accustomed to his girth; it was the length that sent electric thrills coursing up my guts and spine. His blunt cock head pounded against my sensitive prostate.

"I'll fuck your wet pussy all right. I'll fuck it till we both cum!" Grant huffed in my ear. He was gripping my butt as he leaned into my back and pressed his head into my neck. If he imagined he was fucking a pussy, he couldn't have mistaken my big, muscular body for a woman's lush flesh. Obviously, he didn't mind my muscles, as he was pressed intimately against me as he began to pummel my ass with hard, deep thrusts.

"Fuck, fuck, fuck, yeah! What a sweet, tight cunt," Grant muttered over and over.

"Shove that big bat up my hungry cunt! Ram me with it!"

Grant and I lost all sense of time as he savagely drilled my butt with his big salami. I spread my legs as far apart as possible and leaned back into him. I opened up my ass and allowed his cock to slide in and out effortlessly. The soapy friction was heating up my insides and teasing my puckered rim to distraction. He was slamming so hard up into me and lifting my ass up off the floor with each powerful thrust. His hard body clinging to mine was a dream come true. I imagined his lust for me was more than a momentary desire to fuck any available hole, just as he imagined my asshole was a wet pussy. We floated in our separate fantasies, the steam of the hot shower shrouding us in a wet, slick veil as we fucked and fucked and fucked.

His stamina was awesome. After the first few minutes, I relaxed into the brutal hammering and let him do most of the work. I leaned against the wet tiles and bit my lip as his foot-long rammer toasted my guts. His hands on my butt began to massage and knead, pulling my cheeks wider apart as he searched out new depths in my hot fuckhole. I took it with loud gasps and grunts, encouraging him now and then with vulgar pleas for him to keep on pounding my pussy. Grant obliged relentlessly. My own cock oozed pre-cum continually. I was on the edge of orgasm for what seemed like forever.

Then he did a weird thing. Or not so weird, I suppose. His hands on my ass suddenly slid away, rising upward along my sides, pressing my ribs tightly. As he continued to ram me with his cock, his fingers slid around my chest and found my nipples. Suddenly, he was tweaking and pinching them harshly.

"Oh, fuck! Man, oh, man, that feels awesome! Pinch my tits while you fuck my pussy!" I groaned breathlessly.

Instead of answering me, he suddenly clamped his mouth over my neck and began to suck and lick at it. It was unbelievable. The multiple sensations of his big, hard cock reaming my guts and rubbing my ass lips, fingers tugging at my nipples, and a wet mouth sucking on my neck had me writhing in rapturous lust. My own cock was as tight as a drum, and I felt if I just touched it, the head would blow off.

"I'm so fucking horny! This is so fucking sweet! I love your ass!" Grant blurted between loud slurps along my neck.

"Fuck it hard! Fuck my ass with your big, hard, fat cock! Fuck me until I blow jizz all over the place!"

Grant must have read my mind. One of his hands dropped to

my cock just as I finished my outcry. That hand gripped my boner fiercely. It pumped up and down in time to the slamming of dick up my butt. It only took a dozen strokes, and I was cumming like a horny sailor.

"Oh, yeah, blow your load! My hard cock up your butt is making you cum! Now I'm gonna shoot inside your wet hole!" Grant moaned in my ear.

He was still pumping my spurting cock as he rammed three or four times way up my ass and then held his cock there. I was almost lifted off my feet as he went rigid all over and groaned like he was dying. He was unloading up my ass!

We remained like that for a timeless moment. His body was tight against mine as he held me with one hand on my oozing cock and the other on my chest. I leaned into the wall and breathed in deep gulps of air. His fat cock was still planted up my ass, making him feel like a part of me still.

Then it was over. I moved, then he was pulling out of me and pulling away. I turned to face him as he sheepishly tore off the condom over his cock and washed away the jizz in the spray of the shower. His eyes met mine and he grinned at me, but he wasn't saying anything. It wasn't really uncomfortable, but there were no tender words or caresses either. We showered together under one showerhead, our bodies grazing and our eyes meeting now and then. It was actually quite nice. But it was also obvious Grant wasn't going to become a gushy fairy over that one hard fuck.

"Thanks, Darren. I really liked that," was all he said as he dressed and made for the door.

"So did I," was all I said in reply.

He grinned and nodded before he disappeared. I wanted to say, "Any time you want to fuck my ass again, I'd love it." But I didn't.

## HOCKEY FUCK

Grant and I played hockey together a few more times after that, but I'd already decided to move to the city and knew I wouldn't be out to the 'burbs for regular hockey after that. We said our goodbyes like friends, and no mention was made of our one shower-fuck. But Grant's look into my eyes was full of quiet gratitude.

Straight guys. They can be so sweet sometimes.

# BOOTH BUDDY

## TANNER

The night started with six of us, none over 20, new to our first Army post after basic training. Young, dumb, and fulla cum, as our drill instructors had yelled constantly. It was our first Friday night in the civilian world since we'd joined up. We had a few bucks in our pockets and were out for a good time. It didn't take us long to find the street lined with bars, strip clubs, and porno theaters. We were mostly small town boys who found the sin nearly unbelievable, actual naked women dancing on stage in front of us.

I was even hard in the club, but not because of the naked women. I'd always been attracted to guys but never acted on it, aside from jack-off fantasies. And since joining the Army, I'd had some great ones, although I knew it wasn't the place to meet guys or make a grab for someone. If it was even suspected you were queer you'd get the crap beaten out of you and thrown out on top of it. It was the mid 1970s, and while things were relaxed in the all-volunteer Army, we were still years away from even the glimmer of protection offered by "don't ask, don't tell…"

# BOOTH BUDDY

I was hard just from being with the guys I was with. It wasn't much, but it was all I had back then. They were getting so horny over the tits being flashed in their faces. The dicks I'd seen in the shower had to be fully hard and throbbing under their heavy wool winter dress-uniform pants—and that made my own cock throb until I felt the head slick with pre-cum as I shifted in my seat.

As the night wore on we moved from bar to bar, ties askew, our normally neat uniforms rumpled like they'd been slept in. The group kept breaking apart and rejoining as we moved from place to place.

In one late move, Gary, a muscular blond from the upper Midwest, and I were giggling and sharing a cigarette when he nudged me toward the doorway of a porno theater, the kind with a skin magazine shop in the front and quarter booths in the back. I'd never been in one, but until that night I'd never gotten drunk with a bunch of guys or seen bare tits either.

We looked at some skin magazines, laughing and cutting up, my cock achingly hard from being so close to the sexy blond, until the clerk glared at us. I followed Gary into the dark entry of the movie arcade without any clue as to what was about to happen. When he slipped into one of the booths, I stepped in right behind him, closing the doorway to seal us into the tiny dark L-shaped viewing booth.

"So you wanna watch together, huh?" Gary mumbled as he fished into his pocket for change. I made no move to leave and he didn't ask me to; I'd only seen half a dozen R-rated movies in my life and had no idea what to expect. As soon as the grainy reel started to play I thought my cock would explode in my pants. I'd never seen graphic sex; even the magazines we'd been flipping through out front were just T & A. As the straight movie played, I glanced down at the crotch of Gary's uniform, his thick, hard cock clearly outlined as he stared at the screen.

I was in an agony of pain and pleasure standing next to him, my dick pulsing as the small, dark cubicle grew warmer with our bodies pressed together. Stroking a hand down over his crotch Gary suddenly unzipped and pulled out his cock, the slightly curved seven inches or so pulsing in his palm as he grinned over at me, then curled his fingers around the shaft and began stroking lightly up and down its length.

"C'mon, man, it's cool. He cut his eyes back over toward my bulging cock. It was almost too much, and if I hadn't had a couple beers in me, I probably would have bolted and played straight the rest of my life.

As Gary pumped another coin into the machine, I let my right hand skitter over my crotch. The next thing I knew, I had my hard cock sticking out only inches from the hot blond's piece, both of us palming our dicks and looking more at each other than the grainy movie.

Gary murmured "nice" and squeezed my throbbing shaft so firmly, I thought I would pass out. His callused palm felt damp as he closed his strong fingers around my dick. It felt like a thousand volts of electricity had passed through my body once he began stroking the length of my shaft. Then he put his hands on his hips and smiled that electric grin.

"Go on," he said with a nod toward his slick shaft. His cock was about the same as mine in length and thickness but seemed a yard long and foot wide as it stuck out from his body. I slowly curled my fingers around the base and stroked the shaft; the smooth, slick feel of his cock skin against my palm hand almost made me cum right then and there.

"Yeah, that's it." Gary grunted as he leaned back against the wall of the booth.

Our whole company could have been roaming the dark maze of that little movie house and I wouldn't have cared. I had my hands around the meat of one of my fantasies-come-true and wasn't about to let go. Just jacking him was the greatest thrill of my life. As my fingers wrapped around the thick shaft, little moans of pleasure escaped from my throat as I worked him.

"You like that, huh?" Gary said as he slid the knot of his tie down farther, then popped open the buttons of his shirt. "Ever suck one?"

Freezing in mid stroke, I wondered how the hell he knew that was what I wanted to do more than anything. I'd heard of guys who jacked each other off, but that didn't make them queer. Sucking did.

"Go on," he said again, as his shirt flapped open and he smoothed his hands down over the tight white T-shirt underneath, skinning the thin material back up over the flat muscles of his stomach as he used his other hand to flip open the flat metal buckle of his dress belt. Leaning over as he exposed his midsection I licked my lips lightly, my hard cock stabbing up against my uniform shirt as I slowly took the wide head between my lips.

The taste of the young GI's dick—salty, musky, sweaty, hot, and smooth all at once—made me moan low and deep. After a few tentative bobs up and down over the head, I dropped to my knees and rammed as much of the thick shaft as I could into my throat. Gary groaned as he wrapped a hand around the back of my head and pulled me down onto his piece. His uniform pants fell to the floor around his ankles.

"Suck it, man, suck it!" he hissed as I clumsily ate his dick: my first.

I guess I stroked myself as I sucked—I really don't remember. At one point he told me to put more money in the machine since he was out of quarters. I dug a few out of my pocket and managed to pass them into his fist. I kept sucking as he slipped the coins in and the movie whirred back to life.

"Fuck, that feels good," he whispered above me, his hand still holding the back of my head. My knees were numb, and I felt like my cock was going to shoot off my body like a rocket.

Sliding a hand down under my right arm, Gary eased me up, his slick cock pulling noisily from my throat and lip. I noticed he had rolled his T-shirt all of the way up over his flat stomach and chest. His pants were a puddle around his shoes and his wrinkled issue boxers twisted sexily at an angle over his lean hips.

"Lemme fuck ya," he said.

"Huh?" was all I could manage as I wiped my lips with the back of my hand.

"Lemme fuck your ass," he said as he shoved his hands into the waistband of his underwear and pushed the thin material down over his muscular legs.

"No!" I grabbed his slick, hard cock and stroked it again.

We stared at each other as my hand slid up and down the length of his smooth piece, our cocks still sticking straight out and hard as lumber, until a faint grin crossed his sexy face. Gary reached out and stroked my shaft a few times then let go and hooked a hand around the back of my neck and pulled my face in toward his.

It was all over after that. Our lips met in a full kiss, his tongue darting lightly between my lips, and I knew I'd been had. After wanting to suck cock, my next-most-secret passion had been to kiss a guy, especially one as sexy as Gary.

As we pulled apart, my head reeling as fast as the movie next to us, Gary knew he had gotten me. Without a word I turned around and slid my jacket from my shoulders, letting it fall to the floor as he fished in his pockets for quarters to keep the movie going.

I unbuckled my pants and got ready; the gorgeous fuck had found my weakness, and I was paying the price.

I'd played with my own hole enough to know that this was going to hurt, but I also knew having Gary take my cherry would make it a hell of a lot easier. I heard him spit on his palm behind me as I rolled my shirt and T-shirt up around my waist and braced myself against the wall in front of me, my ass tightening as I felt the wide head of his shaft slip down between the smooth cheeks of my ass and settle against my hole.

"Just breathe deep," Gary said as I felt my gut knot. My cock was half slack by then. Gary pressed his hips forward, and the head of his hard shaft slipped into my tight hole as I exhaled.

"Hold it, just hold it…" he whispered as I felt the first searing wave of pain and struggled. "Now push back."

Taking another long breath, I pushed, feeling the thickness of his cock as it slid farther inside. "That's it! Fuck yeah! That's it!" he grunted, holding his arms tight across the flat ripple of muscles low across my stomach and pulled me in.

Another white-hot bolt of pain shot through me, and I made a bucking move to push Gary off me, although I really wanted him planted all way in me as far and fast as he could go.

"Hold on, hold on, it's in." the blond grunted, his arm snaking around my body and clamping onto my hips. I gritted my teeth and let the pain settle into a mere ache as he slowly slipped his dick in and out of my hole an inch at a time.

"So fucking tight, man. So fucking tight…" he mumbled. My cock started to harden again as he stroked deep inside me. It was the most amazing pain and pleasure I'd ever experienced. It hurt like hell, but at the same time I was getting more excited than I'd ever been. I even started pushing back a little as he pumped my ass. Sweat streaked over the back of my legs as he drove his thick cock deep into the slick muscles of my ass.

By the time Gary was sliding his entire shaft all the way in and out of my tight hole, my cock was back to full hardness, slapping up against the flat muscles of my stomach as he rode me. With a series of long low grunts he worked his fingers deep into the sides of my hips and pulled me back onto his thick shaft with a moan. I stroked a hand down over my throbbing cock and held my fingers tight on my slick meat. He pounded into me, then let go when I felt the first thick blasts of cum shoot from the pulsing head of my shaft. Hell, the sweat- and cum-scented air in the tiny hot cubicle alone would have been enough to make me cum.

With his fingers tearing into my hips, I gasped as Gary slid his cock all the way out of my ass. He moaned deeply as the first of his long hot streaks of cum dripped raggedly over the skin of my ass. As he was cumming, the movie suddenly clicked off, the sudden silence deafening. I felt two more searing slashes of his cum splat across the aching cheeks of my just-pounded raw ass.

My mind and body were in total uproar. I took a fast deep breath and slowly eased up straight, feeling the blond's hot cum trickle down over the back of my legs as I squatted slightly to pull up my pants.

"You OK?" he asked as we both began yanking and pulling our uniforms back into a semblance of order.

"Yeah," I mumbled, reeling at the great things that had just happened to me.

The clerk looked up from the counter when we finally came out of the arcade. This time he had a knowing smile on his face. Gary flipped him off with a scowl as we went out the front door.

As we headed back to the titty bar, my mind and body whirling, I sneaked a look at Gary, who was sneaking a look back at me. "You aren't going to tell, are you?" I asked him.

He just grinned.

Gary and I became casual buddies, saying "hey" whenever we passed each other in the barracks hallway and eating at the same table at chow now and then, although we each had our own circle of guys we hung out with. That sexy blond and I spent almost four years on the same base—he would screw me every few months after a visit to a titty bar and a few beers. I never turned him down, and he was a good enough (or horny enough) guy to get me ready for his dick with a little make-out session each time. After a while, I think he started to like that as much as I did.

Right after he got out of the Army, Gary got married to his hometown girl. I didn't go to the wedding, but did I ever envy his bride. And I do wonder, all these years later, if he still thinks about me now and then the way I still think about him.

# EL ANILLO

**MOSES O'HARA**

I've always had a soft spot in my heart for towel boys. And the first time I met Silavio, he was on his hands and knees picking weeds out of the half-assed garden in front of the club. "How's it goin'?" I asked, flashing him a big, friendly grin.

He looked at me with total contempt. "All right. Sometimes."

Damn. And I would've fucked him right there in the parking lot if I'd had the chance.

There was just something about him. That Silavio.

The next time I saw him, he was dripping with sweat, unloading what seemed like a staggering amount of hot, white towels from the industrial dryers in back of the locker room.

"Hey. Looks like they moved you inside." Big smile. Suffice it to say I should have just shut up.

So the next time I saw him I didn't say anything. Not a fuckin' thing. I just took my two fuckin' towels from him and split. Fuck you. Asshole. Then, on my way out, I shook his hand and tipped him 10 bucks. "See ya next week." And I smiled. 'Cause I'm just that fuckin' nice.

Towel boys.

When I was a kid my major ambition was to be a towel boy—
or a doctor, because then you could give guys naked exams. But
mostly, for all the obvious reasons, I thought being a towel boy
would be just fuckin' great. So, like I said, I've always had a soft
spot in my heart for towel boys. And I always tip with drugs for
Christmas—to those inclined. It just seems in keeping with the
season. That year the towel boys got dope.

And those were the circumstances of our connection. We
connected.

The bridge was made. We crossed, Silavio and I. Unlikely
allies. Future fuck buddies.

He knew shit about me, and I knew shit about him, and we
knew shit about each other that nobody else knew. We got each
other. Very cool. Silavio—*and* he was straight.

I swear to God.

If there is a straight. Which I'm not at all sure there is.

He had four tattoos. First and foremost, the Virgin of Guada-
lupe exploded across his back in a major blaze of electric glory.
It was in Technicolor; it was…a vision. Second, a vine of thorns
and roses wrapped around the middle finger of his left hand.
Thirdly, ARIEL (his wife's name) sprawled across his heart. Last
but not least, a toe-ring—which was totally unexpected—was
etched his big toe.

He had a goatee—sometimes. And three kids. And he was, like, 26.

There's nothing like showering with a guy to really break the
ice. Silavio got off early on Tuesdays—4 o'clock. Then he did
laps, then he took a steam, then he took a shower. And then we'd
get stoned out on the roof. Every Tuesday.

"Didja see that guy checkin' out my dick?"

"Ya mean the one starin' at it the whole time we were in the
sauna? Nope. Didn't notice him."

Everybody checked out Silavio's dick. Silavio had an awesome dick, balls—crotch in general. Primal admiration. Adoration, whatever. Guys notice each other's dicks. Some more than others—dicks, I mean. And Silavio had one of those dicks.

He soaped up his abdomen and looked over at me.

"Hey, you ever do a guy?"

"Sure." And I left it at that. Didn't even flinch.

Intimacy is an elusive thing. And watching the way a guy handles his own equipment can be mind boggling. Silavio slid his fist up over his dick, then used his thumb to massage its head. I practically fuckin' blew. Big beautiful fuckin' ass—*muscular*—and a major set of forearms... And he liked that we were both guys, so it was no holds barred. I was totally into him, and he was totally into that, you could tell. .

Another time we were swimming and he boosted himself up out of the water and swung around in a single motion, slamming his bare ass down on the edge of the pool. That gorgeous, fuckin' muscular ass. I came up between his legs. (By this time he was closing on weekends—and selling X to half the members under 50.) I dragged my tongue up the inside of his thigh and along the hair on the back of his balls. Then I licked the hell out of his asshole.

"Moses...man, you are fuckin' insane." And his eyes rolled back in his head.

I pride myself on that—the abandon. I learned it from a guy a long time ago. He used to come up behind me and hold my dick when I was taking a piss. I mean, how sexy is that? Purely a man-to-man thing, no translation. And there's nothing like driving your tongue up a guy's asshole to say "I get it." Wives don't do that. Not most wives anyway.

Not any wife you'd want to be married to. Not Ariel. Definitely not Ariel. And that was just fine with me. Ever really go to town on a guy's ass? Sends him right over the fuckin' edge.

He spread his legs even wider apart.

And the weird thing is he would've let me fuck him. Which was totally out of character—like the toe ring—but I didn't want to go there. It would've thrown off the dynamic too much, and the dynamic was working just fine. I wanted things to stay the way they were—like that could ever happen. And besides, it left him wanting me on a very specific level. So everybody was getting what he wanted. At least that's the way I looked at it.

I love the smell of chlorine. It smells clean and masculine to me. I also love guys' armpits, so go figure. Silavio was straight so he maintained himself like a straight guy—no frills. Decidedly not overly trimmed. And I like that in a guy. I also like a guy who wants me. Wanting me is a definite turn-on. I like that look that a guy gets in his eyes. When you know he's really fucking there with you. Silavio ended up blowing my fuckin' mind, and that was perfect for him—it wasn't even cheating. I was a guy. It was a guy thing. An understanding.

And he could give head like a motherfucker sometimes—when he was in the mood or on X. Or both.

Watching a guy go down on your dick is an extraordinary pleasure.

And if it's the most forbidden thing the guy doing it could be doing—and he's doing it. And he's really fuckin' into it—well, then it's poetry. Actually, it's beyond poetry. It's fucking…existential.

He liked to give me his own dream blow job, because that's the only thing he knew how to do. And what a fucking dream it was. Based on the expert technique he used on me, Silavio liked getting the head of his dick sucked real slow. God fucking bless Silavio.

I'd say we had roughly 40 encounters over the course of about a year. Two-thirds of them sexual. And I love jism. I love seeing a guy cum. I mean, come on. I'd pay to see that. And I never even had to—so how lucky was that? I never knew which way to go with Silavio. I wanted to cum in his mouth more than just about anything I can remember. It was like "a thing" with me.

And he knew it.

Which only added to the fun.

And at the same time I loved making him cum. And most of the time I didn't care whether I came at all. As long as I got to get him off. Really get him off. Which is why I'm sure he was so into me—and that made me into him.

So everybody was happy.

Even Ariel. And then I met Ariel.

Big mistake. Fate intervening. That one bit of extra information that changes the whole scenario. And she had the kids with her, which only made it worse.

Like I said, he used to close on weekends. Sundays were incredibly slow, particularly at night—and that much more so after closing. That's when you could turn up the music—really loud and then turn down the lights and open all the windows—so the air gets real cold. And you can watch the steam rising off the water. Fog. And Silavio's body in the fog.

And Ariel and I crossed paths in the parking lot. It was just as simple as that.

She was really pretty.

Genuinely pretty—with great tits and these gold hoop earrings. She had a really nice smile, and one of his kids looked just like him.

And suddenly I was the creep.

Moment lost.

But you wouldn't believe the shit I still think about him when I jerk off sometimes. The back of his neck—actually, the back of his ears. And that fucking toe-ring tattoo. The next time you get the chance, really look into a guy's eyes when you're making out with him. Try it. Trust me, you won't regret it.

Obviously you'll never show up again. I mean, if you're cool at all. It's just understood.

Always approach life with an open hand. Let it go: That's my motto. It's not going to help anyway. You're the only one into it; that's the bottom line. You're just too fucking into it, and that's the rub.

I should've fucked him when I had the chance.

# GARAGE TREATMENT

### DREW BOXER

God bless frat boys! I mean, you've got to love 'em: They're young, they're cocky, they're almost always cute, and they live in a houseful of horny guys. All that pent-up energy makes 'em crazed.

You think sex with men doesn't cross their minds? Think again.

Here in Austin—home of the University of Texas—there's this frat bar called Cain & Abel's. I like to hang out there sometimes and cruise for potential new recruits. I'm 29 but can pass for 22, so I fit in. As long as I play safe, my lover Markus doesn't care what I do. Occasionally, he even goes with me and watches as I try to sweet-talk some young hunk into coming back home with me and…well…cumming.

Anyway, in April 2002, I met a guy named Travis at the bar. He was a business major at U.T., about 5 feet 11 inches tall, with a body muscular from weight lifting. His eyes were a translucent green, and his light-brown hair was cut trendily short. He loved to drink Budweiser and the label off the bottle as he drank. I'd seen him in Cain & Abel's several times but had never approached him; it was easier instead to go home and jerk off to some fantasy encounter with him.

The night we finally met, I challenged him to a game of pool, betting him for the next round of brews. Of course, I let him win. The two of us knocked balls for over two hours, trading pieces of personal information and baseball trivia while downing six or eight beers apiece. I was flirting with Travis on and off but doing so in a really low-key way. I don't care how straight a guy thinks he is—give me a few hours and some alcohol, and I can charm the pants off the son of a bitch before he even knows what hit him.

The *g* word never came up that night. (Neither did the *h* word nor the *q* word.) I was too busy playing it cool. Besides, why should I risk scaring him off by tipping my hand so soon? Sex may be an art, but seduction is a *fine* art.

It was almost 2 A.M., and the bar was getting ready to close, so we half-stumbled out to the parking lot. I was going to offer Travis a ride home, but he said his frat house was just a few blocks away and a walk in the night air would do him good. I gave him my business card, wrote my cell phone number on it, and told him to call me the next time he wanted to play some eight-ball. I really didn't know if I'd ever hear from him again. Which was cool.

Fast-forward about three weeks. The phone rings on a Saturday afternoon and it's Travis. We shoot the shit for a while, then he mentions some book he wants to borrow for a class. I guess the title came up during our extended conversation at the bar a few weeks ago—either that or he was just looking for an excuse to stop by.

I give him directions and tell Markus we'll be having a visitor. He tells me he'll be reading in the bedroom and would prefer not to be disturbed. Fine with me, I say.

About an hour later I hear a motorcycle pull up in the driveway; Travis revs the engine a few times and then shuts it off. I walk outside to greet him.

"You never told me you rode a bike, Travis."

"That's right. And there's probably a few things you haven't told me about you. Right, Boxer?"

I grin and try to figure out how far I could take this thing with this hunk of a frat boy.

"I found the book you wanted. It's inside."

"Thanks, man. I've got a paper due next week and I wanted another source. I need an B in this class, or else my GPA's gonna suck this semester."

"I definitely don't miss those days. Hey, how about a beer? I've got your favorite."

"I thought you were strictly a Heineken man."

"I am, but I keep the cheap stuff around for guests."

"Watch it, dude. I love my Bud. Don't make me hurt you for it."

*I should be so lucky,* I muse.

I laugh and grab a couple of longnecks out of the fridge in the back of the garage.

"That's some ride there, Boxer. Is it yours, or are you just the driver for somebody with megabucks?"

I hand him his Bud, and he takes a long swig from the bottle. I can't help notice how he wraps his lips around the grooves of the bottle's head and kind of slurpily coaxes the liquid out of the opening.

"Very funny, college boy," I crack, trying to pull my gaze away from him. "If you ever get to be as successful as I am, maybe you'll be driving one of these babies."

The baby in particular was a brand-new black BMW Z3 Roadster convertible. I love sports cars almost as much as I do my dick—and that's saying a lot!

"You've got to let me drive it sometime, Boxer. I'm serious. I'd totally knock out the guys at the house."

He's walking very slowly around the car, lightly caressing it and looking at it almost lustfully. *How can I get him to make that leap from the car to me?* I wonder.

"Dream on. Like I'd ever hand over the keys to you! You'd have to earn the chance to even sit in it, much less drive it."

At this point, he's standing next to me at the front of the car and seems to be sizing me up.

"So what would it take to let me drive it?" he asks.

"You tell me. What's it worth to you?"

I feel my cock stir in my shorts, since I'm getting off on what I could get Travis to do in exchange for a chance to drive my car. He's directly in front of me now. The heat in the garage is making me sweat; his shirt's lightly stained with patches of wetness from his own perspiration.

Next thing I know, his hand is on my crotch and he's feeling my hard-on.

"How about a nice wax job?" he offers.

"Maybe I don't have any jobs that need polishing," I tell him.

"Satisfaction guaranteed, dude. You've never seen a spit shine as good as the one I give."

"All of that just to drive this car? You're a pushover, Travis." I pause, savoring the possibilities. "It's a deal."

He unzips my khaki shorts and they fall to the ground. My dick is big and hard by this point, standing at attention and ready to rock and roll. He slides down to his knees and begins to tease the head of my cock with his lips and tongue.

No way he hasn't done this before! Damn, it feels good when he takes me in his mouth and starts to suck me off.

He uses one hand to play with my balls and holds my dick with his other hand. By now, I'm having trouble standing up, so I ease myself down onto the hood of the car; he adjusts himself accordingly and goes back to work. Time passes but I lose track, not sure if two minutes or two hours go by.

You know how it is when you hit that moment when you want what's happening to just go on and on and on, but you also can't hold back anymore and just want to cum all over every-thing in sight? No matter how much I try for the first, it's always the second that wins.

I start to see stars and colors, then I shoot my wad right down his throat. He holds on tight and swallows it all. I realize we're both covered in sweat, the smell of our bodies mixing with the gas and oil and greasy scent of the garage. We both look at each other, look around, and laugh.

"How about a cold one to chase that cum?" I ask him.

"Yeah, sure. But you're not off the hook yet."

My shirt is sticking to me, so I pull it off and wander over to the fridge for two more beers. I've never been naked in the garage before. I like it.

"What hook?" I ask as he grabs the Bud from me and drinks half of it before coming up for air.

"You know what I want." He removes his shirt and unbuttons his shorts, which drop to the floor and land in a small puddle of oil. "Fuck me, Boxer."

Never argue with a man who knows what he's after, I always say.

"Let me get something first." I reach into the car, open the glove compartment, and pull out a lubed condom.

"I was a Boy Scout when I was a kid," I tell Travis. "You know: Be prepared."

I rip open the condom package and roll that sucker onto my cock, getting stiff once more as the latex meets my pudge. We stand face to face, our dicks rubbing up against each other. I lick the sweat from his neck, tasting the salt and smelling his musky odor; I bite on his earlobe and run my hands over his tight butt.

Before I get sidetracked and forget my mission here, I turn him around and push him down so he's spread across the hood; his johnson juts out above the car's grill. I knock his feet apart, then shove my cock into his hole. He lets out a yelp but then relaxes into it.

I pump him good and watch my shaft slide rhythmically in and out of his ass. He moans and lets out an "oh, yeah" pretty regularly. I grab his fireplug dick—you know the kind: short but real wide and chubby—and rub my hand up and down the stump. We go at it for a long time and then hit this weird Zen-like fucking motion together.

"Take me, Boxer! Fuck me hard! All the way, man! All the way!"

Hard and deep is what he gets. I grab his shoulders and press him into the metal of the car hood. We're drenched in sweat, and he slips around a bit as I slam my meat up his ass. We cum about three seconds apart—first me and then Travis. As he lets loose, he sprays the hood with jism. The creamy liquid runs down the front of the Beemer and drips to the floor.

We rest for a minute and catch our breath. Looking somewhat guilty and yet very pleased with himself, he says: "I told you I'd give you a good wax job, dude."

I can only shake my head and laugh.

"Yep, you sure did," I answer.

I reach for a rag to wipe up some of the cum.

"You know something else?" he asks. "I think we just invented a new meaning for the term autoerotic." He cracks himself up, then starts to get dressed.

How the *hell* am I going to get all this pecker juice off Markus's car?

I smile and get to work, knowing this is one job I'll never forget.

# PICTURE THIS...

**LANDON DIXON**

I had gone over to my friend Steve's place to catch some rays poolside. He lived in one of those three-story four-building apartment complexes that have a courtyard and a swimming pool in the middle. The day was a mid-summer scorcher, and I lay on my beach towel and let the hot sun soak into my lean, hard body, clad only in a skintight Speedo. I casually propped myself up on my elbows and ogled the two ladies who were sharing the pool with Steve and me. A pair of sunglasses hid my busy eyes. One of the girls, a busty redhead, was doing laps in the pool, while the other, a dark-haired, dark-skinned temptress with a body to die for, was smoothing suntan lotion all over her bronze stomach and chest. Her hardened nipples were shoving against her thin green bikini top, begging to get into something more comfortable—like my mouth.

"What's up?" Steve asked, staring at my crotch and laughing.

"Huh?" I shook my head clear and glanced down at my swimsuit—the outline of my erect cock was clearly visible. I bent my legs, and the redhead in the pool giggled.

Steve's pager suddenly went off, much to my relief. He scooped it up, stared at it a second, then said, "Shit!" and started folding up his towel.

"Problem?" I asked.

"Aw, I got to go into work."

"That's tough," I said. "I'll keep an eye on the girls for you."

"Like hell you will. You're going to have to let the air out of your blow-up toy there and come back to the apartment with me. Guests can only use the swimming pool if they're with a resident. I've been warned twice by the super already."

I groaned, got to my feet, then quickly balled up my towel and placed it in front of my groin so that I didn't get arrested for carrying a concealed weapon. I cast one last covetous look at the two girls and their succulent tits and then followed Steve across the grass and up the stairs to his second-floor apartment.

"Mind if I take a shower?" I asked him when we were inside.

"No problem," he said. "Chad's still sleeping—he's working the night shift now—so don't make too much noise." He grinned. "And don't leave any messy stains in the bathtub. I'll be long gone by the time you're finished."

He was right. By the time I strolled out of the steamy bathroom, he had left, but his roommate, Chad, was up and about. I bumped into him in the hallway. "Sorry, man," I said.

He looked me over. I was wearing nothing but a low-rider towel around my waist. "Slippery when wet," he said and laughed.

I smiled. I didn't know the guy that well—he had only been sharing the apartment with Steve for about two months. He was tall and thin, had short black hair, and was wearing shorts and a T-shirt. Steve said that he was clean and quiet and paid for half of everything—the perfect roommate. "I'll just get changed and take off," I told him.

"Sure," he said. "Use my room. I'm working on the computer in Steve's room right now. I put your stuff on my bed."

"Thanks," I responded, then walked down the hall and into his bedroom. I shut the door and pulled off the towel. I sauntered over to the window and gently parted the curtains a few inches. I had a good view of the swimming pool and the two babes sunbathing there. As I stared at their hot, ripe bodies, my cock rose and tried to peek through the curtains along with me. I stroked it a few times, tugging it to its full seven inches, fondled my nipples, and was really starting to get serious when I heard a noise in the hall: Chad.

I closed the curtains with a sigh and sat down on the side of Chad's bed, figuring that I better take my show on the road. I noticed a glossy magazine partially hidden under one of the pillows. *Chad, you dirty boy,* I thought. I pulled the magazine out and looked at the cover. A naked, blond muscleman with half-closed eyes was getting righteously sucked off by another blond squatting in front of him. The second blond was also a guy.

"Yikes," I said under my breath. Chad obviously liked meat better than fish. *To each his own,* I thought, then looked around to make sure that the door was still closed. Out of curiosity, I started leafing through the well-thumbed magazine. On page 24, the blond Hercules and his suck toy were really going at it—the muscle-bound stud was giving his boyfriend the rump-ride of his life. Their hairless bodies were tanned a golden brown, and sweat glistened on them as they sucked, fucked, and hucked cum all over each other. My own rod remained surprisingly stiff as the action reached its inevitable climax. The last picture was a full-page shot of the two hunks tonguing cum off each other's faces, their long cocks hanging spent in their hands.

"What do you think?" a voice exploded in my ear.

I nearly jumped out of my birthday suit. I jerked my head around and stared at Chad. I quickly bent forward, trying to cover up my swollen cock and the dirty magazine. "Uh, hi, Chad," I said lamely. "You surprised me."

"Pleasantly, I hope," he responded. He quickly walked over and sat down next to me on the bed. His bare knee pressed against mine. He looked at the homoerotic picture for a moment, then flipped some pages over to reveal another pictorial. This one had three rock-hard young cocksmen cavorting in a gym. "This is really hot too," he said close to my ear.

I stared down at the shiny snapshots of the frenzied gay threesome that lay just inches away from the tip of my rigid cock, and I felt Chad's warm breath on my neck. My bronzed body grew goose bumps, and my cock grew another half-inch as it hardened.

"Have you ever tried it?" Chad asked casually, pointing at a picture of a guy lying on a workout bench while another guy sucked his huge cock. The third guy was feeding his own thick dick to the benched guy; there were intense looks on all the guy's faces. Chad's fingers lightly brushed my cock head, then his hand settled on my knee.

My face grew red, and my eyes had trouble focusing. I could feel the heat of Chad's body, and sweat sprouted on my forehead and under my arms. I swallowed hard and my throat clicked. "Uh, nothing like…"

I stopped talking—and thinking—when I felt Chad's wet tongue in my ear. I jumped like I had just been plugged into the wall. He swirled his tongue around my earlobe, then nibbled at it. My breath caught in my throat and I gasped, "Don't!"

"Just relax," he breathed into my ear. "Look at the pictures and think about how good it's going to feel."

I did look at the pictures, and what they showed seared my senses—the guy on the bench taking it up the ass from his buddy, while he swallowed the third guy's cock all the way up to the balls. The sight of all that, coupled with Chad's persistent tongue, was more than enough to destroy my frail inhibitions.

Chad's right arm went around my bare shoulders, while his left hand started playing with my brown nipples. My cock twitched and my nipples hardened. "I love blonds," he murmured in my ear, then licked his way down the side of my neck. He turned my shoulders slightly so that he could lick my Adam's apple, then under my chin. He pulled back, stared at me with his crystal-clear blue eyes and asked gently, "Ready?"

"Yeah," someone using my voice said. I mashed my open mouth against his.

We kissed savagely, our tongues playing together, slapping against one another. It was the first time that I had ever kissed a man and it felt great. His mouth was soft and warm, his lips thick and red, his tongue long and wet and pink. "Yes," I moaned, as he caught my tongue with his teeth, then sucked up and down its slimy length like it was a stiffened cock. His fingers roamed through my hair, held my head in place while he sucked on my tongue.

We devoured each other's mouths, kissing, licking, and sucking hungrily, greedily, urgently. I groaned as he slid his tongue deep inside my mouth so that I could suck long and hard on it. I sucked and sucked, then grabbed his head and licked his lips as I felt him pulling away. The gay porno mag slid to the floor, its job done.

He broke free of my desperate mouth and pushed me back on the bed. I stretched out and moaned softly as I felt his strong hand encircle my cock and begin to stroke it tenderly. "Oh, yeah," I whispered.

He stroked my engorged cock easily and expertly, tugging and pulling on it till I felt harder and longer than I had ever felt before. He spat on my cock, lubricating his hand and my cock so he could stroke faster and faster. Then, just as an explosion was building inside of me, he did the unthinkable—he let go of my cock. He stood up between my legs and quickly stripped off his

T-shirt, his shorts, and his running shoes. His body was toned, tanned, tight, and hairless, except for a small patch of pubic hair just above his tremendous cock. He gripped his perfectly straight eight-inch erection in his right hand and waggled it at me. "You like?" he asked, laughing.

"I want," I replied without hesitation.

His face grew serious, and he lay his body over mine. Our cocks pressed together, and I almost dissolved. He softly stroked my face, lovingly ran his fingers through my hair, and we kissed again and again, swirling our tongues together in an erotic ballet that left me breathless and weak. I wrapped my legs around his narrow waist, digging my heels into his full, round buttocks as our cocks jamming together even harder. I plunged my tongue back down his throat, and he gyrated his hips against me, dry-fucking me.

After a few minutes, he broke contact with my yearning mouth and crawled around on the bed until his long cock was positioned directly over my open inexperienced mouth, his knees planted on either side of my head. I squeezed his firm ass cheeks, took a deep breath, and pulled him down until his cock entered my tentative mouth. I slowly sucked his beautiful shaft into my mouth and felt his body jerk. I began a steady natural rhythm on his cock, taking more and more of it into my mouth each time.

"You're giving head like an expert!" he exclaimed, his hips thrusting in time to my cock sucking.

I answered his enthusiasm by recklessly gulping down the entire length of his engorged cock, shocking both him and myself. My breath whistled through my nose as his fat cock filled my tight throat.

"Oh, God!" he cried, his cock buried to the hilt in my wet throat, the warm tightness scorching his cock and his body. He groaned, then began stroking and licking my own rock-hard member.

"Unh!" I moaned, sending a ripple through his gorgeous body via his mouth-bound dick. I began to slowly disgorge his huge cock, an inch at a time, and he stopped polishing my pole with his hand and tongue long enough to watch in awe as his soaked meat crawled out of my mouth. When his thick cock was completely out, I licked away the drops of pre-cum that had gathered at his slit. I tasted his salty essence, savored it, and swallowed. I wanted more. I nipped at his slick pink cock head, teasing his twitching member until he could stand it no longer and invaded my craven mouth with his manhood again.

While I sucked him, he sucked me. Unthinkable erotic sensations rippled all through me as he deep-throated my raging hard-on. My body quivered uncontrollably, shaken to the core. I frantically pulled his dripping cock out of my mouth and gasped for air. "I'm going to cum in your mouth, Chad!" I warned the seasoned cocksucker, my balls tightening in anticipation.

He raised his head, and my savaged dick slid out of his throat. "No, you're not," he said, licking his lips. "Not until I fuck your sweet ass."

"Do it," I responded, throwing my arms back and closing my eyes. He could do whatever the hell he wanted to me.

He squeezed a couple of drops of cum out of my slit and lapped them up thirstily. Then he abruptly dropped my stunned cock and scrambled back to his feet. I reluctantly opened my eyes and looked up at him. His sun-kissed body was misted with sweat, and his giant cock was moist with my saliva. "Ready to go all the way, baby?" he asked, smiling down at me.

"Do me," I growled.

He dug around in a nightstand, pulled out a condom, tore it open, then rolled it down the stunning length of his glorious cock. My heart thumped heavily inside my constricted chest, and the lower half of my body was heavy, thick, and numb. I swallowed

PICTURE THIS...

hard and tried to prepare myself for my first-ever ass pounding.

He positioned me on the edge of the bed, grabbed his sheathed cock in his right hand, and slapped my ass with his left. "Spread 'em, mister," he ordered.

I lifted my long legs high in the air, resting them on his chest and shoulders, then reached down and spread my ass cheeks as far apart as I could. "Fuck me," I breathed, longing for the forbidden feel of his steely cock up my ass. The air was dense with our man-lust.

He spat in his hand, then rubbed his cock as well as the entrance to my ass. Moving in closer, he slowly began to insert his swollen cock head into my burning pink hole. "Here it comes, baby," he muttered, pushing the first fabulous inch of his cock into my virgin asshole.

"Fuck me!" I yelled desperately, urging him on.

He thrust his hips forward, and I felt his heavy cock slide deep within me. My legs turned to jelly, my head spun, and stars flashed before my lust-clouded eyes. His cock felt great in my ass.

"Just a little more," he groaned, then pressed hard against me. I felt his balls nudge my ass cheeks, and I knew that his rigid manhood, all eight inches of it, was buried deep inside me—where it belonged. He began pumping my ass—slowly at first, then faster, faster, and faster.

I grabbed my tingling, straining cock and began stroking for all I was worth while my new boyfriend banged away at my ravaged ass. Chad closed his eyes, threw back his head, and let out a roar as he slammed his meat in and out of my tight asshole. As his heavy balls smacked against me, a raging fire spread from my ass to my cock, then through my entire body. "I'm cumming!" I screamed, my hand a blur on my swollen dick.

"Me too!" he yelled, and I knew that this time there was no turning back. His face was contorted into a grim mask of boiling ecstasy, and he grunted madly as he furiously plowed into my ass, splitting me wide-open with his battering ram-cock.

"Yeah!" I yelled, jerking myself off viciously while I pinched and rolled my impossibly erect nipples. All of the muscles in my body contracted at once, and I held my breath as white-hot semen roared up from my balls, through my fiery cock, and spurted out my flaming cock head.

"Fuck, yeah!" I moaned, jism rocketing uncontrollably out of my cock and splashing down with abandon onto my sweat-drenched stomach and chest. My body jerked convulsively as I shot line after line of searing jism out of my volcanic dick, as Chad pounded away at my ass with frenzied determination. My mind went blank, and the world went gray as sheer blinding ecstasy gripped my body, tore my senses apart, and drained my immense, granite-hard cock of all its juices. It was man-made bliss of mind-blowing proportions.

Chad pulled his mammoth dick out of my plundered ass, tore off his condom, and began stroking with maniacal recklessness. "I'm going to cum on you, baby!" he cried, then tossed back his head and started raining thick ropes of jism down onto my quaking body. He stroked furiously, his body jerking, his massive cock shooting hot semen over and over again onto my wasted body, until finally his knees buckled and he collapsed between my trembling legs.

I lay totally spent and dissolute, only semiconscious, my torso covered with warm, sticky semen, my newfound lover resting his beautiful head between my legs, his lips absently kissing my emptied balls. What a picture we must have made.

# FUCKED
# AT THE TRUCK STOP

**CHRISTOPHER PIERCE**

With one hand on my crotch and the other on the steering wheel I drove through the night. A breeze blew in through my car's open windows, whispering through my hair and soothing my skin, which was hot from a long, sweaty day on the road.

But no breeze could cool the heat between my legs, a heat that grew stronger with every passing moment. I felt myself through the thin fabric of my shorts, loving the sensation of my cock growing stiff beneath my fingers. It stretched to its full length until it strained against my shorts.

I glanced down and saw a small wet spot at the tip of my dick where a drop of pre-cum had oozed out through the fabric. I rubbed my erect penis from its base to its full bulbous head, savoring the extra friction achieved by the layer of cloth between it and my hand. It felt great, but fondling myself while driving wasn't going to tame the fire in my crotch.

The road stretched out ahead of me. The broken painted lines that cut it in half down the middle streaked together into a glowing smear of yellow. My car's headlights illuminated the terrain ahead, even though there was nothing to see.

Barren, featureless land surrounded me. Every 50 miles or so there might be a town, so small I was through it and out the other side in five minutes. They all looked the same.

I needed to rest.

And get my rocks off.

A sign appeared on the horizon: TRUCK STOP: NEXT EXIT. That sounded good. I could park in a dark corner, jerk myself off, then sleep for a few hours. I pulled my car off at the next off-ramp and followed the signs to the truck stop. It was in a wooded area and had a large flat parking lot with a big restroom building and a small 24-hour convenient store at one end. In front of the store were a few semi trucks, the kind whose drivers drive all night and sleep in their cabs. There were no other cars besides the trucks.

I pulled my car up in front of the restroom, realizing that it had been several hours since I'd pissed. But how was I going to piss with this massive hard-on?

I stopped my car and walked up to the building and through its door. The restroom was big, with lots of stalls. I headed for the long piss trough against the wall. I pulled my shorts down and my cock popped out, hard as a board.

I closed my eyes and willed it to go down.

*Relax,* I said to myself. After a few moments my dick was soft enough to pee, and with a happy sigh I let my urine flow freely.

When I was done, I realized my eyes were still closed. I stuffed my cock back in my shorts, opened my eyes and turned around.

I wasn't alone.

Against the back wall, leaning casually with his arms folded, was a man. He was older than me, probably in his mid 30s, and was dressed like a working man: flannel shirt, dirty jeans, and hiking boots. His jaw was darkened with several days' growth of beard. An old baseball cap was perched on his head.

He was grinning at me.

"Hey," I said, trying to cover my surprise.

"Hey, yourself," he said.

"I didn't know anyone was watching."

"Yeah," the man nodded, "I didn't expect to find anyone in here this late either. I just came in here to piss."

I couldn't stop my eyes from dropping from his face to his crotch. The denim there was well-worn, rubbed white and nearly threadbare. The outline and shape of his cock were clearly visible. My tongue slipped out of my mouth and wet my lip.

"Can I…watch you?" I asked suddenly.

"Watch me piss?" he repeated. "Sure, I guess so."

I stepped to the side, and the sexy man walked over to the trough. He undid his belt and pulled his meat out of his pants. It was hot—big and full, even soft as it was, with a big, dark head and a veiny shaft. He took his dick in one hand and aimed it into the trough. A stream of piss shot out, and the sound of it hitting the porcelain and flowing down into the drain was very loud in the big empty restroom.

The man closed his eyes and tilted his head back a little as he pissed. "Aaahhh…" he murmured. "Do you want to touch it?" he asked. He must have realized I wanted more than just to watch him.

"Yes," I said simply.

"Then go ahead."

Before he even finished the sentence I reached out and grasped that succulent piece of meat in my hand.

"You like that?" the trucker asked.

"Yeah…" I whispered.

"You like holding my big fat cock."

"Yeah…"

He turned to face me, letting me continue to hold his dick in my hand. I felt it start to get hard. It was such a great feeling, so hot.

"But you want to do more than hold it, don't you?" the man asked. I couldn't hide how I felt.

"Yes," I said.

"Then do it." he told me. "Get down on your knees and suck it like you want to."

I obeyed him and dropped down to my knees in front of him. Opening my mouth and closing my eyes, I felt the sexy man shove his cock between my lips. I closed my mouth around it, thrilling to the feeling of it lengthening inside me, filling me up with its strength and power.

He started face-fucking me, pushing his dick deep into my mouth, then pulling it back until it was almost all the way out, then shoving it back in again. I didn't care if someone walked in; I didn't care about the hard floor digging into my knees; I didn't even care that my own stiff cock was staining my underwear with new pre-cum and begging to be stroked. All that mattered right then and there was sucking this man's dick and doing it as well as I could.

"Mmm…that's great," he growled above me. His voice moved through me, and it was as if my blood responded to his pleasure, heating up and rushing faster through my veins. I want-ed to push him over the edge, to make him feel better than he had ever felt before!

"I'm gonna cum, man," he said. "You ready for me to shoot?"

I took my mouth off his cock to answer him.

"Yes, please!" I said. "I want to see you cum!"

I put my face back down between his legs and licked his balls. They smelled fantastic—sweaty and musky from their owner's long day of driving. They tasted just as good, and I massaged them with my tongue, even gently taking one ball into my mouth to roll it lovingly inside. As I did this, the trucker jerked himself off, pumping his cock in his fist. Suddenly, he shifted a little and aimed his dick into the piss trough.

"This is it!" he said. "I'm cumming, man!"

"Go for it!" I said, and as I licked his ball sac again, I felt the churning liquid inside heat up and shoot down his shaft on its way out of his cock. The trucker grunted gutturally as he came, and I turned my head enough to watch his bursts of spunk jet into the trough. His body shuddered for a few seconds, then he was done. He stuffed his cock back in his pants and zipped them up.

"That was fuckin' awesome," he said. I stood up, rubbing my own dick through my shorts.

"You're a stud," I said. "You're fucking awesome!"

"You getting' back on the road tonight?" he asked me.

"I was going to jerk off then catch a few hours of sleep first," I said. "Why?"

The trucker suddenly looked embarrassed and almost shy. I love it when men let themselves be vulnerable; it turns me on.

"It's OK, man," I reassured him. "What is it?"

"Well," he said, "you seem like a nice guy…"

"Yeah?"

"I've been on the road for almost two weeks now, and my girlfriend back home, well, she—"

"Stopped sleeping with you?" I finished. The guy looked surprised that I'd guessed right.

"Yeah," he said. "I don't know what her problem is."

"So you haven't been getting your rocks off." I said.

"That's true," he said, "but there's more to it."

"What?" I asked. Suddenly, the trucker looked angry and pointed at me.

"If you ever tell anyone about this, I'll find you and kick your fucking ass in the dirt, you understand?"

I put up my hands, laughing. "Whoa!" I said. "Take it easy! Who would I tell? This is just between us."

"OK," he said. "The best part of sex for me, after cumming, of course, is the part after, when I got to hold her."

He paused, as if waiting for me to say something, but I just looked at him, listening.

"And tonight there's no chicks around," he continued, "and I was wondering, since you're probably a fag—"

"Gay." I interrupted.

"What?"

"Not fag. Gay. Don't say 'fag,' especially if you want me to help you out tonight."

He looked surprised but nodded and continued.

"I figured, since you're gay you might..." he trailed off.

"Might what?" I prompted him. "Say it. It's cool to say it."

"Let me hold you for a while," the trucker finished without meeting my eyes. "I've got a sleep compartment in my rig."

I smiled at him.

"How about you get me off," I said, "and then you can hold me all fucking night."

"Sounds good," he said, "but I've got some buddies out there. How can I get you to my truck without them knowing what we're doin'?"

"Tell you what," I said, "you take care of me, and I'll take care of that."

I told him my idea for how to get me to his truck without arousing suspicion from his friends outside, and he agreed it was a good plan. Then the trucker took me into one of the bathroom stalls to fulfill his part of the bargain.

Once we were inside the stall with the door closed, he grabbed me and held me tightly, my back against his chest. His left arm was wrapped around my middle, pressing me against him. His right hand grabbed my crotch through my shorts and I jerked in surprise.

"What—?" I started to say, but the trucker clamped his left hand over my mouth and I shut up instantly.

"Sshhhh…" he said softly in my ear. "Keep quiet, little gay boy. I don't want to share you with anyone else." My cock flexed and stiffened under his hand, and the trucker rubbed it through my shorts. Despite the order to be quiet, I couldn't prevent a little moan from escaping my lips,

"This is just what you need, isn't it, gay boy?" he whispered. "You need a real man to take care of you and get your rocks off, isn't that right?"

I nodded my head and said, "Yes, sir," even though it was muffled by his hand over my mouth. The trucker stuck his right hand down into my shorts and grabbed my cock and balls in his fist and squeezed them.

"You need to get fucked, gay boy?" he asked as he started to jack my dick. It was intense and wild, jerked off by a total stranger in a restroom off the open highway in the middle of the night. I nodded my head again. "If I take my hand off your mouth, you gonna be quiet?"

"Yes, sir!" I said into his hand, and he took it off my mouth, letting it drop until it found my left nipple, and pinched it hard. With his right hand he played with my cock, squeezing it and jerking it.

"I'm gonna take you back to my truck," he said, "and I'm gonna fuck you long and hard."

I nodded my head enthusiastically, remembering again his warning for silence. It felt so fucking good to be in his power this way, to be his prisoner. The heat in my balls was burning, and soon enough I couldn't hold back anymore.

I shuddered in the trucker's arms and he aimed my dick into the toilet bowl. My climax roared through me, and squirts of cum shot out of my cock.

"Yeah," he said, "that's it, boy. You need a real man to take care of you, don't you?"

I nodded again, even though I was dying to yell with the pleasure he was causing me. He held me until I stopped quivering, then stuffed my cock and balls back into my shorts. Then he opened the stall door and led me out in the empty bathroom. When there was enough room to turn around, he faced me with a grin on his unshaven face.

As we had agreed, he leaned down toward me and I let myself fall forward over his shoulder. He grabbed onto my legs and lifted me up, hoisting me like a sack of potatoes until he was standing straight up and had me slung over his shoulder.

"You OK?" he asked me.

"I'm good," I said.

"Stay real limp so they believe you're unconscious," he told me.

"Yes, sir," I said, closing my eyes.

The trucker carried me out of the bathroom into the cool night air. He was strong; having a 160-pound man over his shoulder didn't slow him down a bit. It felt good to be carried like that, with his arms holding my legs tight so I wouldn't fall. In some way it was intimate, I guess. Even though what we were doing was technically playacting, it was still cool to be carried by this sexy stud.

With my eyes shut I couldn't see anything, of course, but I could hear the sound of the trucker's footsteps on the concrete, and the sound of several men talking that got louder as we got closer to them.

"Hey, Jim!" one of the guys said, and we stopped. "What the hell is this?" a second voice asked.

"Found him out cold in the bathroom," my trucker said, whose name I guessed was Jim.

"Got any money on him?" a third man asked.

"Fuck you," Jim said. "I'm not a thief,"

"Want me to call the cops on my radio?" the first man said.

"No," said my trucker, "I'm gonna let him sleep in my rig till he wakes up. He might be on the run or something. I want to hear his story before I call the cops."

"He got a knife or anything on him? Might be a crazy fuckin' drug addict."

"No," Jim said, adjusting me on his shoulder. "He's clean. I can handle him. Don't worry."

"OK, man," the second guy said. "You gonna catch some Z's yourself?"

"Maybe. I want to head out early."

"Cool. Later then."

The truckers exchanged goodbyes, then Jim started walking again. After a few steps he stopped, and I heard the sound of him fishing his keys out of his pocket.

He unlocked and opened a door, then lugged me up and into what I figured was his truck. It smelled like him, thick and male, with a trace of sweat and something else that was probably beer. Jim walked a few short steps, opened another door, then took me inside and set me down on a soft surface. I was a little sorry that the carrying was over, but I knew what was coming was going to be even better.

I heard Jim walk back and close and lock all the doors he'd brought me through. Then he came back into the compartment he'd stashed me in and snapped on a dim light.

"They bought it," he said. "It's cool, no one can see us."

I opened my eyes.

The sleeping area of Jim's truck wasn't very big, and the "bed" itself would be tight for two men, but it would be OK. There was more than enough room for what we had in mind.

"Are you going to fuck me now?" I asked, and Jim smirked.

"Well, I sure as shit didn't carry you all this way to talk about art," he said, and we both laughed. "Take your clothes off."

I obeyed him and slipped out of my shorts and T-shirt and kicked my shoes off. The trucker pulled his outer flannel shirt off to reveal two nice pecs clearly showing through a thin undershirt, framed by suspenders. He unlaced his boots and took them off, leaving his socks on. I lay on the bed, naked, looking up at the rough stud who'd carried me like I weighed no more than a bag of laundry.

Everything about him was exciting me.

The dust on his cheeks, the sweat stains on his undershirt from driving all day, the way his cock and balls hung low in his briefs when he unhooked his suspenders and let his dirty jeans fall and stepped out of them.

My cock got hard when I looked in his eyes and saw his hunger for me. Jim pulled his undershirt off and I was hit by the odor released by this. It was like him—striking, musky, undeniably erotic. His chest was hairy, his pecs crowned with big, dark nipples. His stomach was flat and hard. His whole torso was tanned golden brown; I imagined him driving long, sunny days with his shirt off, or fishing shirtless on his days off. Below his tan-line he was just as sexy. From his bush of dark pubic hair grew his penis—long, hard, veiny, the big foreskin pulled back from the flared red head.

I resisted leaning forward and devouring it again as I had before he'd brought me here. I resisted because I knew getting fucked by him was going to be even better than giving him a blow job.

"You look good enough to eat," the trucker said, "I like the way you look up at me."

"You look fucking awesome!" I said. "I need you to fuck me."

"Yeah?" Jim said. "You need me to pile-drive my big cock into your little gay-boy butt?"

"Yes," I said, "please!"

"Beg me," he said with a grin.

I turned over on my back and spread my legs wide for him.

"Come on, man!" I pleaded. "I *need* you inside me! I need you to ram me, stud! Come on, please, *please,* pound me, pork me, take me, *FUCK ME!*"

"Now *that's* what I like to hear!" he said and climbed up on top of the bed. My whole body tingled and vibrated with excitement as the naked trucker crawled between my legs.

I fished a condom out of the pocket of my shorts and tore it open quickly. The trucker said nothing as I unrolled the latex sheath over his formidable meat and squeezed some lubricant on it from a travel-sized tube in my other pocket.

We were ready.

"You set, gay boy?" Jim asked me.

"Yes, sir!" I said, and he got in between them and rested my feet on his shoulders.

I knew this man wasn't going to be big on romantic foreplay, so I just prepared myself for a direct assault. The trucker took his cock in his hand and aimed it until it was pressed against my asshole. I took a deep breath and willed my whole body to relax and receive him.

It worked a little, but when he thrust himself into me it still hurt. But the pain was accompanied by pleasure that was sharp and bright in its intensity.

"Oh, fuck, yeah…" the man inside me said, closing his eyes as my asshole gripped his dick and held it with ecstasy. Jim fucked me hard them, shoving himself into me savagely. It was painful and wonderful at the same time. "Aw…" he growled. "Nothin' like a little gay-boy ass,"

"That's right, man," I encouraged him. "Fuck me like you want to fuck your girlfriend—long and hard and deep! Go on, I can take it!"

"Feels so fuckin' good!" he said.

"Yeah, stud," I answered, "'cause you're so fucking hot!" His thrusts got longer and faster, and I had to anchor myself against the wall behind my head with my hands, or he'd have thrown me all over the bed with the passion of his fucking.

My cock was erect and dripping from the incredible ordeal it was enduring. It was amazing to feel this way, to be reamed and pummeled by a real man, a trucker stud like Jim!

"I'm gonna cum soon, gay boy," he said breathlessly.

"Me too," I moaned.

I thought about how he'd looked earlier, leaning against the wall of the bathroom, his big fat cock clearly visible through his jeans. I thought about sucking that dick, feeling his manhood and power inside me. I thought about him carrying me, how he'd slung me over his shoulder and carried me like I weighed no more than a kid.

But most of all I thought about that exact moment, the sensation of this man making rough love to me, screwing me, fucking me like I'd never been fucked before.

And I came.

My load of spunk shot out of my cock in milky ropes that landed on my chest and abdomen. My orgasm hit me then, blooming inside me like an explosive flower of ecstasy. I felt my asshole contract, tightly clenching around the trucker's thrusting dick.

"Oh, fuck, *yeah!*" he said, and I imagined the pleasure of the contraction sending him over the edge as my butt held him in its grasp of bliss. "I'm cumming, gay boy!" he groaned above me.

"Do it, man!" I urged him, "Give me everything you've got!" The trucker's next groan was wordless, an animal cry of passion, and with a final thrust I knew he was shooting his load deep inside me. I took it all, gratefully, wanting all he had, wanting to give him as much pleasure as I could.

Jim's hands gripped my upper arms, his fingers digging in. In that moment I didn't care about pain. All I could think of was pleasing him, making him feel better than he ever had.

And I thought, just maybe, that I had.

The trucker collapsed on top of me, the last waves of his orgasm washing over him and through him.

We lay there for a while, so long I thought he might've fallen asleep. But then the trucker grunted and raised himself up, pulling his cock out of my butt, which felt suddenly empty without it. With my eyes closed I heard him snap the condom off. Then there was the sensation of something rough and dry on my chest, and I realized that he was wiping my spunk off my body.

When he was done he turned off the light in the sleeping compartment and got back in bed with me. With his strong arms the trucker pulled me close, my back to his chest. He wrapped those arms around me and held me tightly. There was no need for words.

I snuggled against him and rested my head on my pillow. Only then did I suddenly remember how tired I was, and I fell asleep almost immediately, the reassuring feeling of Jim's big soft cock against my butt cheeks.

The next morning I woke up early.

The trucker was still asleep, snoring quietly with a smile of contentment on his face. I got up slowly and carefully so as not to wake him. I moved my pillow into the space I had occupied, and he held it tightly as if it were me.

I quietly made my way back to the truck's cab, and let myself out of the passenger door, locking it behind me.

Walking back to my car, I took a deep breath of fresh morning air and was reading for the new day. A few moments later I drove out of the truck stop and headed back toward the freeway entrance, where the open highway was waiting for me.

# RURAL SUCKFEST

**BRENT HOWELL**

It was one of the raunchiest sexual experiences of my life—
and it was with three straight guys. I was living in rural
British Columbia in the early '80s. One winter night I was at a
neighbor's and we were watching the Playboy Channel on his
satellite dish. There were four of us there that evening, all
friends and all in our early 30s. Although we lived on farms in
the mountains, none of us were really farm boys. We had all fled
to the country in the back-to-the land movement of the '70s. So
we were just city boys with country aspirations. Beer flowed,
and although we weren't really drunk—at least I wasn't—the
evening was getting pretty wild. It was Ernie's house, and he
was the party ringleader with the well-deserved reputation of
being a total slut. It was said he'd fuck anything that walked. In
fact, it was Ernie who first pulled out his cock and began whack-
ing off to the porno on TV.

"I'm getting too hot, looking at all those dripping pussies and
hard dicks," Ernie joked.

"Put it away, you idiot! There aren't any pussies here to get excited over your hard dick—as if that little shrimp could excite anyone!" Gary chortled.

"Brent probably gets hot when he sees a boner." Dean turned to me with a smirk. "How about it? Do you?"

By that time in my life, I was openly gay. The locals frowned on sexual deviation, but these guys were all from the city and much more open-minded. Not that any of them would have admitted to having gay feelings. I didn't mind their teasing that night; we gave each other shit on a regular basis. But something about the way Dean looked at me provoked an unusual response on my part. With my eyes staring straight into his baby blue orbs, I pulled out my dick and began to stroke it hard.

"Yeah, I get hot when I see a boner, Dean. How about you?" I grinned.

The others laughed uproariously, although Dean blushed even as he joined in. But then Gary was the third to join the whack-off party, and took our attention off Dean. The tall, good-looking Gary was the youngest of us all. Slightly inebriated, he stood up and shoved his jeans down to his ankles. He wasn't wearing any underwear.

"How's this for a hard dick!" he announced loudly. His lengthy cock was rising up rapidly into a stiff pole. It looked as if it was at least a foot long.

Ernie and I were seated on the couch facing the television, while both Dean and Gary were sitting on old stuffed lounge chairs. Ernie was close enough to me lean over and drape his arm around my shoulder and leer into my face. "All these boners— does it make you want to taste one? Wanna suck cock?"

Whether Ernie was teasing me or not, I decided instantly I would do exactly what he was suggesting. My head dropped down, and I swallowed his fat sausage to the root. Ernie grunted loudly and shoved his hips upward into my sucking mouth, obviously enjoying it too much to protest.

"Fucking nice!" Ernie hissed through clenched teeth. His hand had dropped to the back of my head, and he was holding my face firmly against his thrusting crotch. He was far from protesting; in fact, he was avidly fucking my mouth.

I hadn't sucked a cock for at least a couple of months, and I was eager to do a first-rate job on Ernie's bone. It was short and fat, and it was stiff and pulsing between my lips as he battered my tonsils with it. I sucked and licked and opened wide for all he offered me. I even got my hands down in his crotch and tickled his ball sac, which made him rise up and slam into my mouth. His pants were down around his ankles, and his lean, hairy thighs were a sexy pillow for my head. I had totally forgotten the others until I heard their raucous jeers cheering me on.

"Suck that fat pork, Brent! Suck it till it blows!" Gary encouraged me from close by. From the corner of my eyes I saw he had walked over to stand beside us, and his pants were down around his ankles. He was beating his meat furiously just above us.

"With an eager mouth like that, you may as well suck us all off," Dean added from the other side. I felt his body next to mine as he sat on the couch beside us. A moment later I felt his hand on my neck pulling my face off Ernie's pile-driving boner.

"Taste this one," Dean muttered as he steered my head to his own lap.

I turned around on the couch and obliged him. Dean was the hottest of my three buddies. With soft brown eyes and curly dark hair, he looked like a handsome cherub. His short frame bulged with muscle, but he also had a roly-poly look, with a touch of fat around the edges to soften the angles of his body. His cock was stiff and drooling. I glanced up at his eyes before dropping down to suck him off. The softness of those brown orbs had gone wet with intensity. He was hot!

I slurped noisily while the other two jerked their dicks around me. I felt like a slut, which added to the excitement of the scene. I really got into it, bobbing up and down over Dean's shaft and sucking loudly as I tongue-bathed his mushroom head. He murmured little words of encouragement that only increased my passion. My head pounded up and down over his lap.

"Suck mine, Brent! Come on, give me a turn!" Gary was practically whining from above.

Although I would've been content to cradle my head in Dean's lap forever, I just couldn't pass up the opportunity to suck off three guys at once, so I rose off Dean's cock and sat up. Gary was right there in front of me, his pants around his ankles. He was pumping his boner in my face. It had to be more than a foot long.

"Can you suck this snake down? Take it to the balls!" Gary begged in a quavering voice. All that noisy cock sucking must have got his balls churning. He was practically vibrating with lust.

I leaned forward and reached out to clasp him by his ass cheeks. He had a tight butt, hairy and solid. Those firm buns were shaking wildly as I pulled him forward into my face. I opened wide and stuck out my tongue lewdly, which brought out gasps and oohs from my buddies. Then with my eyes staring upward into Gary's intense blue ones, I lapped at the jerking head of his boner and felt his butt rock with convulsions under my hands. He was like a live wire, ready to blow any minute. I decided to tease him, licking his tapered cock head with broad swipes of my tongue, digging into the drooling piss slit and sucking up the pre-cum there.

I was putting on quite a show, obviously better than the forgotten porno on television. My mouth was wide open as I licked all around Gary's cock head and shaft, without taking the quivering boner into my mouth. When I dropped down and sucked in his balls, Gary whooped with nervous delight. I toyed with his balls for a delicious moment before tonguing my way up his veined shaft toward the head of his jerking boner. If I hadn't held his hips still with my hands on his butt, he would have shoved his cock right into my mouth. He could barely contain himself.

Then I pounced. My tongue swirled around the flared head when I suddenly wrapped my lips over it and vacuum-sucked the entire thing into my mouth. I held Gary against me as I opened my throat and let his cock slide beyond my tonsils. The hard pole quivered in my mouth and throat, and I felt Gary's body tense up. He was going to blow!

"I'm fucking shooting in Brent's throat!" Gary squealed.

Jizz flooded my throat. I swallowed quickly while letting Gary's cock slide from my throat into my mouth. Then I sucked him dry. Even though I wasn't usually a jizz connoisseur, the situation was so hot that I swallowed all the salty goo Gary had to offer. There was a very powerful thrill to the act of sucking a straight guy till he shot—and then swallowing his jizz. My own cock was aching and stiff in my lap.

That's when I felt Dean's small, callused hand insinuating itself into my crotch. He gripped my leaking boner and began to pump it eagerly. That surprised me. But I wasted no time before searching out my next conquest. As soon as Gary's cock stopped oozing spunk, I let it slide out of my mouth and immediately turned to Dean. With jizz on my lips, I grinned at him and dropped my face to his lap.

Dean moaned deeply and gripped my dick more fiercely. His crotch rose into my face as he tensed his body and drove his cock between my slurping lips. He was intent on fucking my face until he shot. But I had other ideas. I wanted to save him for last. Spitting out his cock, I rose up and winked at him. His look of disappointment was comical.

"Ernie deserves to be next. It's his house and his party!" I joked as I turned around and faced Ernie.

"That's the fucking spirit! Suck my balls dry, like you did with Gary!" Ernie chortled gleefully. His hands came around my neck and he thrust up, even as I dropped down to meet his fat poker.

Gary had stumbled back to his chair and was catching his breath, with his pants still down and his cock still hard. Dean was beside me, his hand still working on my hard cock as his other hand pumped his own.

I opened up and let Ernie fuck my face. He wasn't subtle or considerate. He rammed into me faster and faster while huffing loudly and muttering how sweet my mouth was. I didn't mind; it was a turn-on to have him so excited. I wormed my hands down between his parted thighs and squeezed his ball sac with one of them and even managed to poke the other deeper where I found his tight little asshole spasming and quivering with the force of his face-fuck. I tickled his sphincter while he drilled my face, which had him rising from the couch and practically shouting out with obscenity-spiced joy.

"Fuck! That is so fucking wet and hot and so fucking good and—oh, shit, I'm gonna blow!" Ernie yelped.

I pulled my mouth off his spurting cock and let the jizz splatter my lips and chin. Immediately, even while Ernie was still in the throes of orgasm, I turned back to Dean. With jizz on my lips, I grinned at him and gripped the base of his twitching boner. His look of awed disgust battled with his even deeper feelings of intense lust. His eyes meeting mine, he shoved upward toward my cum-smeared mouth, intent on getting his rocks off just as the others had.

Dean was the best. Once he had managed to insert his jerking bone between my lips, he sat back and relaxed into the couch, spreading his thighs and shoving his pants below his knees. He leaned back and shut his eyes. One of his hands was still under my belly, working my stiff meat. He was almost gentle as he stroked it up and down.

"Looks like you're in cocksucking heaven, Dean!" Gary laughed from his seat. Ernie's breathless laughter joined in. They had shot already and were now content to watch and coach from the sidelines.

I had all of Dean's cock in my mouth. My lips were wrapped around the wide base as my tonsils massaged the broad cap. I slowly rose up until only the head remained inside my mouth, swirling my tongue all over it before I just as slowly dropped back down to swallow all of it once again. I did that over and over, slurping loudly and making noisy smacking sounds with my lips. I didn't want it to end. But then Dean's hand on my cock was just too much. His steady stroking was became an irresistible friction over my hard meat. I humped his fist as I bobbed up and down over his cock.

I shot. It was sudden and intense. Dean felt the warm ball juice spurt over his hand but didn't pull away. He kept pumping even as his own cock stiffened, jerked, and erupted. He lay back with his eyes closed and his mouth open as he spilled his load into my sucking mouth. I squirmed on my belly on the couch as my own seed oozed from my hard cock and Dean's salty stuff filled my mouth.

I rose up and faced my buddies. Gary was staring at us with renewed passion. His hand was flying over his cock. He suddenly erupted, for the second time. I had to laugh at his youthful passion. Twice in 20 minutes!

We cleaned up amidst teasing banter. Ernie and Gary seemed unfazed by the sleazy orgy, but Dean was obviously more affected. He wouldn't quite meet my eyes and didn't join in the laughter as enthusiastically as the rest of us. I didn't mind. I figured it might be hard for him to admit to enjoying a gay sexual experience.

But it was more than that with Dean. I found that out a few months later when he and I were alone. It was the early spring, and we were working on his fence line. He was acting strangely, as if something was bothering him. Then he suddenly blurted out that he couldn't stop thinking about the night I had sucked him off. He looked at me nervously and asked if I would maybe do it again.

I sucked his cock right there in the woods. I got down on my knees in the pine cones and wrapped my lips around his sweet boner and sucked him dry. He shivered and moaned and begged me not to stop. But afterward he was shy and quiet about it.

And that was a pattern we followed for the next two years. Every couple of months, or weeks sometimes, Dean would get me alone and ask me to suck him off. We never went any further, but that was enough. I loved the way his soft eyes got all wet and intense when I looked up at him with my mouth full of his stiff cock. I loved the way he grunted and thrust into my mouth during his spewing orgasms.

Then he got married and moved away. Eventually I moved away as well. We kept in sporadic contact over the years, and I was only a little surprised when he showed up at my apartment almost 10 years later.

"I remember our times together in the mountains. They were the best of my life. You think you could maybe suck me off again?" Dean blurted out after only about 10 minutes of bullshitting.

I was glad to oblige. That was the last time I saw him. He came on my chin, and on my knees I shot all over the carpet.